MW00412786

NOBLE'S
HONOR

BOOK THREE
OF THE CHANGELING BLOOD SERIES

NOBLE'S
HONOR

BOOK THREE
OF THE CHANGELING BLOOD SERIES

GLYNN STEWART

**FAOLAN'S PEN
PUBLISHING**

faolanspen.com

Noble's Honor © 2019 Glynn Stewart

All rights reserved. For information about permission to reproduce selections from this book, contact the publisher at info@faolanspen.com or Faolan's Pen Publishing Inc., 22 King St. S, Suite 300, Waterloo, Ontario N2J 1N8, Canada.

This is a work of fiction. All the characters and events portrayed in this book are fictional, and any resemblance to any persons living or dead is purely coincidental.

This edition published in 2019 by:

Faolan's Pen Publishing Inc.

22 King St. S, Suite 300

Waterloo, Ontario

N2J 1N8 Canada

ISBN-13: 978-1-988035-86-4 (print)

ISBN-13: 978-1-989674-01-7 (epub)

A record of this book is available from Library and Archives Canada.

Printed in the United States of America

1 2 3 4 5 6 7 8 9 10

First edition

First printing: January 2019

Illustration © 2019 Shen Fei

Faolan's Pen Publishing logo is a trademark of Faolan's Pen Publishing Inc.

Read more books from Glynn Stewart at faolanspen.com

1

Someone had clearly thought it was a brilliant idea to put a restaurant on top of a giant spike in the middle of downtown Calgary. Okay, the tower was already there and people were going up it, so feeding them at the top made sense.

I did not understand just what logic went into making the thing *rotate* and turning it into a fancy restaurant.

But there we were. My American immigrant three-quarter-fae self needed a nice place to take my wildcat shifter girlfriend for our first anniversary, and this was where the leader of the local Fae Court had suggested.

It wasn't like I couldn't afford it.

My name is Jason Kilkenny—along with a long list of other names I don't generally admit to—and I am a Noble of the Wild Hunt and a Vassal of the Queen of the Fae.

Both of these come with salaries so large that I have no idea what to do with the money they give me beyond "stick it in a bank and try not to think about it."

These days, I wasn't even openly armed. One of the tricks I'd learned from the Wild Hunt was that not only could I step Between to travel from place to place, I could open a pocket of Between to store my gear.

"Wait, are you scared of heights?" Mary Tenerim asked me with a chuckle as I carefully stepped out of the elevator, trying to ignore the glass that made up much of the floor.

"There is a gap between being scared of heights and a quite reasonable fear of being, what is it, five hundred feet in the air with only *glass* between myself and the drop, isn't there?" I replied.

"It's stood up to a few million people, love," my petite redheaded girlfriend told me. "I'm sure it will survive our feet."

"That's *probably* true," I conceded, still gesturing for her to lead the way. Both of us had dressed up for the night in plain black suits cut for athletics. I towered over Mary, at just under six feet tall, with long brown hair neatly cut around my shoulders to help cover the fact that I had visibly pointed ears.

"Sir, ma'am," the hostess greeted us. "Do you have a reservation?"

"Under Kilkenny," I told her. "For two."

Mary had grabbed my hand as we approached the lectern and leaned against me. It had been...months since we'd had time for anything resembling a date. She helped run the shifter community in town, and I, well...

My job for the last six months had been to turn Calgary into a trap for the enemies of the High Court of the Fae. With myself as the bait.

The rest of that name I mentioned earlier? Jason Alexander Odysseus Kilkenny Calebrantson.

Mom was a mythology major and my father was dead before I was born.

He had also been Calebrant, the Horned King, the master of the Wild Hunt. His only son was target number one for the people who'd killed him.

DINNER LIVED up to the ambience and the price tag, even if the slowly rotating floor threw me more than a little bit. Calgary's downtown was

"Always a joy to see what happens next," I said brightly, toasting her with the glass of sweet dessert wine. "Together."

"You aren't getting rid of me soon, that's for sure," Mary told me. "At this point, I know how to get ahold of your boss."

"Which one?" I chuckled. As a Noble of the Wild Hunt, I answered to Ankaris, the new Horned King. As a Vassal of the Queen of the Fae, I owed Fealty to Mabona, the Queen of Light and Darkness.

"I have phone numbers for both of them," she said sweetly. Further joking was interrupted by the arrival of our waiter, and something about him caught both of our attention.

I felt more than saw his tension. Fae and shifters were predators, even more so than humans, and I could sense the prey instinct running behind his eyes. The young man's shoulders were tensed up and his hands were trembling.

I was about to ask if he was okay when he dropped a black leather folio, presumably our bill, on the table and vanished as quickly as he'd arrived. I exchanged a long look with Mary and opened the folio.

Somehow, I wasn't surprised that it wasn't our bill. It was a note, written on the restaurant's stationery.

If you wish to avoid unnecessary mortal deaths, come to the observation deck. Now.

"Short and to the point, I suppose," I said softly. I glanced over at the kitchen, where our waiter had disappeared. The restaurant was only about two-thirds full, but that was still over a hundred people. We'd come alone, though both of us had panic button apps on our phones that would bring support in a few minutes.

"The type of person who leaves a note like that doesn't have much patience," Mary noted. "Shall we?"

I pulled several hundred-dollar bills from my wallet and tossed them on the table—probably at least twice the cost of the meal, but I suspected the extra tip was going to be needed.

"Let's go see what our mysterious note-writer wants," I agreed. Half-consciously, I was checking my dimensional pocket.

Whipstock, a gift from the Wizard MacDonald that acted as a focus for my power. Check.

a brilliantly lit-up skyline in winter evenings, and the view was definitely worth the price of admission.

"How's Grandfather?" I asked Mary as the servers brought us
desserts and wine. Both of us were more than human and had the
metabolisms to go with it. Dessert was a requirement.

"According to him, his joints hate the cold more and more every
century," she replied.

Grandfather was Enli Tsuut'ina, the Speaker of the Shifter Clans in
Calgary, an old, *old* cougar shifter who'd been born in the region...
before Europeans had ever shown up and called it Canada.

"Has to be at least some downside to being him," I said. "Everyone
in line at last?"

The previous Speaker for the Clans had been Mary's own Alpha
Tarvers Tenerim. He'd died in the political nightmare that had
wrapped the city shortly after my arrival just over a year before. A year
wasn't long as supernaturals counted things, but it was *probably*
enough for the Clans to adjust to a new Speaker.

"Finally," she agreed. "He's taking a bit more of a direct approach
than Tarvers did. He didn't have much choice, not after Fontaine tried
to kill us all."

"And it's not like our side of the political spectrum has been nice
and calm," I admitted. The Fae Court and the Shifter Clans were the
two largest supernatural groups in Calgary, two of the three pillars
around which the supernatural community here orbited.

The fae had basically fought a civil war, related to my own
authority as Vassal of the Queen and the discovery of my parentage.
That had left two of the pillars of the community in flux, though the
seemingly permanent assignment of a troop of the Wild Hunt to me
was helping.

The third pillar was the Wizard Kenneth MacDonald, the demigod-
like Power generally regarded as the city's overall supernatural ruler.
He had his own problems, which meant that the community we both
served had been in a disrupted and dangerous state.

Stability was an ideal, never truly achievable, but we were getting
closer.

Silver-hilted sword with a cold iron blade, the standard weapon of a Rider of the Wild Hunt. Check.

Multiple firearms, ranging from a small nine-millimeter Jericho pistol to the Steyr AUG assault rifle favored by the Wild Hunt—and, not coincidentally, I was sure, by the Irish Army. Check.

Stepping out of the restaurant, Mary turned an eye on me and held out her hand. Chuckling, I pulled one of those firearms out of the pocket—the ugly little machine pistol she favored, already in its shoulder holster. She tucked it under her jacket then looked over at the stairs.

"Well?"

2

I WASN'T REALLY surprised to find the observation deck completely empty of civilians. Nor was I surprised to find it occupied by half a dozen armed men. I wasn't expecting them to be armed with strange curved swords to go with their AK-47s or, well, to not attack me on sight.

All six of the men could have been cast from the same mold. They were evenly six feet tall with dark hair and skin, wearing dark gray suits with big swords strapped to their backs. The hands holding the familiar assault rifles were all gloved as well.

The uniformity was odd…and also a sign that I was dealing with supernaturals of some kind. Just not a kind I was used to.

Before anyone could say anything, a seventh figure stepped out of the shadows. He was dressed similarly to his men but was shirtless under his gray blazer. His revealed physique was spectacular, with muscles on top of muscles…and traces of gold swirling across his dark skin.

He was the only one not carrying an assault rifle, but he held a long, curved sword in his hand. Wave-like patterns glittered in the steel, ringing a faint bell of memory, but my focus was on his brilliant white smile.

"Jason Kilkenny, Noble of the Wild Hunt," he greeted me with a thick but intelligible East Indian accent. "I am Raja Venkat Asi and I am tasked with your death."

"This is oddly formal for an assassination attempt, don't you think?" I asked dryly. I doubted the Indian supernatural was fooled by my lack of visible weaponry.

"There are standards to these things," he told me. "If possible, I wish to avoid unnecessary damage." He gestured to Mary. "The girl can leave freely."

"And if I shoot you in the head?" Mary asked, drawing her machine pistol from inside her coat.

Asi laughed.

"Then you become necessary extra damage," he told her. "I am charged with the death of Jason Kilkenny. I will do whatever is necessary to achieve that."

His men were spreading out, blocking the exits. I tested the links I was using for communication and was unsurprised to find them blocked. This Asi was far more prepared than his casual manner suggested.

"And you're, what, expecting me to kneel down so you can chop off my head?" I demanded.

"That would be such a disappointment," Asi said. "I've never fought a Noble of the Wild Hunt before." He lifted the sword and pointed it at me. "I will permit you to prepare. Draw your blade."

I sighed and gestured. Despite his instruction, I didn't bother with my sword. I had been training, but I wasn't going to pretend I was more than a mediocre swordsman.

Instead, I drew a sixteen-inch-long rod of black wood carved with golden orichalcum runes along its length. It looked like a whip handle without the whip—because that's exactly what it was.

I cracked the wooden stock through the air and conjured faerie fire through it. White-cored green flame snapped through the air between Asi and me, and the other man's grin widened.

"Let's dance."

THE GOLDEN TINGE to the other man's skin lit up as he moved towards me, a soft glow wrapping around him as he charged with a grace and speed no mortal could match. A golden aura wrapped around his hands and extended up over the blade of the sword.

He then proceeded to run into an invisible wall. A projection of my Gift of Force, the chest-high barrier stopped him in mid-step. He bounced backward but reacted quickly by leaping *over* my magical barrier.

My whip met him in midair, the green-and-white faerie flame smashing into the golden aura around him. The aura resisted my magic as I wrapped the whip around him and used it to fling him to the floor.

My whip didn't cut through him, which was a minor surprise, but he couldn't resist its force. He broke free as he hit the glass and bounced back up to his feet.

Grinning.

I hadn't even managed to singe his suit—though it wasn't like he'd even managed to reach me, either.

The sword flickered in front of him in a pattern even I could barely follow, generating a strange sigil of glowing light that then blasted toward me with unexpected speed.

I didn't manage to get a shield up in time, and the glowing symbol hit me like a runaway semi truck. I stumbled back, and a second sword-conjured symbol crashed through my hastily-raised shield.

I went flying and smashed into the glass wall of the observation deck. The lights of Calgary's downtown spread out beneath me, and a chill ran through me. Even a Fae Lord might not survive that fall—and for all of the powers I was still learning, I was still fragile compared to the more powerful fae.

I heard the glass crack beneath me and vaulted back into the main deck. My whip cracked across space. I wasn't aiming for Asi this time. I was aiming for his *sword*.

The Damascus-steel sword wasn't a mundane blade, even before the other supernatural wrapped it in his power. It still wasn't ready to get hit with the faerie fire of a Noble Fae, augmented by a Wizard-forged focus.

Asi's power managed to keep the blade intact. It didn't manage to keep it in his hand, and I flung the weapon away. It slammed into the window blade-first, embedding itself in the carefully designed security glass.

"You fight well," he complimented me. The golden glow around his hands was intensifying. "But the duel is for *my* pleasure. Your death is demanded by a higher call. *Take him.*"

That last was an order to his men, who had spent the last few seconds keeping Mary covered to help convince her not to intervene in the duel. Assault rifles spoke deafeningly in the enclosed space, but I was already moving.

A bubble of force shielded us as I dove for the ground next to Mary. She was raising her own weapon to fire back, but I grabbed her hand before she could object, and *stepped* into the Between, that strange frozen place beyond the world that some fae used to travel.

Among fae, the gift of traveling Between was one of the key markers for recruitment to the Wild Hunt. We wanted powerful fae, Nobles and Gentry and others with power to shake the world...but we *needed* the fae who could step Between and cross continents in mere minutes under their own power.

Few were those who could follow me Between, and I started to take a breath as Mary and I recovered from the stumble into otherness.

And then a golden portal began to take shape behind us.

"THEY'RE FOLLOWING US," I told Mary.

"Um. I thought no one could do that?" she asked.

"No one who isn't fae is supposed to be able to," I replied as I studied the golden light behind us for a few seconds. "It looks like it's taking them longer, but we should really be elsewhere."

"What if they can follow us?"

I grinned at her.

"We had a plan for rogue Hunters," I admitted. "If these guys, whoever they are, want to play on the Hunt's ground, they get to play by the Hunt's rules." I held out my free hand. "Trust me."

"I do," she confirmed as she took my hands. "I just still remember the terrified kid with no idea who he was that saved me in a dark alley a year ago. We've come a long way."

"And we need to keep going," I agreed. With both of her hands in mine, I closed my eyes and *moved*. My Power wrapped around us, sweeping us from the heights of the Calgary Tower to the ground in a moment.

The fact that we weren't in the "real" world helped. Distance Between wasn't exactly a logical thing.

"Yep. Glowing golden guys walking out of the doorway. Just who is hunting us, Jason?"

"I wish I knew," I said as I continued to move us through the strange otherness of Between. "Not fae, not shifters. I can recognize those. Nothing I've ever met before."

"I'm guessing that doesn't narrow it down much," she said, leaning against me as we moved.

"No." The only good thing was that I was relatively sure that, whoever they are, they couldn't catch us Between. They might be able to *follow* me Between, but that was my worst-case scenario.

I opened my eyes as we flew, looking back at the figures following us. They were faster than I was expecting—but still not fast enough to catch us by a long shot.

"We're fine," I said to Mary. "Want me to drop you off? They are chasing me, after all."

"What planet are you from, again?"

I snorted.

"This one," I agreed. "It was worth a shot." We came to a halt at a small glowing crystal beacon in the Between. "Grab that."

Hanging onto me with one hand, Mary scooped up the gem.

"What it this?"

"What it looks like. A beacon. Don't want to give our new friends the idea I went somewhere specific, though, do we?"

She snorted and was smiling at me as we *stepped* again, returning to the regular world.

"Seven guys chasing us," I announced to the dark room we

appeared in. "Not sure what the hell they are, but they glow gold and have AK-47s and swords of some kind."

"Glow gold?" an Irish-accented voice asked. "*Asura*?"

"Indian of some kind," I agree, vaguely recognizing the name as out of Hindu myth. "Not Hunters, but they're coming through after me."

"Well, get yourself out of the killing field, if you please," the voice of Damh Coleman, the commander of the Hunt troop assigned to me, continued. "I'd prefer not to accidentally shoot you, boss."

IT TOOK LONG ENOUGH for the asura to arrive that my eyes had adjusted to the darkness of the warehouse we'd set our trap in. It didn't take fae nearly as long to adjust as humans did, and we could adjust to far less light.

I don't know what the asura were expecting when they came out of Between after me, but I'm guessing it wasn't an even dozen assault rifles opening fire at point-blank range. Four of the gold-skinned attackers went down before they even knew they were under attack, and the other three never left the portal.

Raja Venkat Asi wasn't among the first wave and apparently had the sense to cut off a bad plan before it killed too many of his people. Damn it.

We waited for several minutes to see if any more of the asura followed, then Coleman snorted.

"All right, give me some light."

This warehouse was our space now, which meant that the lights had been tuned for a far dimmer default than most human spaces. It was more than enough for me to pick out the dozen men and woman lurking in the space.

Coleman himself was about as obviously Irish as anyone I'd ever met, a gaunt redheaded man who looked in his early forties. Of course, Coleman was a Rider of the Wild Hunt, a special type of fae Gentry with the immense physical capability of a Gentry *and* the ability to step Between.

He was clad in civilian clothes in a mix of dark green and black that basically *was* a uniform. The other seven Hunters of the half-troop deployed tonight wore different clothes in the same colors.

Three of Coleman's subordinates were "true" Hunters, fae of various levels with the ability to step Between. The other four were Companions. In another time, they would have been lesser fae or even mortals transformed into horses by powerful magics.

These days, "Rider" was more metaphorical and the Companions were volunteers, Gentry and fae, who made up roughly half of the Wild Hunt's numbers. These four were all Gentry, since Lord Ankaris had assigned a powerful troop to my command.

Ankaris was the Horned King, a member of the Fae High Court, the current master of the Wild Hunt...and, as it turned out, my cousin.

My other allegiance was shown in the other four fae in the room, a group of young women with liquid Welsh accents. Like myself, they were Vassals of the Queen of the Fae and sworn to Mabona's service.

All four were water nymphs, members of a pseudo-religious order dedicated to Mabona in Wales. They had an otherwordly attractiveness —that thankfully didn't work on most supernaturals unless specifically turned up to maximum—combined with inhuman grace and speed.

Like the Wild Hunt troop, they had been assigned to my protection. Part of the trap laid for the fae who would hunt me to undo my father's final spell. If they got their hands on me, they would once again be able to kill gods. If we got our hands on them, well, the long cleanup of that particular war would finally be over.

"Anyone injured?" Coleman demanded, looking around. Most of his attention was on Mary and me, though.

"We didn't stick around once they started shooting," I told him. "Asura, huh?"

He nodded, walking over to the four fallen attackers and checking for pulses.

"Damn. They're all gone. I was hoping for answers," he observed, then looked back at me. "AKs. Swords. Asura...it seems our masked friends decided to outsource. To the best."

The Masked Lords were the fae rebels who had killed my father.

They apparently possessed one of the ancient artifacts of the fae —*Esras*, the Spear of Lugh—and had used it to create a ritual that could kill even the Powers themselves.

Like my father, the previous Horned King, Calebrant.

Unfortunately for them, Calebrant had used his life's essence to bind *Esras* to his bloodline. Only two people in the world carried enough of Calebrant's blood to wield the spear now: Ankaris, the Horned King...and me.

I was many things now, but chief among them was bait. It looked like the Masked Lords had realized that, though.

"The best?" Mary asked.

"*Asi* Warriors," Coleman told us. "They're asura mercenaries—out of India, obviously. Some kind of ancient Hindu cult tied up around the supposed 'first true sword.'" The Hunter shook his head. "Asura are tough, but thankfully, they're as vulnerable to bullets as anyone."

I shook my own head, stepping over to stand next to him. We'd been expecting fae, so the guns had been loaded with cold iron.

"Cold iron wasn't needed, I take it."

"No, but armor-piercing rounds would have been if we weren't using cold iron," my subordinate told me. "Their skin is like elephant hide and they're fast and strong. The word translates as *demons*."

"So, they're hunting me because someone paid them?" I asked.

"Bingo. The Hunt knows them of old; we've clashed a few times over the years." Coleman sighed. "They don't give up easily, though they do *eventually* give up. No one has ever worked out what criteria they use for giving up on a contract, though."

"Because it almost never happens," one of the other Hunters pointed out. "We'll need to keep a closer watch on Lord Kilkenny. If the *Asi* are after him..."

"I'll keep that in mind," I promised. I wasn't the one running this show, after all.

Or so I kept telling myself, anyway.

3

ONCE, fae had traveled Between for discussions and meetings. We'd been more able to communicate than regular mortals had, but it still took time and arrangements and was a general pain.

Magically encrypted videoconferencing might seem strangely mundane for a gathering of powerful supernaturals, but it was definitely convenient.

"Asura," Lord Oberis, the master of Calgary's joint Fae Court, noted aloud. "I'll admit that I didn't expect the Masked Lords to hire mercenaries. They seem to have enough resources among our own people."

"But we were expecting our people," Ankaris replied. The leader of the Wild Hunt was one of the people on the big video screen in Oberis's office. "Most of our defenses were rigged around any attacker being fae, so…"

"So they worked around it," Mabona agreed. The Queen of the Fae was a tall and statuesque presence. Like Ankaris, she wasn't physically present. Unlike Ankaris, she had a projection of herself in the room instead of using conference software.

Probably to hide where she actually was. I could tell, for example, that Ankaris was in a castle of some kind. That meant he was almost certainly in Europe, probably in Ireland. Since Mabona was simply "there," there was no background to her image.

The fifth member of the impromptu conference was also linked in by videoconferencing, though he could have been there in person if he chose. The view behind the Wizard Kenneth MacDonald was of downtown Calgary, and Oberis and I were in the hotel that hosted the Fae Court, a western-themed "inn" along one of the city's main southern thoroughfares.

"Your plans and measures were a success nonetheless," MacDonald pointed out. "I am concerned that they entered the city without triggering any of *my* alerts. There are few who can circumvent the wards of a wizard."

"The Asi Warriors have a lot of practice," Ankaris told him. "I'm not even certain how long they've been around, but they are very good."

"There were Asi Warriors when I became queen," Mabona said. "They have always existed among the asura. Few of the asura or deva leave India, though." She snorted. "They can't travel far from their sacred rivers for long, to the benefit of the rest of us."

"They're about as physically powerful as Gentry," I said. "Plus some degree of protection and magical powers different than I've encountered before."

"Raja Asi and I have met," Mabona noted. "He's one of their senior strike leaders. Possibly the only one that operates outside of the subcontinent." She shook her head. "I met him in World War One, I should note. He is at least as old as I am."

"And I'm guessing good and uninclined to give up?" I asked. "At least they care enough to send the best."

"How do we get them to give up, short of killing them all?" Oberis asked. "I'm unenthused with foreign mercenaries in my city, people." He snorted. "At least, ones I didn't invite."

The Wild Hunt weren't the only strangers in town these days, after all.

"They've got some criteria on which they'll break contracts," my Queen replied. "I've heard of them doing it after losing a single warrior...and I've heard of them pursuing contracts for years and losing dozens before they finally brought down their target. We have to keep stopping them until they give up."

"*I* have to keep stopping them," I said, then sighed. "I'll be good, people. I'll keep my escorts with me. All I wanted was *one* private night."

The half-dozen other Vassals Mabona had sent now shared three apartments in my building. I didn't know where the Wild Hunt were staying, but there was usually at least one with me. Oberis himself had several Gentry assigned to a rotating guard duty around me, and his grand-nephew Robert, a Fae Noble, kept showing up at random times.

It was irritating and comforting at the same time.

"All it takes is one mistake, Jason," Ankaris told me. "You're a Noble of the Wild Hunt, yes, and less vulnerable than we once feared, but you are still the easiest target of Calebrant's blood. If the Masked Lords can take you, then the High Court itself is at risk."

"*Every* Power is at risk," MacDonald noted. "My enthusiasm for your rebels and their ritual is limited, Lord Ankaris, Queen Mabona. I will aid in defending this city, but I will be much relieved when your little civil war is *done*."

———

THE VIDEOCONFERENCE ENDED SHORTLY AFTERWARD, leaving me in the room with Oberis and the projection of my Queen. Mabona looked…unhappy.

"You need to be more aware," she snapped. "You are no longer alone, undetected by our enemies. So long as your blood will unlock the Spear of Lugh, the Masked Lords will hunt you. You are stronger than I dared hope—but you are still our weak point."

"I hate to pile on," Oberis said dryly, "but people look to you for leadership now. A troop of the Wild Hunt, a handful of our Queen's other Vassals, several of my own people… They may not owe you fealty, but you have been placed in command of them.

"Respect that authority or *they* will not."

I sighed and nodded. I wasn't used to being in charge of anyone except myself. My fealty to Mabona put me outside most ordinary chains of command in the fae world, so hierarchy and authority were not my strong points.

"I know," I admitted. "Not used to it. I don't like being surrounded by guards."

"*Get* used to it," Mabona told me. "I hated it at first myself, but I go nowhere without escorts now. Even for a Power, there are risks untold to this world. You are not a Power, yet you are hunted by people who have killed them."

She shook her head.

"We can protect you, Jason, but only so long as you are sensible about things. You must act for your own security as well…not undermine the security we have put in place."

"I *know*," I repeated. I was trying not to sound like I was whining, but from the way my Queen's eyes flashed, I failed.

"Impertinent child," she sighed. "We are supposed to be working together here, Jason, but you cannot ignore the fact that the linchpin of all of this is you."

"I have a team waiting for me outside," I reminded her. "Last night was a wake-up call I didn't expect to need. Things had been quiet for long enough that I thought *one evening* would be safe."

I shook my head.

"I was wrong. It won't happen again."

"We will find an end to this, Jason," Oberis promised me. "This cannot endure, my Queen. Not for him. Not for anyone else."

"*I* am not the one who controls that," Mabona told us. "Ankaris seeks the Masked Lords in other ways, but using Jason as bait remains our best route to victory. Assuming you don't get yourself killed."

"Believe me, my Queen, I have no intention of doing so!"

TO MY SURPRISE, Robert was waiting for me when I came out of the meeting. He was chatting up one of my water nymph bodyguards and, from her body language, was being more successful than many would have expected.

Robert was a slim and tall man with shoulder-length brown hair.

He and I could have passed for cousins, but there was something *more* to the other fae. And if Nobles weren't supposed to sleep around outside their own ranks, well, Robert was an example of both that rule being broken and why it wasn't necessarily a good rule.

The theory was that keeping the bloodlines "pure" would result in more Nobles. Someone like Robert, whose father was a Noble and whose late mother had been Gentry, usually didn't manifest the higher-tier powers.

In his case, though, trauma had required his father and me to work together to save his life. Surviving cold iron had awoken the young man's true gifts...which was *not* a trial I would recommend to anyone.

"So, are you doing another random checkup on me, specifically hitting on Kristal, or do I owe the pleasure of your presence to something else?" I asked Robert as I reached him.

He blushed, *hard*. Kristal Sayer, to her credit, just laughed—and then tucked a piece of paper I presumed to be the petite raven-haired woman's temporary Canadian phone number into Robert's shirt pocket.

Robert coughed again and shrugged helplessly at me.

"I was actually looking for you," he told me. "My father is in town. He wanted to meet with you."

Talus was the senior Noble of Oberis's Court, which meant he spent most of his time in Fort McMurray. Thankfully unknown to the humans, one of the by-products of their oilsands extraction processes was a material called heartstone. Mixed with other materials, it became key components of all kinds of magical materials.

The runes carved into my Wizard-forged whipstock were made of it mixed with gold. The small vial of what was effectively a powerful fae combat drug hanging around my neck was heartstone and mercury. Mixed with silver, it was bane—a deadly weapon against shifters like Mary.

Calgary's various supernatural communities all had exclaves in Fort McMurray that controlled its production and distribution, and Talus led the fae team there. It kept him busy.

"I can make time for Talus," I told Robert. "I need to go home and touch base with Mary before she heads to work herself, but I'm free after that."

"He said to tell you to meet him for a late lunch at the steakhouse," the youth replied. "Two PM? I'll be there as well. Mary's invited if she's free, I think this is mostly social."

Nothing was *entirely* social when you were a Fae Noble. I was still getting used to the fact that that category included me now.

"I'll check with her," I promised. "I'll definitely be there. Kristal?"

"Car is waiting out front; Riley's with it," she told me. "Hitting the road?"

4

AN EIGHT O'CLOCK meeting in Calgary was a midafternoon meeting in Ireland—and I didn't pretend to know where Mabona was hiding out. If I focused, I could use our blood bond to locate her, but if I didn't *know* where she was, I couldn't betray where she was.

Since the supernatural community only approximately runs on the same time frames as the human world, Mary hadn't left the apartment yet by the time I returned. She was dressed in a crisp black business suit—with the distinctive cut I recognized now of a suit designed to go over guns and body armor—and smiled as she saw me.

"Wasn't sure how long your meeting was going to take," she said after we embraced. "I'm heading out to the office soon enough, but I have time. What's up?"

"I'm missing a few strips of skin," I told her. It was probably well deserved, if I was going to admit it, too. "We should never have been caught unescorted like that. *I* should know better."

"I have a text from Grandfather in much that vein, yes," she admitted. "We made more of a show than anyone likes, too."

I winced. I hadn't even thought of it, but we'd cracked up the observation deck even *before* the asura had opened fire with assault rifles.

"How bad?" I asked. "Cleanup didn't get mentioned in my meeting."

"I don't know details, but if no one talked your ear off, I'd guess it was handled," she told me. "Gunfire in the Calgary Tower, though? We're lucky they shooed everyone out before giving you that note."

"The asura don't want to blow the big secret anymore than anyone else does," I said. "We all find being invisible *much* preferable to the alternatives."

"That we do." Mary tucked herself into my shoulder. "I imagine Grandfather will dump as much of the cleanup on me as he can," she noted. "That's his style."

"That it is," I agreed. "If you can break free for a late lunch, I'm meeting Talus at his steakhouse at two. Not *officially* business."

She snorted.

"What, two Nobles in the meeting?"

"Three. Robert will be there," I admitted.

"So, it's business and you need the girls to play cover," Mary replied.

"He didn't *say* Shelly was going to be there," I said. "But I'm guessing she will be."

Shelly Fairchild was Talus's mortal lawyer and girlfriend. The noble certainly hadn't learned any greater ability to follow the rules of his station in romance since Robert's birth.

"I *also* want your point of view on whatever he's bringing up," I told her. "You still know Calgary a dozen times better than I do, *plus* you grew up outside the mundane world. I didn't."

"Stop trying to make me feel better," she snapped, breaking our embrace and stepping back.

I paused, considering her for several seconds.

"I'm sorry," I ventured. That seemed like a good starting point. "I wasn't trying to make you feel better; I was telling you why I wanted you there."

She inhaled and then nodded sharply.

"Fair," she said in a rush. "Sorry. Just feeling twitchy after last night. The kind of enemies you've acquired, Jason... I don't feel like

I'm in my weight class anymore. I'm just a wildcat shifter. I worry that I'm putting you in danger."

"I think the evidence goes in the other direction," I reminded her. "Your enemies, after all, didn't just break up our first date in weeks. Those guys were after me." I paused. "If you want to...protect yourself, I'll back you..."

I was pretty sure what I was saying, even if it hurt. If Mary didn't think it was safe to be with me anymore, then...well, I'd do everything in my power to make our separation painless.

"And if I want to protect *you*?" she demanded.

"How much cold iron is in the gun you're carrying?" I asked pointedly.

"Triple-kill rounds," she said slowly. "Cold iron, rock salt and silver."

"I don't need you to be my bodyguard, Mary," I told her. "I need you to be my partner, my second set of eyes—the person with a brain, because Powers know I'm not sure I have one some days!"

She chuckled. It was a somewhat forced thing, but I thought I'd made my point.

"I know what you mean, though I think you do better than that *most* days," she allowed, then checked the time. "I've got to get going. I'll make lunch unless I can't; will text you either way."

Mary went from stiff and angry at me to kissing me goodbye in her usual tempestuous whirlwind.

Living with a wildcat was an experience, that was for sure.

———

Two o'clock rolled around surprisingly quickly, and my current cavalcade arrived at the restaurant Talus owned. Technically, it was part of a chain and Talus didn't own the restaurant itself.

Technically. I don't think anyone was under the illusion that Talus's various tentacles stretched throughout the business didn't give him control. Certainly, he always had a private room in the restaurant, and the staff ushered my party into it.

Kristal and Riley were today's guard contingent, a Welsh water nymph Vassal of the Queen and a Hunter Gentry from somewhere in Scotland. Neither was visibly armed, but then, neither was I.

Mary was already waiting for me and gave me a quick kiss as she indicated a chair by her for me.

"It's getting crowded in here," Talus observed behind me. "I forgot that everyone comes with bodyguards these days."

I hadn't actually *noticed* the werewolf standing unobtrusively in the corner. Barry and I went back a long way, by my standards. The big dark-haired shifter was one of Clan Tenerim's enforcers, and part of his duties had always involved protecting the Clan's "little sister."

With Mary's involvement in the Speaker's administration, that role had apparently become more full-time.

Talus himself was escorted by his son and his girlfriend-slash-lawyer. It wasn't so much a bodyguard business, in Robert's case, as a "watch each other's backs" business. Talus was more powerful than his son, but that was by criteria that only mattered amongst Nobles.

Those criteria were confused by me. By some standards, I didn't even qualify as a Noble. By others, I was actually more powerful than Talus himself. Seventy-odd years of experience made up any effective difference, though.

Talus was more clearly Oberis's nephew than Robert was Talus's son. He was taller than Robert, with long blond hair and golden eyes. There was a lithe, unconscious grace to him that even I was inclined to term as *fey*, a grace that Robert and I were still decades away from mastering.

"Kristal, Riley," Talus continued with a nod to my two escorts before turning to Mary's. "Barry Tenerim.

"You are all welcome here, of course. Realize, however, that we speak of the business of blood and Fealty. Betraying our confidence today would have dire consequences. If you are bound by oath or other fealty to pass on what you hear, I suggest you have lunch in the main restaurant."

He smiled with the easy charisma of a man who has commanded others for most of a ninety-year life span.

"We know that loyalties are easily divided. It will not be held against you."

The room was silent for long seconds, then Barry Tenerim chuckled.

"I don't know about fae, but shifter oaths don't work like that," he reminded us. "I am tasked with Mary's security. That includes her secrets and confidences, or I'd make a shitty protector."

"My Fealty is to the Queen, but while Master Tenerim has phrased it differently than I would, I agree with his point," Kristal added.

Riley took up a solid leaning post against the wall, the Gentry surveying the room with a sardonic expression.

"Hunters don't have Fealty," he told us. "We have chain of command. And my chain of command says I work for Jason Kilkenny, which means what he wants killed gets killed. What he wants kept secret stays secret."

Talus laughed.

"All right. Then I'll have more chairs brought in," he told the bodyguards. "I have no intention of making anyone stand while we chatter on."

———

THE STAFF at the restaurant knew the nature of the meals and attached meetings that took place in Talus's private room. They took our orders, brought us drinks and then completely disappeared to allow us to talk in privacy.

"How is your elevation to the nobility treating you?" Talus asked as he swirled the wine in his glass. "You've come a long way from the changeling who showed up on a bus without a penny to his name."

"I had at *least* five dollars to my name, I'll have you know," I replied with a chuckle. "It's taking some adjustment; you're right. I had some time to get used to people listening to me when I was working as Mabona's arbitrator here in Calgary, but being in *command* is still new to me."

"How about being bait?" he continued.

I sighed.

"That...that I could live without," I admitted. "It's been almost six months. Somewhere out there, there is an entire conspiracy of Fae

Lords that want my blood. Literally. Somewhere *else* out there, there is a Pouka Noble who wants me dead."

I shook my head.

"This isn't exactly heartwarming, though the friends and allies that have gathered around to help me definitely *are*." I made a toasting gesture with my Coke as my pair of bodyguards chuckled.

Kristal, I noted, was making *very* intentional eye contact with Robert. The young Noble didn't appear to be certain what was going on, but he wasn't objecting, either.

To be fair, I'm not sure *I'd* have known what was going on in his place. Mary's approach to flirting was best described as "apply gold brick wrapped in sock to idiot male's head."

It was easier to pick up when it was directed at someone else.

"We do what we can," Talus told me. "Which brings me to a point that I want to keep very quiet."

I straightened, eyeing him.

"I can get you out," he said softly. "We have a few tricks that can shield your signature, make you impossible for the Masked Lords to track. You'd probably have to go hide in a mortal life somewhere, but I could make sure you and Mary were set up for at least a mortal lifetime down in the Caribbean or some such."

"I volunteered for this, Talus," I reminded him. "I'm not trying to run."

I reached for Mary's hand and squeezed it under the table.

"Mary?" I asked. "*I'm* in this fight for the long haul, but…"

She squeezed my hand back…and kicked me gently.

"I have no intention of being your mistress, put up in a beachside apartment somewhere safe and protected," Mary said sweetly. "I'm here, and I'm staying."

I snorted and arched an eyebrow at Talus.

"You didn't actually expect me to take you up on that, did you?"

"I wanted to be sure you knew the option was on the table," my friend replied. "It's easy to agree to fighting a war when you're talking to members of the High Court—and you think it's going to be quick. Six months of waiting for them to strike wasn't what you signed on for."

"I won't let my father's killers escape justice," I said quietly. "And even if I was willing to let that happen, the Masked Lords have already caused enough damn trouble. If I can lure them in and stop that, I will. I owe that to the fae. To our people."

Talus saluted me with his wine glass.

"Good," he told me. "But remember that the option is there. I have the resources to make you and Mary disappear. So long as I'm still breathing, Shelly and I can smuggle you to safety."

I glanced at my bodyguards. They looked surprisingly unbothered by this entire discussion about me abandoning my oaths and duties. Fae were…mercurial, I suppose.

"That's not all you wanted to talk to me about," I guessed.

"No," he agreed. "I was approached, back in the fall, by several unknown parties. There was an extended period of feeling each other out, as they were testing me and I was testing them."

He smirked.

"Or playing them, as the case may be. I suspected from quite early on who I was dealing with."

"The Masked Lords," Mary guessed.

"Give the werecat a prize," Talus agreed. "I wanted to know what they were up to. They wanted to know what my price was. They guessed wrong."

"Your price for what? Becoming a Masked Lord?" I asked.

"No. I don't think they thought that was ever a possibility." Talus leaned back, sipping his wine as he studied me. "They were smart enough not to offer me Calgary, either. They knew I'd never turn on my uncle.

"They wanted me to deliver you, Jason. In exchange, they offered me overlordship of North America's Seelie Fae. All of them."

I whistled silently. There was no such role, which meant that the Masked Lords were continuing their plans to completely rebuild fae society to their vision. An idealized vision of the world before the High Court.

"They're mad." I barely realized I'd spoken.

"They're powerful and they want more power," Talus replied. "They don't want to be bound by the High Court anymore. They want to decide what Covenants and oaths they follow, not be bound by fealty to the race."

"That way lies chaos and the breach of the Covenants of Silence," Mary objected. "We can't hold together a global supernatural community if one faction goes off on their course."

"Exactly," Shelly agreed. "That's what I told Talus after he told me. Speaking as one of the mortals who help keep that particular Covenant..." She shook her head.

"I don't know what would happen if humanity found out what was hiding behind the curtain," she admitted. "I'd like to think we could adapt, that humanity would just absorb you as another branch of themselves, but..."

"Racism gets ugly enough when all that's involved is skin color," I said bluntly. "What do you think is going to happen when they realize some people can conjure fire and break walls with their bare hands?"

The silence that followed was long enough that the arrival of lunch interrupted further conversation.

We all knew that the world the Masked Lords wanted would be doomed from the moment they took power. The Covenants between the races existed for a reason, after all.

5

ARBITRATION. Mediation. Facilitation.

Whatever label you wanted to hang on it, it was a large chunk of the job I actually did for Mabona when I wasn't being bait. Since I owed Fealty directly to a member of the High Court, I was neutral in affairs between the various lower courts.

I went straight from the lunch with Talus to my scheduled meeting. Four fae were waiting for me in the rented conference room in downtown Calgary, *very* clearly divided into two different groups.

Two Seelie, two Unseelie. All from Vancouver. The Seelie had sent a pair of Gentry. The Unseelie had sent one of their Gentry and a hag.

The hag was using a glamor to make herself look just as perfect and gorgeous as the Gentry. She'd probably have been quite upset to realize I could identify types of fae at a glance. The same with most other supernaturals, too.

I'd once thought all fae could do that. I'd once been very uninformed.

All of them rose as I entered. My two shadows took up residence on either side of the door and I looked around the room.

"I presume this room has a security camera?" I asked.

"It's suffered a strange mechanical failure," the older of the Seelie

Gentry told me with a grin. "I believe our Unseelie…acquaintances brought a white-noise generator?"

The hag snorted—but produced what looked like a glorified iPod and laid it on the table. It began emitting a frankly irritating noise that would render our conversation unintelligible to any recording devices.

"All right," I said, then pulled the silver-hilted sword of a member of the Wild Hunt out of thin air. Four sets of eyes focused on the weapon as I laid it in the center of the table to make sure I had their attention.

"Your Courts have appealed to Mabona for arbitration in a deal gone sour," I stated aloud. Powers that are, my job was surprisingly mundane for all of the strange and fey politics wrapped around it. "I've reviewed the documentation you provided, but why don't you summarize your positions for me."

All four of them started talking at once and I let them continue for several seconds before giving in to the melodramatic urges that ran in every fae's blood.

An invisible telekinetic hand *slapped* the table, almost loud enough to sound like a gunshot. All of them were suddenly quiet and I smiled.

This wasn't a job I'd have chosen for myself, but I was turning out to be surprisingly good at it.

"You." I pointed at the Unseelie hag. "The Unseelie Court's position. Quickly and concisely, if you please."

I had no illusions about any fae's ability to go on and on *and on* about politics if given the chance.

"Both our Courts partnered to create a joint venture three years ago," she told me calmly. "The intent was to use our position in Vancouver to assist Chinese supernaturals in acquiring property despite the mundane government's rules on foreign property purchases.

"It went well, but the fae managing the venture turned out to be both doing deals on the side, using our resources without including our fee, and skimming off the top when doing deals openly.

"Two months ago, this was uncovered and he fled. We have established the total loss and it can be borne by the joint venture. That, as far as we are concerned, is the end of the situation beyond continuing to locate Vadim Argyll."

I was impressed. She'd managed to sum up the situation in under two minutes and done so firmly enough that the Seelie hadn't managed to interrupt her. I'd been expecting to have to shut the other party up to let her finish.

"Okay." I pointed at the older Seelie Gentry. "And what part of this is the Seelie Court up in arms about, again?"

"What Ms. Ornat Clarkson is not mentioning," the Seelie told me, "is that Vadim Argyll is an Unseelie Noble. Her summary of the basic events is fundamentally correct, but we have grounds to believe that Argyll was working with the full knowledge and support of the Unseelie Court, and that the money he stole was being funneled back to Lord Sherburn."

Of course. Why blame one person when you can blame an entire Court, after all?

"Since the Unseelie Court was involved in Argyll's theft, Lady Belrose believes that Sherburn's Court should compensate us for our portion of the losses incurred."

"And as my Lord has told your Court, Ocean Woodrow, that is unacceptable," the hag snarled. "We are equally wronged here, and you would have us be wounded twice!"

I raised a hand to stave off the argument before it could continue. Once again, they listened to my silent command and calmed down. Or, well, at least quieted down.

Sooner or later, I might get used to that. Maybe.

"I have reviewed the files you both sent," I pointed out. "It's an interesting tangle. Despite being an Unseelie, Argyll was recommended by Lady Belrose to lead the joint venture. That is correct, yes?"

Woodrow nodded sharply.

"We were the ones driving the setup, but we needed the Unseelie's people and money," he admitted. "By recommending an Unseelie chief officer, we knew we'd get Lord Sherburn on side. We didn't expect him to rob us!"

"I should note, Mr. Woodrow, that I have a significantly greater degree of access to the Vancouver Unseelie Court's finances than you do," I told him quietly. "One of my requests when this file arrived on my desk was that a Covenant-bound neutral auditor review Lord Sherburn's files."

In this case, that had meant borrowing people from the accounting firm used by Vancouver's shifter population. They'd been inside the Covenants of Silence but not involved in fae politics.

"So?" Woodrow demanded.

"Lord Sherburn agreed to that review *immediately*," I said. "It was clear in my communication with him that I was requesting an unusual degree of transparency on his part but that he valued peace with Lady Belrose above the usual privacies of a fae court."

I shook my head at the Seelie before he could try to interrupt.

"There is no evidence that Lord Sherburn or his people received any of the money that Vadim Argyll stole."

Woodrow looked rebellious but then sighed.

"Would we be able to see the auditors' high-level report, at least?" he asked.

"Lord Sherburn has agreed to provide a copy to Lady Belrose," I told him. "However, before anyone starts cheering…" I turned back to Clarkson with a grim smile.

"Regardless of Lord Sherburn and his Court's knowledge or benefit from Argyll's actions, the fact remains that he was Lord Sherburn's man. Argyll is of your Court and bound by Fealty, which leaves Sherburn with a responsibility for his actions and his crimes."

Now I had everyone's attention.

"It is not equitable to demand that Lord Sherburn bear the full responsibility for a theft he did not benefit from," I noted. "It is *also*, however, true that Sherburn and his Court do bear some responsibility for Argyll's actions."

Of course, along with everyone's *attention* came everyone's rebellious glares, and I smiled at them.

"My *suggestion* is that Lord Sherburn compensate Lady Belrose for half of the Seelie Court's portion of the loss," I concluded. Technically, after all, this wasn't a binding arbitration.

Of course, refusing the suggestions of the Queen's Vassal tended to result in pointed commentary from the Queen herself. No one wanted to be on the receiving end of Mabona being sarcastic.

"I also suggest that both Courts combine their information on Argyll's activities and see if they can track him down," I told them. "If the funds can be retrieved from Argyll, then they should be distributed as per the new ratio applied to the losses.

"Does this seem reasonable?"

They didn't really have a choice, but both Woodrow and Clarkson seemed relatively mollified. My job wasn't to make everyone happy… my job was to make sure no one was going to go to war. Minimizing the dissatisfaction was useful, but *satisfying* everyone wasn't required.

"I will consult with my lord," Clarkson told me. "But I believe that should be acceptable."

"I will speak with my lady as well," Woodrow agreed. "It should suffice."

"Thank you for being reasonable," I replied. "It's always a pleasure for these conversations to be so straightforward."

Clarkson chuckled at that, but I wasn't entirely joking. It wasn't often that "split the difference" was actually the right solution.

I was about to close out the meeting when my cold iron sense exploded. I could feel our kind's ancient bane at any distance less than about ten meters—there was no way it was suddenly five feet from me.

The second Seelie Gentry had just dropped a bag on the table and opened it. It was linked to a pocket of Between…and it held a cold iron–laced bomb!

———

I'D LIKED it a lot better when my abilities were a surprise to my enemies. They'd tended to be a surprise to me at the time as well, but using an enchanted bag to sneak a cold iron bomb up to me wasn't something the Masked Lords would have done if they didn't *know* I was an Iron Seeker—though it had also got the weapon past my body-guards outside.

"Down!" I bellowed, force flashing out from my hand as I tried to close the bag. Everyone was staring at me as I moved and I threw out force with my other hand.

Clarkson, especially, could have stopped me if she'd been prepared. The Gentry could probably have resisted my power, too. I was rushing —but I was rushing with enough power to send everyone around the table crumpling to the floor as I failed to close the bag.

Against almost any other device, I could have used my Gift of Force to block the explosion. Cold iron, however, would go right through any force field I raised. What I *could* do, though, was hold something *else* in place.

Like a table that wouldn't normally stop an explosion on its own. I started to flip the conference table into the air, sending the bomb sliding away from me.

And then the bomb went off with the table mere centimeters into the air. I kept it moving, absorbing the force of the bomb as it went off, holding the table together against the iron hammering into it with the force of my will.

I was fast enough. Somehow, I got the table rotated under the exploding bomb to use it as a reinforced barrier to stop the cold iron shrapnel. Some debris still scythed around the room, and Clarkson's Gentry companion went down.

But he looked like he'd live. The bomb had failed…and now I had a *bomber* to deal with. I was turning toward the Seelie Gentry when an unfamiliar popping sound echoed through the room.

Repeatedly.

And three tranquilizer darts materialized in my throat and chest.

"Nobody move, please," the young Gentry said calmly as I staggered. He studied me for a moment, then fired a fourth tranquilizer dart into me.

They weren't succeeding in knocking me out, but they *were* doing a damn good job of disabling my powers and my ability to think as I stumbled, half-paralyzed.

"I don't want to hurt anyone else. I'm here for Kilk—"

Everyone in the room had forgotten my sword. It had slid off the table when I'd reacted and skidded across the floor—landing by Ocean Woodrow's feet.

Even fae tended to forget how fast Gentry were. Woodrow kicked the sword up into his hand as his friend started speaking and was across the room in the time it took to start saying my name.

The tranquilizer pistol went flying and the Gentry dodged backward. He was going for another weapon…but he never made it.

Ocean Woodrow cut off his head with a single blow.

6

THE RENTED conference room was very, very quiet.

"I need to call Eric," I said softly as I looked at the wrecked table, the wounded Unseelie and the dead Seelie. The tranquilizers were already fading from my system, but everything was still a bit foggy. "We need a cleanup team and a doctor."

Clarkson was already at her companion's side. The glamor that made her look young and beautiful was fading, revealing the natural appearance of a hag—that of a woman in her late eighties, withered and worn with years the fae hadn't necessarily experienced.

From the glow around her hands, she was one of the roughly half of all hags with healing magic. Her companion was in good hands, but a doctor wouldn't hurt.

"You do that," Woodrow told me. He laid my sword on one of the chairs. "I apologize for borrowing your sword, Master Kilkenny. I know it is a...touchy matter for the Wild Hunt."

"It is," I agreed. "But seeing as how you just *saved my life*, I think the only response I have is 'You're welcome for the loan.'"

That got a small forced smile out of the Seelie as I reclaimed my sword and returned it to my dimensional storage unit. As I did so, I was pulling out my phone and dialing Eric, the city's Keeper.

The Keeper was in charge of the neutral ground amongst fae, the Manor. He stood outside the Court politics and was, therefore, in charge of the small group of professionals tasked with making sure that the Covenants of Silence were kept.

"Eric, it's Jason," I said quietly. "I need backup at my meeting. Someone just tried to bomb us and drag me off to the Masked Lords."

The gnome on the other end of the line was silent for several seconds.

"Well, fuck," he said bluntly. "I can have people there in about thirty minutes. Can you cover that long?"

"We'd already screwed any video or audio recordings, and I *think* the room is soundproofed enough to cover the bomb," I told him. "I'll talk fast if anyone has questions, but the room is booked for another three hours."

"On our way."

Eric hung up on me and I turned my attention back to Ocean Woodrow. He was kneeling over the other Seelie Gentry's body, gently patting at the dead man's clothes as if to sort out the inevitable mess.

"Are you okay?" I asked.

"I've known Harrison Avery for longer than you've been alive, Master Kilkenny," Woodrow said very quietly. "We weren't close, but I'd have called us friends for over two decades. I...would never have thought he'd turn on me like that. What the *hell*?"

"I have powerful enemies," I told Woodrow. "Their reach is long and their resources are vast. I won't say every man has his price...but it seems my enemies found Avery's."

Woodrow inhaled sharply and nodded.

"We'll need to bring his body back to Vancouver," he said. "I will need to inform Lady Belrose of his actions and his fate." Fae or not, he was on the verge of shock. "This was..."

"This is civil war," I said. "It's messy and ugly and I hate it, Mr. Woodrow. We'll find the people behind this. They'll pay. I promise you that."

He nodded grimly and looked back up at me.

"I'll hold you to that, Master Kilkenny."

———

ERIC VON RADACH, Keeper of Calgary's Manor, was a gnome. Roughly three and a half feet tall even in platform shoes, thick white hair, recessed eyes and a hooked nose made him one of the fae who found moving around mortal society somewhat difficult.

Despite that, he arrived with the cleanup team himself. They were all casually dressed, nothing to draw attention to the half-dozen fae as they swept into the conference room. The apparent leader of the team, a tired-looking older man with a faint green tinge to his skin, studied the space for several long seconds, then gestured.

The glamor the dryad conjured recreated the room as it had existed before we'd entered. It didn't replace anything that was lost, but it gave the team a solid idea of where things needed to go back to.

"Nothing ever goes smoothly with you around, does it?" Eric asked me calmly as he studied the room. "Davies, the table's a write-off. Get a model number from the wreck if you can and text it to Langdon. We *should* have something he can make look right."

I shook my head.

"I had the whole arbitration handled, a relatively agreeable solution decided—and then someone working for the Masked Lords pulls a cold iron bomb out of a Between pocket."

The gnome grunted. He opened a pocket similar to the one Harrison Avery had just accessed, and pulled out a chair that matched the ones wrecked in the meeting room.

"How many chairs, Davies?" he asked.

"Three are repairable here," the dryad replied, watching two of his subordinates do just that. "The other five are wrecks."

"All right," Eric said. A gesture opened his pocket wider. "Toss the wrecks in there while I work on seeing what Langdon can pull together. There were only two in the warehouse."

It had taken me weeks to learn to create a pocket of Between I could store my gear in. Gnomes did it instinctively and could do far more complicated things than I could. They could, for example, create a shared warehouse that Langdon, one of Calgary's other gnomes, could stock with whatever furniture the cleanup team needed.

A gnome could also create a pocket someone else could access.

"I guess it's not a surprise that the Masked Lords have at least one gnome," I said quietly. "Andrell had gnome-forged arms, after all."

"They're the leaders and right hands of courts across the world," Eric pointed out. "If Oberis asked me to make him a portable pocket, I wouldn't ask him what it was for." He snorted. "Well, I might now. It's been a messy year."

"You've got this under control?" I asked, watching the team go through the room with practiced efficiency.

"Completely," he confirmed as he checked his text messages. "Just waiting on Langdon to find the right table. We'll have the place looking like nothing happened in twenty minutes. When do you have to give it back?"

"A bit over two hours now. You have time," I said. "Eric...what do we do?"

"You volunteered as bait, kid," Eric pointed out. "This is what that looks like. The Masks won't be coming at you with an army from the front, not unless they run out of other ideas. Mercs and bombers? That seems about what I was expecting."

"Wonderful." I shook my head. "I'll have to check in on people. Let me know if you find anything unusual in the clean-up."

"Will do," the Keeper told me. "The real clues, though, will be back in Vancouver. I'd put a bug in Lady Belrose's ear, if I were you."

I sighed and nodded. My job required me to arbitrate between Fae Lords. That didn't mean they weren't still terrifying to me.

"LADY BELROSE," I greeted the Fae Lord who ran Vancouver's Court as politely as possible. I was hoping it was easier to avoid giving offense over a phone call than in person. My experiences with Fae Lords were mixed, after all.

"This is Jason Kilkenny."

"I know who you are," she said sharply. "Your decision should be carried to me by my representatives. What is the purpose of this contact?"

"Harrison Avery attempted to murder everyone at the meeting," I told her flatly. If she wanted to cut the Gordian knot of fae conversation, well, two of us could do that.

There were several seconds of silence.

"That is impossible. Avery is one of my longest-serving retainers. What *happened*?"

"He pulled a cold iron bomb after I'd laid out my decision," I told her. "He'd concealed it Between and was probably relying on my iron sense to preserve me, since he was apparently tasked to deliver me to the Masked Lords."

"The Masked Lords," she repeated. "They're gone, Kilkenny. Calebrant defeated them."

"Oh, I wish," I sighed. "Calebrant defeated them, yes, but they have merely regrouped. Lord Andrell was one of them. I presumed you had been briefed on that."

The call was silent.

"I do not necessarily, Master Kilkenny, assume everything that the High Court says is true," she warned me. "The Masked Lords are a bogeyman that has been used to justify a thousand sins over the last few decades. Why should I regard this as any different?"

"Ask Woodrow," I replied. "Then see if you can find out how they got to Avery. Right now, Lady Belrose, I would worry about the security of your Court, not conspiracies in the High Court."

"You are extraordinarily naïve, young Noble," she told me with a chuckle. "From that alone, I think I can believe you for now. I will investigate our Avery. I will learn who turned one of my most loyal servants against a Vassal of our Queen.

"But I do this for my own reasons, Kilkenny. Don't expect updates."

The call cut off before I could say anything more and I sighed. If nothing else, the Vancouver Court probably wasn't going to be a source of future threats. Even if Belrose was a Masked Lord herself, Avery's actions had embarrassed her.

And the *last* thing Fae Lords tolerated was being embarrassed.

7

I WAS HOME EVEN LATER than usual, trading off bodyguard teams when I left the conference room that had become a battlefield. The inevitable cascade follow-on from that occupied my entire afternoon and evening, and it was easily past eleven by the time I arrived at my apartment building.

"You guys go check in with the rest of the team," I told my passengers and escorts. "I don't think I'm going to get jumped between the parking lot and my apartment."

"You realize that just by *saying* that, you made sure we have to escort you?" Isaac MacAlister told me. The dark-haired Scot Hunter was grinning as he said it...but he was also entirely serious.

"Fine," I told him. "Send Alissa up to check in and you can walk me to my apartment door. If you insist, MacAlister."

The bodyguards chuckled...but Alissa Perry headed upstairs and MacAlister fell in beside me as I headed down into the basement.

My Queen had called my apartment "a hole in the ground" to my face once, and she wasn't entirely wrong. It was the end unit in the building's basement, down a set of stairs and along a windowless corridor.

No monsters jumped from the shadows to ambush us and MacAlister left me at my door with a grin and a slight bow.

I wasn't sure what my neighbors thought of my stream of assorted gorgeous men and women escorts. If they didn't know I lived with Mary, they probably thought *I* was an escort or something.

I shook my head as I stepped into the apartment, opening the door quietly in the hope of not waking Mary if she was still up.

"I'm in the kitchen," she greeted me. "I only got home half an hour ago myself. Can we go *one* day without kicking up a crisis?"

I stepped around the corner into our tiny kitchen to find that she'd brewed up an entire pot of hot chocolate and was already pouring me a mug.

I was an extraordinarily lucky man.

"To be fair, we had a couple of months with nothing major," I said as I took the cup. "You're incredible, you know that?"

"Yup," she agreed. "Most of today's bullshit wasn't even your fault. Cleanup on the asura attack, yeah, but also soothing tensions over a nine-way fistfight at the Lodge."

The shifters' Lodge was equivalent to the fae's Manor, neutral ground between Clans. Fistfights weren't supposed to happen there—and Calgary only *had* nine shifter Clans.

"That messy, huh?"

"Yeah." She shook her head. "Apparently, a couple of grudges dating back to this time *last* year and the mess around Tarvers's death, plus the usual alpha-male bullshit over girls. Shifters were bad enough on that garbage *before* pop culture gave them an excuse!"

"And they say the fae are the ones with melodrama for blood," I said with a chuckle.

"Hey, our guys at least just had a knock-down fistfight that everyone walked away from," Mary told me. "You guys would have had a formal duel with seconds and swords!"

I made a vague handwavy gesture.

"Or a back-alley knife fight," I replied. "Could go either way."

Hanging onto my hot chocolate with one hand, I began massaging her neck with the other. "Everything got sorted, though?"

"Yeah. And *then* someone told me that someone tried to blow up my boyfriend. You okay?"

"Yeah," I echoed. "The Masked Lords are finding a lot of ways to come at us sideways. We've got a hell of a trap laid out here for them, but if they don't walk into it, we're going to have to think of another plan.

"Almost wish my enemies would just...come at me head-on."

I should have known better than to say anything like that.

———

THE FIRST EXPLOSION knocked my hot chocolate from my hand. It hit the floor and shattered, but that mess was irrelevant as a second and third explosion rocked the apartment building. Part of the *ground* around our living-room window, a relatively thin gap at the top of the wall, disintegrated through the wall as the explosives pulverized the concrete structure of our basement.

The screaming started even before the third explosion, and Mary and I were already running. I could smell the fire starting, too.

"At least one incendiary charge, multiple demolition charges," she reeled off as we dodged our neighbors. Then she grabbed my shoulder before I could charge up the stairs. "Jason, the main entrance is on fire."

I caught her meaning. The rest of the people here were headed for the stairs as well, but if the main entrance was on fire, that wasn't an escape route.

"Everybody, stop!" I bellowed. "The fire's in the main hall. We need to go out through the windows; the evac route is blocked."

I managed to get enough of everyone's attention that they slowed, then someone else shouted.

"Unit two's wall collapsed under the window; we should be able to climb out there," they told the crowd. "It isn't perfect, but it's safer than running through fire and faster than going through any of the windows down here."

"Go, go, go!" I told everyone, standing aside to let the crowd rush past as I reached into my arsenal of superhuman and just plain weird senses.

"No cold iron," I murmured to Mary. "Building is still standing, so..."

"They weren't trying to bring the building down," she concluded. "Set it on fire, wreck it in the long term, but without causing *too* much collateral damage... Someone's trying to draw you out."

I grimaced. The thought of my entire apartment building being attacked just to get at me rankled. But Mary was also probably right.

"Okay."

The last of our neighbors disappeared into unit two and I grimaced.

"Through the fire?" I asked.

"Seems the last place they'll be expecting us. What about your guards?"

"They'll have retreated Between if their apartments were threatened," I told her. "At least one should be outside watching everything, though. If there *are* attackers out there, we'll have reinforcements pretty quickly."

"Can't you do the same?" she asked.

"I could," I admitted as I drew my whip and sword from Between. "But I'm not going to. Whoever these bastards are, they just set an apartment building on fire to draw me out. I can't let that pass."

The asura might even be waiting Between, too.

"You know they're counting on that, right?"

"I know," I agreed. "And I'm going to go fight them anyway. You don't have to come with—"

"Fuck that bullshit," Mary snapped, producing an assault rifle I hadn't realized was concealed in our apartment. "I'm with you. I just wanted to make sure you knew we were walking into a trap."

———

I COULD CONJURE fire out of nothing, but that didn't give me any great deal of control over *existing* fire. My Gift of Force, however, was easily turned to creating a shield that allowed us to walk through the burning front entrance of my apartment building without even feeling the warmth.

There were sirens in the distance, but somehow, I was certain they weren't going to get here before the current situation was resolved. I wasn't even sure, yet, who my attackers were, but I was sure they'd made arrangements to make sure they could kill me without, at least, uniformed witnesses.

I barely even registered the sniper shot. My shield stopped the bullet despite its cold iron tip—barely—and Mary returned fire almost on instinct.

It was harder to miss the sound of a 5.56mm assault rifle going off over your shoulder. Mary was a better shot than any human could reasonably manage, and the sniper fire stopped after the second round.

The people setting this up had almost certainly not expected a sniper to take me out, but some efforts had to be made.

I wasn't surprised, however, when a familiar-looking cluster of broad-shouldered Indian men materialized out of the crowd.

"I don't suppose they're here for a Bollywood dance number, do you?" I asked Mary.

"No. Do you want to talk?"

Whether or not *I* wanted to talk was rapidly rendered irrelevant as a dozen or so asura mercenaries produced AK-47s and opened fire.

One heavy slug, even tipped with cold iron, wasn't a threat to the shields I could muster now. A dozen assault rifles firing cold iron tipped rounds…that was an entirely different story, and I swept Mary forward with me as I used Force to lift us out of the line of fire.

I threw off her aim and only one of the mercenaries went down to her fire. They'd probably live—the Indian supernaturals apparently had super-tough skin and regenerative capabilities—but the man was down.

The one I caught with my whip was less lucky. I sent fire twisting around at waist height, cutting through his weapon, his hands and his torso in a single strike.

More gunfire answered and I left Mary behind cover as I bounced off the ground and charged the asura.

She shot down two more of them before I reached them, but they were *fast*. By the time I was into close range with them, the AKs were gone. Curved long swords replaced them and I charged into a blurring labyrinth of steel.

A golden glow lit up around their swords and hands as I met them. A shield of Force knocked away the first asura to charge me, and the silver-hilted Hunter's sword impaled the second one. Fire flashed around to knock the second pair who came at me to the ground, and Force augmented my backward dodge as more tulwars came slicing at me.

There were more asura here than when I'd started my charge, and I was starting to realize this might have been a bad idea. I skipped Between, dodging around a trio of stabbing blades and reappearing behind the attackers.

Whip and flame smashed across their legs and that trio went down.

Then Raja Venkat Asi was there himself, a glittering shield of golden light suddenly separating me from his men.

"You're better than I was told," he said calmly to me. "I should have asked for more money."

"You shouldn't have taken the damn job," I replied. "I don't like people trying to kill me."

"I am a weapon in the hands of those who call upon me," Asi said. "I am not responsible for the choices and actions of those who purchase my services."

That was...fucked up.

"So, who's responsible if I cut you in half?" I asked sweetly as I drew power around myself. Asi's golden bubble had separated us from everyone—almost certainly buying time for his people to retreat.

"That won't happen," he noted. "But if it were to, responsibility would fall on those who hired me. I am but a tool. Theirs are the hands that wield me."

"Right. So, that philosophy is fucked," I told him. "You just blew up a building. I'm pretty sure I'm going to hold you responsible for that."

"You are not required to agree with me," Asi replied. "All I ask is that you die in an orderly fashion."

"Not going to happen."

He smiled.

"I didn't think so."

We both moved. Even my senses had a problem keeping up with him, but I managed it. I parried his first strike, then his second.

By the fourth parry, I started to realize I was probably outmatched. I was managing to keep Asi away from me, but that was *all* I was managing.

By the time we'd been going back and forth for about ten seconds, I realized he was toying with me. Both of us were capable of nonphysical attacks, but I was simply too busy fending him off to try anything else.

He…wasn't.

I dove sideways, letting him thrust through where I had been standing, and brought the whipstock around in a vicious blow. White-green fire flashed across the golden bubble he'd conjured and hammered into a shield of shimmering light gathering around Asi's free hand.

He smiled.

"Not bad. I am, however, running out of ti—"

The golden bubble disintegrated under a hail of gunfire, and Asi dodged backward as half a dozen Hunters stepped out of the shadows. The asura were either down or fleeing, and fire and fury surrounded Coleman's people.

A new golden shield deflected the rounds that came near him, and Raja Venkat Asi bowed to me.

"It seems I underestimated your preparations. We are hardly done, Sir Kilkenny."

Before I could say more, the golden shield flashed inward on him and he was gone.

I stepped forward and poked at the ground where he had been standing and shook my head.

"Damh?"

"Sir?"

"Take any of them that are still alive prisoner," I ordered. "Then we all need to get the hell out of here." I pointed to the oncoming sirens.

"I'm guessing Asi's people held up the fire trucks, but we need to be gone before they arrive."

And that meant, sadly, that I wasn't going back to my stuff.

Fortunately, I kept my arms and armor Between. Everything else, though…

Yeah. Mary was going to be pissed.

8

"Are you okay?" were the first words out of Mary's mouth as she passed through the rough cordon of Hunters.

"I'm fine. Unfortunately, so's Asi," I said bitterly. I turned around to look at the ruined building behind us. "Someone's going to pay for this."

"Later," Coleman replied. "Riley's bringing your car around. You need to get going yourself."

"I do," I agreed, watching as my big Cadillac whipped out of the parking lot, the driver cavalierly ignoring the still-burning building. He brought the SUV the Queen had bought for me to a halt in front of us.

"Mary, Damh, in the car," I told them. "Everyone else, go Between to the warehouse. We'll meet you there."

There were a series of nods and then the Hunters began to blink out. None of the Companions or other Vassals were there tonight, but I was going to need my car—and I needed to talk to Damh Coleman.

And it wasn't like there'd actually been any prisoners. The asura had taken anyone alive with them when they'd retreated.

The three of us piled into the back of the SUV and Riley took off, barely exiting one end of the street as the fire engines finally arrived on the other.

"Police are still about a minute out," the Hunter driving told us, the earpiece he was wearing obviously linked to a police scanner. "I'm guessing the half-dozen accidents holding everybody up were anything but."

"Raja Asi told me they'd made sure no one interfered," I agreed. "I'm guessing they were about as careful to make sure no one died in those as they were with the fire."

Mary winced.

"I can't tell if everyone made it out," she whispered.

"Neither can I. And there was enough gunfire going around that I'm not sure there weren't casualties from that," I admitted. I was trying to stay calm, but I *wanted* Asi's head. On a platter. Potentially in pieces.

"We didn't lose any of our own, but a couple of the Hunters and Companions got burnt pretty badly," Coleman told me. "Your brother's treating them right now, Mary. Thank you for putting us in touch."

"Not many doctors who can treat supernaturals," Mary said. Her brother, another wildcat shifter, was the main doctor working for the shifters in Calgary. Oberis had his own doctor, but the Hunters would go with whichever of the pair could get there first.

"No. And your brother may be the only reason one of them lives," the Hunter captain replied. "We'll thank him appropriately, too, but you put us in touch."

She nodded, leaning her head heavily against my shoulder.

"What now, Jason?" she asked.

"Damh, we need to stop playing defense," I told the Hunter. "Can you pull together a meeting of our main contacts at the warehouse in the morning? Asi and his people are somewhere in the city. If MacDonald can't find them…"

"If he could find them, he'd have already told us," Coleman pointed out. "You can shield from a Wizard's Sight, and the asura clearly are doing so. I'll make the arrangements, Jason, but I don't know what else we can do to find them."

"We'll find something," I insisted. "One apartment building fire is enough for this mess."

———

"THE WAREHOUSE" was the same facility we'd jumped Between to at the first asura attack, a facility in one of Calgary's smaller and quieter industrial districts. Officially, it was owned by a company in Ireland that was looking into toy distribution in Canada.

A different toy distributor in Ireland paid my salary as their "Vice President of Sales, Western Canada." I'm not certain that there are any toy companies in Ireland or the United Kingdom that Mabona *doesn't* own.

There were half a dozen or so racks of shelving filled with boxes claiming to be toys. Only the first rack actually held toys—Fisher-Price would have been *quite* upset to find out what we'd replaced the contents of their boxes with.

Toy makers generally didn't sell custom-machined cold iron bullets, after all.

Two Companions were waiting at the front door, non-Hunter Gentry with the Steyr AUGs acquired via the Defence Forces of Ireland. They opened the doors to allow us to park the Cadillac inside, then closed them behind us.

"Corpses and gear are being moved to Sector D," the guards told us as we got out of the car. "Dr. Tenerim is in Sector B."

"Thanks," I replied. "Riley, get the car into the lot, then find somewhere to crash. We'll need a plan soon enough."

Coleman and Mary trailed behind me as I headed into the southwest corner of the warehouse—Sector B.

Clementine Tenerim was stripping off a pair of operating gloves and washing his hands outside a clear plastic tent in that corner. Through the plastic I could see a Wild Hunt medic checking in on our two burn victims.

"They're going to be fine," he told me, then shook his head. "The asura didn't need my help, thankfully. Connor wouldn't have made it without assistance."

"Thank you, Doctor," Coleman told him. "We'll see that you're well compensated for your service."

"I came because you asked, not because of money," Clementine replied, but he nodded his acceptance as he said it.

"I know," I said. "But the Wild Hunt pays our debts, my friend. Thank you."

He hugged Mary and then me. He wasn't normally physically affectionate, but I returned the hug regardless. It had been a scary evening.

"Do try not to die, Jason," he ordered. "I don't want to have to deal with Mary grieving. It would just all around *suck*."

I chuckled, shaking my head at him.

"Staying alive is high on my to-do list," I replied. I turned to Coleman. "You have somewhere Mary and I can crash?"

"We do," he confirmed. "We're a little strained since we just lost the three apartments we were using to keep an eye on you, but we always figured we'd need the space to pull everyone inside the defense in an emergency."

"Good call. Get that meeting set up, Damh. We need a plan."

"Not least, boss, we need to find you a new place to rest your head." he told me.

Mary sighed.

"And, apparently, we're going to have to send someone shopping once we've got a home."

I squeezed her hand. I didn't have much of real sentimental value. Not even a picture of my mom, even before the fire. Most of the real loss in the fire for us would be hers.

And there was nothing I could do to make that right.

9

THE NEWS in the morning was hard to watch.

Four people had died in the car accidents to keep the fire department away from the apartment building. Seventeen had died in the fire itself, and another twenty had needed to be rushed to the hospital to save their lives.

Two more had been wounded by gunfire, and the police were giving grim speeches about gang violence. Twenty-one dead and over twenty people in the hospital…all in an attempt to murder me.

"This cannot be allowed to recur," I said grimly.

This time, the entire conference was taking place via video. I was alone in an office in the warehouse with several screens set up around me, with Oberis, Mabona and MacDonald on the screens.

"About the only value I saw in your hole in the ground was that it seemed securable and unlikely to be traced," Mabona told me. "Surrounding yourself with mortals was never a good idea."

"It was what I could afford. And then I had never had time to move elsewhere," I admitted. "But this kind of attack can't be allowed to recur. Not just the deaths but also the risks to the Covenants."

"The asura have paid heavily for their attacks here," Oberis pointed out. "Surely, they will stop."

"They have accepted a contract. They will complete it," I said. "Or at least, we don't know what will *make* them stop."

"You can't stay in that warehouse," Mabona told me. "I will talk to Eric; we'll find somewhere to put you. Somewhere more defensible and secured than a mortal apartment building."

"If you insist," I allowed. I knew when I'd lost an argument, after all. "But we need to find these asura."

"They are shielded from my Sight," MacDonald said grimly. "I'm starting to get quite sick of people shielding. I *enjoy* having near-omniscience in my territory."

"These Asi Warriors have hunted some of the planet's most powerful creatures over the decades," the Queen noted. "They know many tricks and have many games. They will reinforce and try again. I do not know if you can avoid that, Kilkenny."

"They have to be based somewhere," I argued. "We have to find where."

"I have people looking," Oberis told me. "I have seen nothing to suggest a hiding spot yet."

"Then you must prepare a new trap," Mabona instructed. "We must find you a base of operations they will not have to threaten mortals to engage, and one where we can gather a significant force for your protection."

"That's assuming we can trust anyone we can gather," I said. "Even fae from Vancouver have turned out to be working for the Masked Lords. Is there a force we can draw on that isn't at risk?"

"No," Oberis said calmly. "But we have sufficient forces we can trust to keep you safe. I must admit, I am concerned by the Masked Lords' lack of direct activity. I wonder what other plans they may be acting on."

"There are many possibilities," Mabona noted. "I will pass the thought on to Ankaris." She shook her head. "For twenty years, they have hidden unnoticed. I fear we may not be able to track their operations now."

"We need to," I replied. "Or we may find we've missed another attack coming at us sideways."

"The Wild Hunt will find them if anyone can," Oberis concluded. "We will do what we can to keep you safe. You remain our best bait for their main striking forces."

———

THE TINY SIDE room that had been put at Mary's and my disposal was silent when I reentered. She was there and she was awake, but she was sitting quietly, looking at something on her phone.

"Mary?" I asked.

"Hi." She shook her head. "Clem says he has a copy of the picture of our mother I lost. Not sure what else I can duplicate, though."

"I'm sorry."

"Don't be. You didn't pick this fight," she reminded me.

"I didn't?" I snorted. "I seem to remember at least one plan involving having me parking my butt in one of the old forts in Ireland that we still control. Put an army of fae between myself and the Masked Lords, with no mortals in any kind of danger at all."

"And if I hadn't come with you?"

"You'd at least have been safe."

She sighed and gestured for me to join her on the bed. Wrapping her arms around me, she pulled my head down on her shoulder.

"If I'd wanted to be safe, I could have left you, too," she pointed out. "There were always options. I decided I wanted to be with you more."

I nodded against her shoulder.

"I'm not *happy* with what I lost," Mary admitted. "But your stuff was there too."

"I'd lost anything of real value by the time I made it here," I told her. "I don't even have any pictures of my mom."

"You didn't?" she asked. "I hadn't realized that. I should have."

"I don't talk about it, love," I reminded her. "It is what it is. I'm sorry your stuff got caught up in this. I'm sorry *you* got caught up in this."

"I seem to recall you getting dragged into at least two fights and rescue attempts because I asked," she pointed out. "We're here for each other, Jason. If these fuckers come at us, they're going to come at us. There's nothing we can do about that.

"I wish I'd kept a few things somewhere else, but..." She sighed again.

"I spoke to our landlady. She was glad to hear we were okay, but she says the building is a total write-off. The firefighters aren't even letting people back in to try and get their stuff. It isn't safe."

Mary smiled sadly.

"I told her we would be fine, we'd already made arrangements. I didn't want her to worry; she was always so sweet."

I chuckled and squeezed her gently. Our landlady, Rhonda, had been the sister of my first boss when I'd moved to Calgary. I'd spent a few months working for a courier company, and they'd helped me get set up in the city.

My duties for Mabona had eventually forced me to leave, but they'd been good to me.

"I'm glad you spoke to her," I admitted. "I'm not sure I would have remembered, and you're right. I wouldn't want her to worry."

"Have we made longer-term arrangements than this?" Mary asked me. "There are nicer places we can crash with the Clan if we need it."

"Talus can put us up in his goblins' spare units if we're that desperate," I said.

Talus had helped evacuate a goblin clan from Vietnam during the war. They now owned a townhouse complex in the northeast of the city, where they kept a few units free for Talus's friends.

They'd made for a reliable safehouse in the past and would again in the future, I was sure. Even if the goblins *weren't* inhumanly sneaky and strong, a number of them had trained with Viet Cong guerillas before they'd left Vietnam.

I wouldn't want to tangle with their defenses.

"We could do that," Mary agreed. She'd always liked the goblins— as had I. They were secretive, but they were good people.

"Shouldn't be necessary," I told her. "Mabona asked Eric to take care of it."

Mary raised an eyebrow at me.

"Well, that should be interesting."

"What?"

"Last time Mabona asked Eric to take care of something for you, you ended up driving a *Cadillac*, Jason."

Right. That…could definitely be interesting.

10

ERIC JOINED us at the warehouse a few hours later, the gnome looking particularly pleased with himself.

"And just what canary did you swallow, Master Keeper?" I asked as he entered the lounge area I was waiting in and dropped into a chair.

"I don't know if *canary* is the right word, but I've arranged a meeting for you that I didn't expect to manage," Eric told me. "There aren't a lot of Indian supernaturals outside that subcontinent—something to do with the sacred rivers.

"But where a people go, their myths follow," he continued. "And some of the deva are less bound than the asura, for whatever reason. There is a deva family in the city, but they are *very* insular."

"Why didn't anyone mention them before?" I asked. "When the asura showed up, we should have been talking to them immediately!"

"Because pretty much no one knows they exist," Eric told me. "That I'm in contact with Pankaj Gupta is a gesture of extraordinary trust. The deva who have left India are...inherently vulnerable. Without access to their sacred waters, they lose much of the invulnerability many of us supernaturals take for granted."

"So they get paranoid," I said with a sigh. "But he agreed to meet us?"

"Agreed to meet you. *Only* you," Eric said with a raised palm. "He gave me the address of a temple in the northeast and said to send you there for three this afternoon."

He paused.

"Jason, Gupta is…a deva-sura, the equivalent of one of our Fae Lords. He gave up a *lot* by leaving India, and I've never worked out why he left. He's not as powerful as he once was, but he demands the respect due his blood."

"And his family?" I asked quietly.

"Born here, except his wife. Two generations of deva who don't even know what their sacred waters feel like. So far as I know, they've never gone back."

"Which suggests that he can't go back. That he's an exile."

"The highest deva-sura are Powers. If they banned him from the sacred waters, then they thought they were killing him," Eric pointed out. "My research suggests that there are only three deva-sura outside of the Indian subcontinent and that Gupta was the first to leave.

"He is very old, very well informed…and, as you say, he is an exile. Tread carefully, Jason."

"Then why are you sending me to him?" I asked. That was a lot of warnings.

"Because if anyone in this city understands these Asi, it's him. If anyone knows how to turn them away without killing them all…"

I sighed and nodded.

"He's probably not going to try to kill me, right?" I asked.

"Almost certainly not. He's paranoid, not hostile."

"Wonderful." I checked the time. "I guess I should get going. What about you?"

"I'm here to grab Coleman," the Keeper told me. "I want his opinion on the defensibility of the house I'm getting you."

I sighed.

"Is it too much to hope for something low-key?" I asked.

"It will be low-key, I assure you," Eric replied. "And defensible. *And* worthy of your status."

I glared at him, but I wasn't sure it got through to him. Eric wasn't *that* thick-skulled…he was just very certain in his view of the world.

———

THE HINDU TEMPLE in Calgary's northeast was quiet on a weekday afternoon. There were only a handful of cars in the parking lot of the gray-and-red brick building, and no one challenged us as I parked the SUV and headed up to the door.

"Stay here," I told my bodyguards. "I'm supposed to meet with Gupta alone. If there's a problem, well, I'll make my way back."

Kristal and Riley nodded and split apart to flank the door. Jumping Between from inside a building to the front door wouldn't take me very long.

A young man in a conservative black suit was waiting inside the door as I entered, bowing slightly as he saw me.

"Mr. Kilkenny?" he asked.

"That's me," I confirmed.

"Follow me, please."

I nodded and fell in behind him as he led me deeper into the building. The office he guided me to was roughly what I expected: a normal-looking administrative space, with paintings and statues in keeping with the nature of the organization it administered.

Pankaj Gupta was sitting behind the desk and dismissed the young man with a gesture, studying me as the door swung closed.

I returned his study levelly. Gupta was a tall man, broad-shouldered and heavily built. Like Raja Asi, he wore his hair dark and long and there was a golden tone to his skin that was ever so slightly different from the more natural dark tones of the man who'd shown me in.

"Lord Gupta," I finally greeted him, bowing slightly. "I appreciate your willingness to meet with me."

He grunted.

"Sit down," he instructed.

I sat, waiting for the older supernatural to speak. If he was as old and powerful as Eric suggested, respect was an absolute necessity. If he wasn't…well, it didn't hurt.

"So. The Asi have targeted you." His words were slow and deep, though he had less of an accent than I would have expected.

"Yes. Eric said you knew about them?"

Gupta grunted again.

"As much as anyone," he told me. "The organization is older than I am, though they lose enough young and old warriors alike that I doubt they have any members of my age."

I waited.

"They are the guardians of *Asi* itself, the first sword," he continued after a moment. "Their mercenary activities are an extension of that. They believe they are descended from *Asi* when it took the form of a man."

Okay, even for supernaturals, that was stretching it. A sword who'd turned into a man and spawned a line of supernaturals to be its guardians?

"Are they right?" I asked.

Gupta chuckled and smiled for the first time since I'd arrive.

"I don't know. Their origins pre-date me, and those few who are old enough to say do not talk of the past."

"How do I get them to stop hunting me?"

"You kill them," he said bluntly. "Kill enough of them, and they will walk away. Of course, what qualifies as 'enough' changes from year to year and century to century. Certainly, Raja Venkat Asi is one of their more determined commanders, with the influence to bring vast resources to bear."

He shrugged.

"Your enemies knew what they were doing when they hired him. If he cannot kill you, there are few people on this world who could."

"I intend on frustrating him," I said drily.

"So have his previous enemies. I wish you luck, Mr. Kilkenny. You will likely need it."

I sighed.

"So, what, I just keep killing them as they come? That seems…time-consuming, if nothing else."

"Once they have accepted a contract, you cannot outbid it. You cannot defer them or negotiate with them," Gupta told me. "They were once charged to drive me from India." He grimaced. "Clearly, they succeeded. They are asura, demon warriors."

"I was hoping for something more useful, I'll admit," I told him.

Gupta snorted.

"I will reach out to Raja," he said. "I doubt I can buy you anything, not even time, Mr. Kilkenny. But I will talk to Raja and see."

"I appreciate that. But...why?" I asked.

"Because I can," Gupta told me. "And sometimes an old man wants to feel useful."

That didn't seem like enough to me, but...I wasn't going to turn down his help.

11

I MET up with Mary again for lunch and she looked tired. I hugged her wordlessly and she squeezed me hard.

"So, my morning was weird," I told her without letting go. "How was yours?"

"Fortunately, my boss has seen *everything* over the years," she replied. We each dropped into our seats at the restaurant we'd picked basically at random. "On the other hand, a firefight outside a burning building... We're swamped today with cleanup."

And the Shifter Clans hadn't even really been involved. I wasn't entirely sure *how* Eric was finding time to house-shop for us.

"Eric should have left the house-shopping to us," I concluded aloud.

Mary shook her head at me.

"Oberis is probably running the cleanup for your side," she pointed out. "And Eric doesn't trust your sense of your own importance."

"The last thing I need is a mansion somewhere like Eagle Ridge," I said. Eagle Ridge was one of Calgary's more upscale communities, full of the type of house that just *reeked* of pretentiousness to me.

"You can afford it," Mary reminded me. "And it might be more defensible, which is pretty important these days."

I sighed and nodded, the arrival of the waiter temporarily suspending the conversation.

With our drinks and meals ordered, the young man disappeared and I leaned heavily on the table.

"The whole plan of being bait to lure the Masked Lords into a mistake sounded a lot better on paper," I admitted. It had been *my* plan, sadly. Mabona and Ankaris had wanted to hide me in a fortified bunker somewhere.

"A lot of people are dead, Jason," she half-whispered. "We didn't anticipate that, but that's not really your fault. Most of us keep things quiet."

"We weren't expecting them to attack the apartment building to get at us," I agreed, shaking my head. "I don't know what Eric's criteria are, but we need some place isolated enough that *when* the asura come for us, we're ready."

Our food arrived then, cutting off further conversation—and then my phone buzzed before we finished our meals. Eric was texting me.

Found a place. Can close the deal tonight, want to take a look?

"He's got a place," I told Mary. "Are you free this afternoon?"

"Yeah, Grandfather told me to go clothes shopping before I came back to work," she said, then snorted. "I *hate* clothes shopping, but I literally have what I'm wearing at this point."

"Well, let's meet up with Eric and see what white elephant he wants to hang around my neck. Then we can go clothes shopping together."

Mary chuckled.

"I suppose being ogled while I change will make the process more pleasant, won't it?

I had the grace to blush. That hadn't *quite* been my intent...but it hadn't been far from my mind, either.

————

WE MET Eric in one of the southwest's larger shopping centers. Signal Hill was spread out across a dozen square kilometers of stores of various sizes. It wasn't even a shopping area set up for walking; you needed to drive if you wanted to get from the grocery store on one end to the bookstore on the other.

It was often very obvious that most of Calgary had been built after cars became a thing and before people started to think driving less might be a good idea. Eric was sitting on the hood of his Land Rover, in front of the Starbucks and with a tray of three steaming cups balanced on his lap.

The gnome seemed utterly unbothered by the subfreezing weather. He waved us over and then passed the coffees through the window once I'd parked the Escalade next to him.

I'd spent time living in a Seattle independent coffee roaster's café, the Manor in that city. I was only somewhat reconciled to drinking Starbucks still...but it was *cold* out.

"You already found a house, Eric?" I asked.

"Hey." He spread his hands wide. "I'm good. And I found something worth the effort, too, my boy."

I rolled my eyes.

"Should we follow you or hitch a ride?" I asked.

"Hitch a ride," he told me. "There's going to be enough vehicles running around the house over the next few days. Every car less we can swing around will draw that much less attention."

"All right." I held the back door of Eric's Rover open for Mary, who hopped in ahead of me. My usual trailing shadows slid in the other side. "How ridiculously over the top *is* this place, Eric?"

"To be fair, I was more concerned about security and privacy than I was about making sure it was fully worthy of your rank and authority," he told me. "It'll keep you safe. Everything else was secondary."

Secondary. Right. That wasn't a good sign.

"It's your show, Mr. von Radach," I sighed.

————

I HAD a few minutes of hope that Eric had found something reasonable as we drove north into a relatively normal-looking suburb.

Then, however, we turned down a street and the suburb rapidly gave way to a surprisingly dense forest of evergreens. My phone happily told me there was more city in every direction, but we were now in an area of roughly two or three square kilometers of forest.

Calgary has plenty of greenspaces, so this wasn't entirely unusual. Given our current mission, it sent a shiver of suspicion down my neck.

A shiver proven entirely correct as we pulled off the road into a gravel driveway leading up to a closed gate. There was nothing fancy or particularly ostentatious here, but there were very few gates inside the city.

"Hold on a second."

Eric got out and plugged a code into what looked like a garage-door-opener keypad on one of the gate's stone posts. It was a very solid-looking gate, with a two-meter fence stretching into the forest in either direction.

The code worked and the gate swung open. Eric hopped back in and drove us through, waiting a few seconds to make sure the gate closed behind us.

"We've got a few prefab structures in our warehouses," he told me. "We'll set up a guard post by the gate with a remote. Everyone who comes in will be checked."

"Fenced perimeter?" I asked carefully as we drove up the gravel driveway.

"Partially. We'll lay motion sensors initially, complete the fence when we have time," Eric explained. "It's about a three-acre lot, so secluded, private and securable—while still inside the city and about ten minutes from Signal Hill."

I could see the value of that. The security point of view I agreed with, at least. We could even do it subtly—the fae courts had a *lot* of experience doing subtle security. Once we got our hands on a property, it rarely passed out of fae hands.

We had a habit of ending up with buildings that were much bigger on the inside, after all, and that was hard to explain in the real estate listing.

Halfway down the driveway, there was a bump and I looked out the window again to realize the road had changed. What was visible from the road remained gravel, but we were now on a neatly paved driveway leading the rest of the way to the house.

A carefully stacked array of paving stones showed that the driveway was a work in progress, presumably a refit from the original driveway. That was all the warning I really got about the house itself, too.

From the outside, it looked large but not spectacular. An older—by Calgary standards, anyway—two-story estate home occupied the heart of the wooded lot. It was bigger than most of the suburban homes we'd passed, but still quite compact.

The roof and siding were new. I could even see the spot in the snow where the dumpster had been sitting until a few days before.

Eric stopped the Land Rover in front of the house and gestured for us to get out.

"Owner is a house-flipper," he told us. "The house and grounds were pretty run-down after the previous owner died. They bought it, installed a better gate, renovated the house and were starting to shop for a buyer as they finished the landscaping."

"You said we could close it tonight?" I asked as I glanced over the building.

"No one is living here. I mean, technically, we'll be renting it for the first twenty days or so while the papers go through, but we *are* paying cash for a multimillion-dollar property." The gnome grinned. "That opens a *lot* of goodwill, in my experience."

"Multimillion," I echoed, feeling a bit faint.

"Why don't we go inside?" Eric told me.

———

IT RAPIDLY BECAME clear that the flipper had completely gutted the interior of the house. I don't think many fifties-era farmhouses were entirely open-plan, after all.

Part of the upper and main floors had been cut away to create a three-story open living space that dropped into what had once been the basement, with a grand staircase leading down from the front entrance. The kitchen was tucked away in one corner but still open to the main living area, and two galleries allowed access to what I assumed to be bedrooms on the higher floors.

You could go directly from the main entrance onto the ground-floor gallery, but the stairs to the second floor were on the opposite side of the house.

"Master bedroom is at the back on the second floor," Eric told me cheerfully. "There are four smaller bedrooms on the main floor and three more upstairs. Probably intended for kids, but we'll set them up with a couple of beds apiece and use them for your guards.

"The master suite has its own sitting area, but the main area is designed as a 'great hall'–style space. If we get the right kind of furniture—and we will—you can move tables and couches around and either have a big dining area or a comfortable living space."

The design of the house was super-modern but the esthetics were the same kind of rustic country estate the outside evoked. A stone fireplace and chimney climbed one side of the wall, and it seemed like everything was done in gorgeously matched hardwoods.

"Multimillion," I repeated. "Eric...this is too much."

"It's not just for you," he pointed out. "We're housing a troop of the Wild Hunt and a half-dozen other Vassals, *plus* Grandfather informs me that Mary is getting her own team of bodyguards going forward."

I looked over at my girlfriend.

"He told me," she admitted. "I'm trying to argue him out of it."

"I'm not going to say you can't veto it," Eric admitted. "But it checks all of our boxes. It's in the city, it's convenient to everything, but it's isolated and securable. It's private, it's quiet and no one is going to be poking around, asking questions." He snorted. "You probably won't even get trick-or-treaters."

"What are we going to use this space for?" I waved around.

"There are a couple of spaces in the basement that can be set up as either media or meeting rooms," the Keeper replied. "You can do your arbitration work from here, and you'll have an appropriate setting to meet petitioners."

He sighed.

"Remember, Jason, you are now a Noble of the Wild Hunt as well as a Vassal of the Queen. People will look to you for decisions, for guidance, for *authority*. You must project that when you meet them.

Having a space you can bring people to that is entirely secured, entirely under the control of *your* people..."

"Talus doesn't live like this," I pointed out.

Eric shook his head at my intentional unworldliness.

"Jason, Talus lives in the full-floor penthouse apartment of a mixed residential and commercial building downtown that he owns *outright*. He lives like this, yes."

"Can I even afford this?"

"Nope," he told me brightly. "You could afford the mortgage, truthfully, but for now, the Queen is buying it and *lending* it to you. It's not a gift and we'll sort out the paperwork for some kind of rent-to-own agreement and taxable benefits and such later."

"And if I veto it?" I asked.

"We probably end up shifting outside of the city to find something equally securable," Eric replied. "This one's available right now, checks off all of the security items *and* is worthy of your rank and authority."

I sighed and met Mary's gaze again.

"Am I going to win this argument, love?" I asked.

"Let's go look at the master suite," she suggested. "If it has the kind of bathtub setup I think it does...no, you're not winning this argument."

————

THE BATHROOM MANAGED TO BE, at once, both utterly over the top and surprisingly unostentatious. There was a massive bathtub, clearly designed for two people and also possessing that rarest of features: sufficient length for my nearly six feet in height to lie down in.

There was a massive shower, with two separate showerheads. There were dual sinks. All of this was done in glass and a muted white ceramic. Or possibly granite. I wasn't sure and I didn't *want* to be sure.

I sighed as I surveyed the suite. That was definitely the right word. A surprisingly normal-sized bedroom centered it, but that bedroom was accessed via a good-sized living room area and had *two* walk-in closets.

Plus the bathroom.

"Eight bedrooms," I noted aloud. "Meeting rooms. Multiple acres." I glared at Eric. *"Why?"*

"You've had the lecture," he replied. "All of the reasons you need it. I've already set up the deal, but Mabona insists you sign off."

I looked at Mary, who was inspecting what looked like it might be some kind of hydrotherapy setup in the bathroom.

"All right. What about furniture?"

"I'll take care of it," Eric promised. "I have an interior designer friend; I'll unleash her on the space tomorrow. Give me two days, and you'll be able to move in."

"Give the asura two days and they might burn my damn warehouse down around my eyes," I replied.

"It's possible," he agreed. "But that's why you have guards and the Wild Hunt. We'll all keep our eyes open, Jason, but we need some time to get this set up."

He smirked.

"Even *I* don't have prefabricated security setups and luxury furniture hidden in my little interdimensional storage space."

"Let me know what you need from me," I told him. "Otherwise, I think Mary and I need to go clothes shopping." I shook my head. "The Asi Warriors owe me. A lot."

"The Masked Lords hired them," Eric said. "Never forget that, either."

"I won't," I said, stepping out on the second-floor gallery and looking out over the main living area. "I'm only going to wait so long for them to come for me, Eric," I admitted. "Once these asura are dealt with, it might be time to saddle up."

"You're a Noble of the Wild Hunt," the gnome reminded me. "You were born for the hunt, for the chase. I don't think *anyone* expected you to be bait forever."

12

To my shock, our shopping trip passed without any interruptions. Mary and I picked up a small wardrobe of new clothes each before returning to the warehouse to check in.

Coleman had an array of screens set up in his command center, news on about three screens and security feeds from across the city on others. The rest of the troop was scattered around, sleeping or checking in on their gear.

"Eric says you saw the house," he greeted us. "Serves our needs nicely, doesn't it?"

"And then some more," I replied. "You encouraged him, didn't you?"

Coleman chuckled.

"A private lot we can secure and fence off, with trees all around so no one is going to wander in by accident? Hell, yes. This way, the next time someone comes at you, there'll be no collateral damage."

"Next time, huh?" I sighed.

"You're a Noble of the Hunt," the officer replied. "Someone will come for you, even if we deal with these asura. That's the nature of what you are, what you do. We make enemies, Jason."

I looked around the room and came to a quick decision.

"Let us drop off the shopping, but then are you free for dinner?" I asked. "We need to sit down and go over some of our plans, just the three of us." I gestured to Mary as well.

"I can manage that," he agreed. "I'll be bringing some extras, though. I'm not an escort all on my own."

I snorted. Damh Coleman wasn't a Noble, but he *was* a full Hunter, a Greater Fae with the Gifts of Between and Force, as well as well-beyond-human natural abilities. I'd back him against most people coming after me—and I'd back him and me together against just about *anything*.

"If you insist," I allowed. "This will be quiet."

"Fair enough." He shrugged. "Speaking of escorts, Ms. Tenerim?"

"If you call me *miz* again, Damh, I will leave claw marks all over your face," Mary said sweetly. "You know my name."

He laughed.

"Fair enough, Mary. Do you know who's going to be heading up your detail? If you're going to be under guard, we're going to need to coordinate. We may as well put together a combined command that answers to you two."

What Coleman was suggesting was basically a multispecies Court. That was going to be…interesting. But he was also right.

"I believe Barry volunteered for the job," Mary told him. "I think he figured I'd put up with one of my adoptive big brothers doing it better than I would anyone else."

Coleman laughed again.

"Probably. I'll get in touch with him later. We'll combine resources, make sure that you and your house are secure."

I met his gaze and shook my head.

"These asura aren't to be underestimated," I warned him. "The Masked Lords even less so."

"I know," he confirmed. "And it's my job to make sure they don't get to you. Any of them."

———

ONE OF THE things I'd learned while living in Calgary was that most neighborhoods had at least two pubs, usually more. Only one of them would actually be good, but that one would be pretty good.

Coleman and his team had been operating out of the warehouse for just over four months now. They'd identified the good pub and we descended on it for a working supper.

The back corner table we grabbed was directly under the speakers, an annoyance but a necessity to keep our conversation secret. We ordered food and beer and I leaned back in the seat, holding Mary's hand under the table while the news continued to prattle on about a terrorist attack in Pakistan.

"Any more sign of the asura?" I asked.

"Nothing. We've been looking and reaching out to everyone," Coleman replied. "They're *here*—we can confirm that Raja Venkat Asi hasn't left Calgary—but they're a lot better at keeping their head down than we'd prefer."

"I'd rather they happily wandered out into free-fire killing zones," I admitted quietly. "They're not my favorite people right now."

"I'm hesitant to lay the blame for mercenaries on the mercs themselves," my subordinate said. "I mean, they're far from innocent, but if the Masks hadn't hired them…"

"I think we're reaching the end of this plan being viable," I said as the food arrived. The waitress disappeared back into the kitchen and I shook my head. "Trapping the Masked Lords required them taking the bait, and apparently I'm not tempting enough."

"I think they figured out we were waiting for them," Coleman noted. "Hence the asura. They'd love to have you delivered to them, but they're not going to challenge the High Court on ground of our choosing."

"Any idea where we'd find them if we went looking?" Mary asked. "What, do we wander around various Fae Courts and poke through closets for iron masks?"

I chuckled at the mental image but shook my head.

"The masks themselves have some kind of spell allowing them to hide Between," I admitted. "Searching closets wouldn't help us, but I swear that's the best idea I've heard lately."

"The Wild Hunt has been keeping an eye out for these bastards for, well, as long as you've been alive," Coleman told us. "If they weren't good at hiding, we'd have taken them down years ago."

"I know." I sighed and stared into my macaroni and cheese. "We have to be able to do something, though, Damh. If they don't come after me…"

"You're the only weakness they've had in a quarter-century," he pointed out. "Your bloodline is the key to their weapon. They have to come to you, sooner or later."

"Then why aren't they?" I asked. "These Asi Warriors are here to kill me, not take me captive. What exactly are they going to do then?"

"Collect your body and use your blood to unlock the weapon. Somewhat more literally than normal," Coleman said with a sigh. "Look, my lord, I don't know what the answer is. I'd rather be on the road, taking the offensive against these bastards. But we don't know where they are, so all we can do is wait."

"And at least knowing they need me gives us something to work with," I agreed, sighing myself. "We'll see what trouble pops up as we get the house ready, I guess."

"I'll admit I'm hoping they think we're *vulnerable* while we're setting up the new place," Coleman said with a wicked grin. "Because if they do, I have some *lovely* surprises waiting for them."

All three of us chuckled. If the Masked Lords came for us, we'd be ready. My biggest problem was that my enemy didn't seem to want to play.

13

THE BIGGEST SURPRISE, however, was that we heard nothing for three days. The move into the house went without incident and Eric's interior-designer friend utterly outdid herself.

I didn't ask what the budget had been and I didn't want to know. She'd acquired us everything from couches to art to kitchenware. Well, the kitchenware was *probably* Eric. Probably.

A prefabricated guard post went up at the gate, just out of sight of the road. Several others were scattered through the woods, and I'd spotted several of Talus's goblins working with my people to lay out motion sensors and traps amidst the trees. We were going to need regular briefings on the defenses to keep everyone from blowing themselves up!

I could swear, though, that every time I turned around, there was another door and another room in the house. We weren't even playing games with space and Between yet.

That was an important point, too. I wasn't quite sure *how* to start adding extra space to a building, but I knew enough to know that I could. The Calgary Court was hidden inside, roughly, one meeting room and a side corridor of the hotel Oberis owned. Its actual square footage encompassed half a dozen meeting rooms, what was basically a throne room, several offices...

If I stayed in this house, I could already tell we were going to end up somewhere similar. I'd brought sixteen Hunters and Companions. Kristal and her fellows were another half-dozen Greater Fae.

Talus had lent me a security detail as well, another half-dozen goblins and Fae.

Exactly twenty-four hours after we'd moved in, I answered a knock on the door to find Barry Tenerim standing on my new doorstep accompanied by five other walking walls of muscle. Grinning.

"Barry," I greeted him. "You're looking for Mary, I assume?"

"More on the order of checking in," he admitted. "*Nice* digs you're putting my cousin up in, Jason. I might have to start approving of you."

I shook my head disapprovingly at him.

"Come on in," I told him. "If you're staying around here, *you* get to arm-wrestle with the Wild Hunt for rooms. We'll add more, given time, but right now, we've got about seven bedrooms to play with."

"You'll...add more?" Barry asked as he looked around the massive open space occupying half the building. "With what, renovations? It looks pretty well done up already."

"I'm a Fae Noble, Barry," I reminded him. "I'm not exactly bound by linear space."

He snorted.

"I keep remembering the half-dead changeling we peeled off the pavement with a spatula after he leapt to Mary's defense," he said. "Times change, don't they?"

"They do," I agreed. "Mary's taking a shower. Coleman's in meeting room three; he's in charge of security."

"And what are you in charge of?" Barry asked with a chuckle.

"Everything, apparently," I told him, shaking my head. "But it's starting to look more and more like I may be in charge of fighting a war."

The werewolf paused.

"The Masked Lords?" he asked. "Like Andrell?"

"Exactly like," I confirmed. "You know the spiel by now, but it's looking more and more like they aren't coming directly at me. Sooner or later, I'm going to have to go hunting them."

Barry snorted again.

"You won't be counting Mary out," he warned me, "so count me and my boys here in."

"It's not your fight," I said.

"You're Clan Tenerim, Jason Kilkenny," Barry said with a smile. "Might not be blood, but you're clan. It's our fight."

———

I WAS FIDDLING with my office set up when Eric showed up later that day. It was a make-work project, really, since my "office" consisted of a desk and a laptop for the moment. I'd almost certainly upgrade it in the long run, but so long as I had a connection to the Fae-Net—the set of unregistered and magically concealed websites the Fae used as a dark internet—I had what I needed.

"Coleman said you'd be in here," Eric greeted me from the door. The office was on the main floor, exactly opposite the main entrance. There *was* a dedicated office included in the design right next to the entrance, but that was now a guard post and where Coleman usually hung his hat.

The gnome looked around the room and at the single chair.

"I thought Mikayla had done every room," he noted. "This looks pretty sparse."

"She had this one set up as a bedroom, but we needed an office on the inside of the last layers of defenses," I admitted. "Now we have a spare bedroom set in the storage downstairs, and I have an IKEA desk I pulled out of Between."

Eric snorted and pulled an overstuffed recliner out of Between himself. He dropped into the chair, crossing his legs to look even *more* like a child with gray hair and a beard, and studied me.

"You sound tetchy," he observed.

"Coleman didn't even need to argue with me on putting my office back here," I said with a sigh. "I'm getting far too used to being behind security. And this whole place?"

I gestured around me.

"This isn't a home, Eric. This is a fucking miniature Court."

"So is the office underneath Talus's penthouse," Eric reminded me. "Robert is still working on putting together his own space and allies, but his house has a security detail. Most of them are his father's people, but he's building his own team.

"It's what Nobles *do*, Jason. It's part of the value and service you provide to the community, above and beyond simply being more powerful than most."

I sighed.

"I'm still getting used to the idea of being a Noble," I admitted.

"So's Robert. He has his father. You have Mabona, Ankaris and me," Eric told me. "And given that the High Court only has so much time, most of the backing you up as you build your own space is falling on me."

"You're saying you don't help Robert?" I asked.

The gnome chuckled.

"Oh, I help Robert," he confirmed. "But Robert has his father and Talus has as many resources as I do. Possibly more, though in the case of helping you, I have access to other resources as well.

"It's in everyone's interest to see you in control of your own faction with your own resources and power," he concluded. "Well, everyone except the Masked Lords, that is."

I nodded and pulled a bottle of wine and two glasses out of Between.

"Drink? I think I need one."

"Sure." Eric took a glass and I filled it for him.

"What brings you here tonight?" I asked. "I can't imagine you're here just to remind me that, yes, I *am* supposed to be putting together a miniature version of a Court."

"Touching base with you is always a good idea right now," Eric told me. "But you're right. I got a call from Pankaj Gupta. He wants to speak to you again."

I raised an eyebrow at him.

"He told me he was going to try and track down information on the

Asi Warriors, I suppose," I said. "I didn't actually expect him to *do* it." I shook my head. Plus, why wouldn't Gupta just email us?

"Gupta didn't tell me what it was about," Eric said grimly. "I don't like it, Jason. Something doesn't smell right. The asura go silent suddenly, and then Gupta wants to talk to *you*?"

Eric...was not wrong.

"It's not like I can turn him down, though, is it?" I asked. "We need whatever information he's gathered. If he knows how to get these asura off my back..."

"Then you've got to meet him," Eric agreed. "That's why I'm here. But...he wants to see you alone, which isn't unusual, but somehow I don't trust it this time."

"I'll have a Wild Hunt team on standby and an alert on my phone," I promised. "I'm not looking to get knifed in the back by an old Indian warlord."

"We don't want to offend Gupta, but that makes sense to me," the gnome told me. "If worst comes to worst, I *think* you can take him in his reduced state, but...I wouldn't count on it, Jason."

"So, be ready to run," I concluded. "I'm used to that one. When does he want to see me?"

"Midnight tonight, at the same temple."

"All right. I'll go see what our friend Gupta wants."

———

"So, you're telling me you *know* it's a trap and you're going to walk into it anyway?"

Coleman sounded more amused than anything else.

"We need the information he's offering badly enough to take the risk," I told my Hunt leader. "I need *you* to have a fire team ready to drop into his temple through Between if this does go sideways."

"I always have a fire team ready to go," Coleman told me. "We haven't finished relocating our main trap from the warehouse, but that's in the process. We've got enough space for it here."

"And it's even more isolated from civilians," I agreed. We'd talked it over, at least. We'd probably end up putting the trap in a pit some-where in the "backyard," but we could keep it secure.

"Agreed. What happens if Gupta expects you to expect a trap and accounts for it, though?" my subordinate asked.

"I'll take Kristal and Riley. They'll wait in the car and get the same alert code you do," I told him. "If he blocks Between somehow, I'll still have backup on hand—and at that point, we're in pure 'get the hell out of Dodge' mode."

Coleman chuckled.

"I see you're learning."

"I'm in charge," I told him. "That means I have to. I need to meet with Gupta...but I also need to live through it. Think we can manage that?"

"Yes," he confirmed. "We're the Wild Hunt, after all."

14

THE HINDU TEMPLE was even quieter when I arrived this time. There were no other vehicles in the lot as I parked the Escalade next to the entrance. The lights in the building were out and only the streetlights illuminated anything.

"Okay, so, this is creepy," Riley noted. "What do we do?"

"Lock and load," I ordered. "Stay in the car but watch for an alert. It looks like the place is closed, and the lack of bystanders suggests all sorts of ugly possibilities."

"Lock and load yourself," Kristal suggested. "You were supposed to come alone, not unarmed."

"I'm never unarmed, and I doubt Gupta thinks otherwise," I replied. Nonetheless, she was right. My sword, whip and pistol materialized out of Between, and I strapped holsters, scabbard and harness under my coat.

In many ways, the weapons were almost *less* accessible this way, but it also made a point.

"We're out here waiting," Riley told me as he checked the safety on his AUG. "You call us, we'll be through the door in thirty seconds."

"Let's hope it doesn't come to that."

I strode over to the main doors, my eyesight sufficient to see clearly even in the dim and snowy night. The doors were closed and locked, a chain on the inside rattling when I tested them.

I shook my head and stepped Between, emerging on the other side of the doors and heading toward the office where I'd met Gupta before.

The building was empty and dark. Creepy as hell, but nothing jumped out at me before I reached the deva-sura's office and knocked on the door.

It swung open instantly, revealing there was *a* light inside the temple. A single lamp on Gupta's desk lit up the room in a mix of light and shadow that was more confusing to my sight than complete darkness would be.

"Mr. Kilkenny," he greeted me calmly. "Thank you for coming."

"I don't suppose we're going to turn a light on," I answered. "Or is the creepy haunted house factor part of the point?"

Gupta chuckled.

"Allow an old man his foibles, Mr. Kilkenny." He rose from his chair, revealing for the first time that he *towered* over my own near-six-feet in height. The old Indian warlord was at least six inches taller than me and he looked like a walking brick wall.

"Come with me," he instructed.

"You asked me to meet you here," I pointed out. "Care to explain?"

"I have the answers you sought, Mr. Kilkenny," he told me. "I know how to end your little war, but you need to trust me. I ask no more of you than I have of others tonight. This is not a safe game we play, you and I."

"And if I refuse?" I asked.

"Then you leave," Gupta replied. "You never find out why I called you here and you face your enemy without whatever aid I would provide. Does your fear overcome your curiosity, Mr. Kilkenny? Does it overcome your *responsibility*?"

"What responsibility?" Fear wasn't really the issue. Caution, definitely, but I wasn't *afraid* of Gupta.

"The world has changed in the last seventy-two hours, Mr. Kilkenny. Have you felt it?"

"I have no idea what you're talking about," I told him.

He snorted.

"Then if you do not come with me, you may doom not only yourself but the High Court you are sworn to serve. Tell me, Mr. Kilkenny. Are you prepared to risk that?"

"You could be a lot clearer about what's going on," I said. "Then I'd be much more willing to play."

"I made a promise, Mr. Kilkenny. I will keep it. I will promise you this: you will not be harmed by my hand or my inaction. Does that suffice?"

If Gupta was as powerful as Eric implied, his protection would be enough against many problems.

"All right," I allowed. "Lead the way."

GUPTA PROCEEDED out of his office and through the unlit corridors with an easy confidence that told me he had even less need for light than I did. We passed through the main worship area into a set of private cubicles, where he proceeded into one of them and pulled aside a tapestry depicting several of the Hindu gods having a discussion around a fire.

There was, unsurprisingly, a door behind the tapestry. He produced a key that unlocked it and held it open for me.

"Creepy dungeon basement. Right. And you want me to go first?" I asked.

He sighed.

"Fine."

Handing the door over to me, he went down the stairs first and I followed. For all that the space was at least somewhat hidden, it wasn't quite as bad as I assumed. The stairs were still the same tile as the main floor and had safety grip lines. There was a railing and even lights.

The lights were *off*, but that had been par for the course tonight.

At the bottom of the stairs was a midsized storage room, filled with furniture, carpets and tapestries. Since I doubted that Gupta wanted to show off his collection of fine Indian carpets, I followed him deeper through the maze of debris, to another door.

This one was also locked, but when he opened it, there were lights on the other side. I followed Gupta through and instantly realized we weren't alone.

It took me a few moments longer to realize that the other man standing just inside the door, clearly illuminated by the lights, was Raja Venkat Asi.

I went for my whip—and found myself frozen in place the moment I had the weapon out.

Gupta had a hand raised at me. He also had a hand raised at Asi, and I could *feel* his power suddenly dominate the room. If this was a deva-sura *reduced* by lack of access to the sacred waters of the Ganges…I didn't want to meet one at their full power.

"You are both powerful men, warlords of the supernatural with Gifts and armies at your command," Gupta said harshly. "But *I* am deva-sura. And I command you to *listen*."

I waited a few moments, to demonstrate that I wasn't struggling, then sheathed my whip while I studied Asi.

"You told me you had a way to end this fight," I told Gupta. "I'm guessing this has something to do with it."

Raja Venkat Asi exhaled. He wasn't wearing his suit jacket from earlier, so the motion was *very* visible in his bare and well-muscled chest.

"Our fight is over," he said flatly. There was something else to his voice, some tone that hadn't been there in our previous conversations. He sounded almost…broken.

"That seems a little out of the blue," I pointed out.

"You were never my enemy," he told me.

"You tried to kill me. That seems pretty enemy-like. Plus, you *did* kill a lot of people trying to get at me."

He closed his eyes, almost wavering on his feet.

"Bhagavan Gupta, may…may we sit somewhere?" he asked. "This is going to be hard enough."

"If you two promise not to draw on each other," Gupta replied. "I have promised both of you your safety. Even if I hadn't, I will not permit violence in this place."

"I'll hear him out," I promised slowly. "I can't offer more than that."

"It's...enough," Asi said. "I mean no one here harm anymore."

————

THERE WAS QUITE the complex underneath the Hindu temple, as it turned out. Raja Asi had been waiting for me in the main entrance hall, and he now led us to a side office. I got a glimpse of a well-lit corridor and what looked like small dorm rooms along it.

I could also see other asura down that corridor, broad-chested men and long-haired women with noticeable golden auras over their skin. Somehow, I knew this hadn't been where they'd been hiding when they'd been launching their operations against us, but they'd retreated here at some point in the last few days.

Asi dropped heavily into a chair and studied me.

"Your enemies, Lord Kilkenny, are evil," he said quietly. "Understand that I have seen and spoken to many that others would call evil. Some were evil. Some were...simply focused.

"Some would argue that our own mercenary ways were evil. But these Fae Lords, these Masks...I would call them evil."

"Is this supposed to be news to me?" I asked.

"No," he admitted. "But I will admit that we regarded a civil war among the fae as...not our problem. We were prepared to take their money. Had you approached us first, we would have taken your money. Temples and fortresses aren't cheap to maintain, especially if you must be prepared to defend against any mundane or supernatural power of the world."

Gupta busied himself in one corner of the room, and it wasn't until a warm scent of spices and milk drifted back over to me that I realized what he was doing.

There are rules that cross supernatural communities, ones that were never formalized in Covenants but are even more ironbound because of that. If Gupta was making tea for the three of us with his own hands, I was safe.

I'd been relatively sure of that already, but the extra reassurance was helpful.

"Why am I here, Asi?" I asked. "If we're done…then go home."

He was very quiet for several seconds, and then Gupta dropped cups of steaming milk tea in front of each of us.

"Tell him, Raja," he ordered. "I arranged this meeting. I'm not explaining your situation for you."

"We were betrayed."

His words were very soft. I'm not sure a human could have heard them.

"Betrayed?"

"The contract to kill you was a trap. They knew we would not succeed and would concentrate too much of our forces here to complete it," he continued. "Then, when half our warriors were here… they attacked our home."

Okay, so I could see why the contract was void now.

"They stole *Asi*, Lord Kilkenny," he told me. "They murdered our brothers and sisters who remained to defend the fortress. They murdered our spouses and children. Our order, our mortal allies, our families…all dead. The fortress-temple of the Asi Warriors is ash and dust."

"Sacred Powers," I swore. "Wait, *Asi*?"

"The first sword," Raja Venkat Asi told me. "The weapon I and our order are named for. An ancient weapon of immense power we were sworn to defend into eternity. Now your Masked Lords have it…and I and my strike team are all that remains of its defenders."

The description of *Asi* lined up disturbingly closely with the description I'd been given of *Esras*. I didn't know enough to be sure, but it sounded like the Masked Lords might no longer need the spear that was bonded to my blood.

That ruined the plan around me being bait.

"I appreciate the warning, Raja Asi," I said slowly. "But you understand that you murdered innocents to kill me. My sympathies for your own plight are limited. I will permit you to leave Calgary and return home, but that is all."

He sighed.

"I cannot return home," he said flatly. "My wife. My children. My grandchildren—and beyond, even. I am *old*, Jason Kilkenny, and seventeen generations of my descendants served the Order.

"They are all dead. I cannot return home. I *must* avenge them before I no longer can."

"You share an enemy now, Lord Kilkenny," Gupta told me. "I would not turn aside his aid if I were you."

"I am no lord," I replied. "And I have no need for murderers."

They would be powerful allies, but...there was too much blood on their hands.

Asi rose and sank to his knees in front of me.

"I owe you a debt of honor and blood," he whispered. "My family is gone, but my enemies are your enemies, and I have done much harm in my pursuit of you. I could blame others, and I lay the lion's share of the blood guilt on the Masks, but I owe you a debt.

"I would pledge you my service and that of my asura," he told me. "I would swear fealty and place my arm at your command."

I stared at the kneeling asura.

"You have to go back to India, don't you?" I finally asked. "Without your sacred waters, don't you get weaker?"

"I will." He held my gaze. "But I will remain in the West, and diminish, and pass into legend. The last of the golden-handed warrior kings. I cannot go home and look on the ashes of all that I loved.

"But before I fade, your enemies are my enemies, and I cannot fight them alone. I will pledge you a sword that has rarely known defeat, a power that has known few equals, and all that remains of my order and my blood."

I sighed.

"I can't make that decision right now," I told him. "This is all very fresh."

"You must," Asi said flatly. "Three times, Lord Kilkenny. I pledge you Fealty, my life and sword and gifts, yours to command."

Three times. Yeah. Raja Venkat Asi knew the fae, all right.

"Thrice offered, I cannot thrice deny," I said slowly, the formal words coming to me almost instinctually. I rose from my chair, laying my tea aside as I placed my hands over his.

"You and your asura understand that among fae, this pledge cannot be undone?" I asked. "If I command your Fealty, *you are mine.* There will be no more innocent blood shed. No more mercenary contracts. I cannot take you to the sacred waters. I cannot even promise that I will find the Masked Lords."

"But you will try." His voice was soft.

"I will try," I confirmed. "There are other debts to be paid here, Raja Venkat Asi. If you pledge your Fealty, you will follow me to a hundred wars, only one of which will be yours."

"I swear it," he told me. "I pledge you Fealty, my life and sword and gifts, yours to command," he repeated. "Unto death. Unto eternity. Until I diminish and pass into myth."

"So be it."

My hands closed around his and power flared in that room.

I was a Noble of the fae. He was a warlord of the asura.

Beings such as us do not—*cannot*—swear oaths lightly.

15

"YOU HAVE GOT to be fucking *kidding* me," Coleman exclaimed.

He, Mary and I were sitting in his front guard-post office in the house as I explained the situation.

"You want me to just...blithely allow these asura to join us? To *trust* them?"

"Damh...they owe me Fealty," I said quietly. "Technically, *you* don't owe me Fealty. And that's as meaningful and unbreakable an oath for them as it is for us."

I shook my head.

"I understand, for all that, and I don't expect you to trust them," I continued. "I'm assuming we can pull some prefab barracks or something out of storage and set them up on the lot? Keep them outside the house, at least initially."

Coleman continued to look at me like I was crazy, then looked desperately over to Mary for support.

"Don't look at me, Hunter," she replied. "Shifters don't do the fealty thing. We do clan and oath and loyalty, though, and even *I* know that a fae swearing or accepting fealty is a big deal."

"Thrice-sworn Fealty," I told Coleman. "Asi wants his revenge. The

Masked Lords wiped out his order. The twenty-two asura here in Calgary are all that's left of the Asi Warriors."

"I understand Fealty," he allowed. "I'll make it happen if you insist. I may not owe you Fealty, but you are my chain of command. I answer to you regardless."

"I appreciate the faith, Damh," I said. "And trust me, I want you to keep a *close* eye on them. I'm reasonably sure Fealty means much the same to them as it does to us, but I can't be certain."

"I'll check in with Eric, get a barracks set up, and then you can get them over here." He shook his head. "We're going to need a damn motor pool if this keeps up. The garage attached to the house only holds five cars."

"Set it up with Eric," I told him. "We need more than just my Escalade and a couple of sedans. Once the asura move in, we'll have over forty people living on the lot."

"It's a big house and a big property, but that's going to start attracting attention," Mary pointed out. "Not to mention getting crowded."

"Don't worry about the crowding. I'm going to do some expanding on the lower level before we move the asura in," I promised. "Oberis has been promising to train me on that particular trick for a while, and now we need it."

It was apparently an odd merger of the Gift of Force and the Gift of Between, creating space where there hadn't been space before. Oberis also possessed the Gift of Glamor, which meant he could literally create entire invisible wings to buildings, already decorated and furnished.

I was pretty sure all I was going to be able to create was space, but even if we had to install floors and walls ourselves, the house was going to need expansion.

Apparently, being a Fae Noble came with multitudes.

"That's...so damn weird," Mary told me. "I kind of want to watch."

"Apparently, there are shifter shamans who can do it, but they're few and far between," I said.

She chuckled.

"You just described shamans in general, Jason," she reminded me. "There aren't any in Calgary. At all."

"I could give suggestions there, but I know when I'm outside my bailiwick," I said with a grin. My understanding, backed up by the High Court's files, was that the *potential* to be a shaman was more common among shifters than they thought.

But unlike most fae powers, there was no instinctiveness to the use of that set of Gifts. Another shaman had to find the potential and train them. Which meant that so long as Calgary didn't have any shamans, Calgary would continue to lack shamans.

"And what about this sword?" Coleman asked. "That strikes me as concerning."

"More than concerning," I admitted. "I'm going to need you to double- and triple-secure meeting room one. Cut off from all non-magical communications, blocked off from Between access if you can manage it."

He swallowed.

"Just...who are you contacting?" he asked.

"I need to talk to the High Court," I said quietly. "I think the Masked Lords just did an end run around our entire plan."

———

When I say "the High Court," I usually just mean Mabona and Ankaris, and this time was no exception. There were seven other members of the High Court, but I'd only met the Unseelie Lord.

The Seelie Lord, the Ladies of the Seasons, and the Puck were strangers to me—and I didn't want to get tangled up in the affairs of more Powers than I had to.

Mabona was my Queen, however, which meant reaching out to her was easy. As her Vassal, we had an almost unbreakable link. I could contact her through it, though it wasn't great for communication of any level of detail.

As a Noble of the Wild Hunt, I had a similar but weaker connection to Ankaris. I could let both of them know that I needed to speak with them without so much as picking up the phone. Videoconferencing and telephones were great, but sometimes the most secure way of communicating was to step entirely outside the mortal world.

The mystical connection apparently carried at least some of my urgency with it. A projection of Mabona appeared within moments, and Ankaris's projection arrived before she'd even finished saying hello.

"Kilkenny," Ankaris greeted me, with a nod. "Mabona. I presume there is a reason that we aren't having this conversation via the internet. What happened?"

"The Masked Lords have stolen *Asi* from the order of asura who guarded it," I told them. "I don't know enough about that weapon or about the ritual they used *Esras* for, but I can't help feeling they would only have stolen it if they had a reason."

"The Asi Warriors guarded that blade with their lives, inside a temple-fortress with everything from swords to *tanks* ready for its defense," Ankaris said slowly. "*How?*"

"The Masked Lords hired them to kill me and I was too stubborn to die," I replied. "So, they'd lost too many and deployed too many over here. I don't know what they hit the fortress with, but according to the asura, the order of the Asi Warriors is no more. The only survivors are here in Calgary."

"And have sworn you Fealty," Mabona realized aloud. "I wondered who, when I felt you receive those oaths."

A Vassal never truly kept secrets from their liege. I was still surprised to realize that my Queen had felt me receiving the asuras' fealty.

"So, the Masked Lords now have *Asi*, the first sword of the deva." Ankaris sighed. "That's…that's bad. You're correct, Jason. *Asi* is just as old, just as tied to power, as *Esras*. The hands that wielded it were Adityas, not Powers of the High Court, but the end result is the same."

"They can use it to fuel their ritual," I said.

"Exactly. Our attempts to keep you out of their hands just became redundant." He turned to Mabona. "We need to gather the Court. If the Masked Lords now possess another artifact of that potency, then we must prepare for true war."

"Damn them." My Queen's voice was tired. "Arrange it, Ankaris. I will attend."

"What about Jason?" Ankaris turned his attention back to me.

"You are no longer the target you were," Mabona told me. "But your power and rank remain the same. I will lend you my guards for a while longer, but I suggest you begin recruiting your own retainers." She smiled. "The asura are a good start, though they have their vulnerabilities as you've seen."

"You remain a Noble of the Wild Hunt," Ankaris said with a sigh. "Coleman and his troop will remain with you. You may have insight or opportunities we have not realized—but even if you do not, know that you *will* be called to war.

"If the Masked Lords wish to take down the High Court, then they will face the Wild Hunt. That is our duty. That is our *purpose*."

"I am sworn to serve," I told them both. "What do you need of me?"

"For now, keep your head down," Mabona told me. "Just because the Masked Lords have *one* artifact doesn't mean they won't prefer to have two!"

16

MY LUNCH MEETING was surprisingly quiet, with the collection of locals and imports I'd gathered staring into the cups of coffee that Coleman had made for us. The pasta dish Mary and I had put together was growing cold, but no one was really feeling up for food.

"So, that's it?" Oberis asked finally. The city's Fae Lord was looking unusually informal, lacking anything resembling a suit jacket or tie with his slacks and dress shirt. "Now we know the Masks have an artifact, you're basically left to your own devices?"

I waved a hand at Coleman and Kristal.

"Coleman's troop is apparently sticking with me, though I'm on notice that Kristal's team will be moving on sooner or later."

"If it's war, then we have other battles to fight," she agreed. "I can't imagine you'll be sitting on the sidelines for long either."

"A Noble of the Wild Hunt?" Coleman snorted. "No, you'll be in the thick of it soon enough, Kilkenny. And my troop and I will be right beside you. You have my oath on that."

"And I was told that, too," I confirmed. "The High Court has no choice now but to prepare for war. If the Masked Lords have an artifact that can fuel their ritual, then our Powers are vulnerable."

"And since they're the only target we've ever known the Masked

Lords to be after, everything goes to hell now," Oberis agreed. He swallowed his lukewarm coffee and passed the cup to Robert. "Grab me some more coffee?"

The young Noble nodded and rose to obey.

"War." The word hung in the room like an anvil as the youth passed the cup back. "What does that even entail when it's fae against fae?"

I looked over at Oberis.

"I don't even know, myself," I admitted. Robert and I were roughly the same age, as young by human standards as we were by supernatural. "Given that, apparently, the last one was literally right before I was born."

"It's quiet and it's ugly," Calgary's Fae Lord told us. "We're talking assassinations and small-squad ops. We're at a disadvantage since we don't even know who our enemy is. Our own right-hand people could turn out to wear a Mask. Lord Andrews's reputation and power base were shaken by the revelation of Andrell's treachery."

Lord Jon Andrews was the Lord of the Unseelie, the highest-ranked member of that group and their voice on the High Court. Andrell, who had been tasked to create an Unseelie Court in Calgary and blown a lot of things open along the way, had been one of his chosen troubleshooters.

"So, what happens now?" Mary asked.

"Well, for one thing, we bring Raja Venkat and his people into our fold," I told them. "They swore fealty to me. I don't know if I trust them yet, but I have to honor that.

"They're in my service with the intention of fighting the Masked Lords, so I'll be keeping my own eyes open. There has to be an answer we're missing, some way we can use the link between me and *Esras* against them still."

"I don't suppose the Asi are sufficiently linked to the sword to track them through it?" Robert asked. "That should be possible, shouldn't it?"

"They'd need a far closer link than anything they have," Oberis replied. "For me to track the sword through them, one of them would have had to have carried it for months. Possibly years—and recently, too.

"A Mage might be able to do more with less, but…" He shrugged. "We don't have that kind of link to work with."

His words rankled in my brain like a loose tooth. I was going to have to think about that.

"More than anything, I think we need to start going over global news," I told my team. Oberis and Robert were guests, not subordinates, but they were also smart enough to know I wasn't giving *them* orders.

"The destruction of the Asi's temple-fortress made the news; it was a big terror attack. I don't think any of us registered it as relevant to our interests…so what else have we missed?"

I grimaced and sigh.

"Who else have the Masked Lords killed without us realizing they were coming at us from the side?"

"It wasn't your duty to see this coming, Jason," Oberis pointed out. "You were tasked to lay a trap and be bait, and you did so quite well."

"Well enough that our enemies used that trap to their advantage," I said. I shook my head. "They used *me* to set this up."

"And it was Ankaris's job, not yours, to see that coming," Coleman told me. "Your task was here. The grander war was his responsibility."

"Well, right now, the Court I am sworn to defend is vulnerable and my father's murderers are running around free," I reminded them. "So, I am *making* this mess our responsibility, do you understand?

"I may not have been given a task, but I have authority and I have resources, and I will be *damned* if I let them go unused now!"

———

Raja Venkat Asi looked more than a little out of place amidst the blowing snow. Despite the subfreezing temperatures and the snow beginning to pile up on the driveway to the house, the asura warlord was still shirtless underneath a long leather trench coat.

His two companions were more appropriately dressed for the

weather, every inch of the men covered in cloth against a temperature they clearly weren't used to.

Asi bowed to me and then again to Coleman after exiting the car, taking in the trio of Hunters that just *happened* to be in position to watch the meeting while armed, with a small grin.

"Ah, it's good to see that the man I've sworn allegiance to isn't a fool," he told me. "Lord Kilkenny." He turned to Coleman and offered his hand. "And I believe this is Captain Damh Coleman of the Wild Hunt, yes?"

"Yes," the Hunter said coldly. He didn't take the proffered handshake. "We've got a prefabricated army barracks set up for you and your people."

Asi glanced past us to the green not-quite-tent set up behind the house.

"It'll serve," he said cheerfully. "It's not a windowless basement, after all!"

"Your eventual quarters in the house are currently, well, lacking in such amenities as floors and walls," I told him. I'd spent several hours learning how to fold space with Oberis after lunch, but the space I'd created currently resembled a hole in the basement wall.

It would, once I was done, have windows. Right now, it looked more like a cave with concrete walls.

"My home is ash and I'm currently in an old enemy's emergency shelter," he pointed out. "Even a tent is an improvement, and I'm familiar with the US Army's prefabs. It'll be warm enough."

"Says the man who isn't even wearing a T-shirt in minus eight," I replied. "How are you planning on getting your people here? We don't exactly have a bus service, and we can only run so many vehicles in and out before people start asking questions. It's a quiet street...but I'm not sure it's that quiet."

"Since I doubt your Hunters are prepared to ferry my people around just yet, we'll filter them in over the next few days," Asi explained. "We've got four vehicles between us, but that's not enough to move everyone."

"Make it work," I ordered. "Coordinate with Coleman; he runs security. That means he's in charge around here if I'm not here."

"I understand completely," the asura said with a nod. "We will need to prove our loyalty and trustworthiness. We were foes until very recently."

"And the speed you switched sides is making me very twitchy," Coleman told him.

Asi closed his eyes and inhaled deeply.

"Seventeen generations, Captain," he said very, very quietly. "That is how many *generations* of my descendants were in our fortress when the Masked Lords burned it down. My children and their children and their children for seven hundred years. Gone. Dead. Murdered by our shared enemy.

"I swore fealty to Jason Kilkenny, but I would hunt this enemy regardless. I will have blood, Captain Coleman." He opened his eyes again, and for a single instant, I almost pitied the Masked Lords.

"I will *wash this world* in blood if that is what it takes to avenge my children. But I think a more targeted approach is wise, so I join you in Kilkenny's service."

Coleman nodded once, sharply.

"I didn't say I didn't understand," he told the older supernatural. "Just that it makes me twitchy. We'll find them, Raja Venkat Asi. Together."

"I know we will." Asi sighed sharply. "I know we will."

17

THERE WERE enough people coming and going from the house—we were going to have to come up with a better name at some point—that someone interrupting me while I was folding space to expand the basement was inevitable.

"Hold on one moment," I said to the person who had knocked on the doorframe behind me. My focus managed to hold through the interruption and I concentrated. Move *this* piece of the Between *here*, fold a layer of Force *there*, twist *here* and...

Everything popped into place with a suddenness that still surprised me, and the section of unfinished basement I was working on was twice as large. Another five hundred square feet of bare concrete was now squeezed into the underground space of the house.

That done, I turned around to see who had interrupted me. I was *not* expecting, I had to admit, one of Talus's goblins.

A moment later, however, I recognized her.

"Hello, Lan Tu," I greeted her. Lan Tu was in the service of the Magus MacDonald, one of the handful of servants he'd taken on after his magically augmented Enforcers had betrayed him.

"Greetings, Lord Kilkenny," she told me with a small bow. Her face was uncovered here, in supernatural territory, and the five-foot-tall goblin managed to be adorable even bald and with tusks.

Or perhaps because she was bald and had tusks. It was hard to be sure.

"I apologize for interrupting, I did not realize you were Working."

I could hear the capital W there. That was a Wizard's phrasing, not a fae one, but I recognized it anyway. Lan Tu's boss, it seemed, was rubbing off on her.

"I am done for now," I admitted. "I'm still learning this trick and it's tiring. How may I help you?"

"My *trùm* sent me to find you," she said. "He wishes to meet with you at your earliest convenience."

Trùm was Vietnamese for boss or master or something like that. I'd only ever heard Lan Tu use it to refer to the Magus MacDonald—and regardless of my own new rank and power and the supernatural politics of the city, there was no question that Calgary remained Kenneth MacDonald's city.

Earliest convenience meant *right now.*

"Of course," I told her with a bow. "Do you have a vehicle here?"

She looked surprised.

"Yes, of course."

"Give the keys to Coleman; he'll make sure it gets back to the Tower. You and I are going a different route," I said with a smile.

––––––

LAN TU CLUNG tightly to my arm as we stepped out of Between into the one area of MacDonald's Tower that wasn't blocked against that kind of travel.

There were ways around his barriers—I had a small vial of quicksilver, mercury mixed with heartstone, hanging around my neck that would allow me to overpower them, for example—but none of those ways were subtle.

If someone bulled past MacDonald's security, he'd know. And if they didn't, well, there were two goblins and two kami in body armor with assault rifles guarding that entrance.

"Identify," one of the kami snapped in Japanese-accented English.

"Jason Kilkenny and Lan Tu," I told them. Even from several feet away I could feel the cold iron in their guns. They almost certainly were loaded with triple-kill rounds—silver, cold iron, and rock salt. Or possibly silver, cold iron and garlic distillate. There were a few versions of the bullets, depending on what your three most likely hostiles were.

"Ah." The kami guardian bowed. I could see the rippling aura of his *other* body shifting around him as he did. "Welcome to the Tower, Lord Kilkenny."

I winced.

"I don't actually hold that title," I pointed out. I'd told Lan Tu this before, but the Wizard's staff were apparently stubborn.

"You are close enough for those who are not fae," the kami told me with a chuckle. "Magus MacDonald is in his office. You know the way?"

"I do," I agreed. "Can you get Lan Tu something warm to drink? Between was a bit more of a shock to her system than I expected."

The goblin woman was shivering despite being dressed for outside in a Calgary winter.

"We can do that," one of the goblins, almost certainly a cousin, told me. "You should get to the Magus."

"Of course," I agreed. "But I want to be sure she's taken care of."

If she suffered any side effects from traveling Between, that was my fault.

"I am fine, my lord," Lan Tu told me with a smile. "I appreciate the trip and the concern, but my master is worried. I have not seen him this afraid before—please, go to him."

Afraid? Magus MacDonald was a *Power*, a being capable of rewriting reality around him at a level even other supernaturals could only dream of. What could scare him?

"Very well." I passed her over to her cousin and gave the rest of the guardians a nod.

———

MacDONALD'S OFFICE was on the top floor of one of the tallest skyscrapers in downtown Calgary, with one wall made entirely of windows allowing him to look out over his domain. The office tower was tall enough that we were actually looking *down* at the Calgary Tower and its touristy rotating restaurant.

MacDonald had a heavy desk with the absolute top of the line in electronics, links to Fae-Net and presumably half a dozen equivalent subsections of the dark web. It was all shut down and dark right now, and the Wizard stood by the wall of windows.

"My lord Magus?" I asked hesitantly.

"Kilkenny. Come here," he instructed.

I obeyed. You didn't argue with Wizards. I'd been known to occasionally whine at MacDonald, in particular, but I didn't *argue* with him.

It wasn't until I approached him that I realized he was holding a bottle of rum in his right hand, open and almost half-empty. MacDonald was apparently drinking—hard.

"To forgotten times and remembered friends," he said aloud before taking another swallow of the liquor.

"My lord?"

"Your war has spilled wider than I ever feared," he told me. "To where it cannot be permitted to spread."

He couldn't possibly mean...

"Sandhya Patel has stood guardian over the River Ganges for five hundred years," the Wizard told me. "She has been a neutral arbiter between deva and asura, colonizer and colonized, for all that time. She was one of the oldest of us, though far from the strongest."

"Was?" I asked. That was impossible. Mages did not die except by their own choice. Except...

"Your Masked Lords apparently decided to test if their stolen sword could duplicate what the spear once did for them," he said quietly. "Patel was the closest Power they knew they could locate. She has always been open to the people of the land she watches over. Her monastery is a point of pilgrimage for both mortal and supernatural alike."

He sighed.

"Or was. It's far enough out of the way that the mortal news hasn't caught up yet, but every pilgrim there is dead. Mortals, super-naturals, deva, asura, fae…even vampires; Patel did not judge those who came to her so long as they observed the truce in her monastery."

"And her?" I asked quietly.

"Murdered. *Asi*, it seems, can serve the same focal purpose as *Esras* did, and their ritual works as well against my kind as against the Powers of the High Court."

The office was silent.

"We have a rule, us Magi," he finally said. "If one of us dies, three of us descend upon the perpetrators. We destroy them. It has been made very clear over the centuries, and Patel is only the third of us to ever be killed."

"And?"

"The Masked Lords knew of our rule," MacDonald concluded. "They killed *everyone*, Jason. Anyone who might have been able to tell us who they were. Even if anyone had survived, we already know their masks block our scrying.

"They have made enemies of the Magi and they *do not care*. What monster has incubated hidden in the structures of Court and Fealty? Are they not bound by their oaths as the rest of you are?"

I sighed.

"There are ways to break Fealty," I noted. I wasn't aware of anyone ever actually *using* them, but the mere fact that we knew they existed meant someone had. "I imagine the Masked Lords learned those first, long ago. Before any of this even began.

"They have broken their oaths and shielded their crimes behind masks and magic. We already hunt them, Magus MacDonald. Any aid we can provide the Magi we will gladly give."

"Will it bring back our dead sister?"

I let the office fall to silence again.

"You know that is beyond even the Powers," I finally told him. "We cannot do anything you cannot. If they can hide from your scrying, we can only find them in the same searches we have carried out since I was born. Our hope was to lure them into an ambush, but…"

"But they found an alternative to *Esras*," MacDonald murmured. "I must wonder, Kilkenny, if they will still come for you. For revenge, if nothing else."

"Then I will have surprises for them. I don't believe the asura who have entered my service would miss the opportunity for their vengeance."

He snorted.

"You must eventually bring those before me; you know this."

"I do. Right now, we're working on making sure they have somewhere to live and that my people don't kill them," I admitted. "I'm guessing they didn't present themselves when they first arrived."

Calgary's particular set of rules said that everyone was presented to the Wizard when they arrived. That was how I had first met MacDonald, long before.

The asura, though, had snuck into the city and hadn't cared about our Covenants. They would learn them and obey them now. Fealty went both ways, after all, and if they broke Calgary's rules, *I* would be held responsible.

"I will give you leeway," he told me. "The situation is unusual and you have earned that much trust. As for the Masked Lords..."

"I will advise the High Court of what you have told me," I said. "Anything we learn will be passed on. We would be fools to decline the aid of such powerful allies against our now-mutual foe."

"I wish it had not come to this," MacDonald replied, turning back to the window and drinking more rum. "The wars of mortal men are dangerous enough, but if we turn the wills of Powers upon each other? I do not know what this modern world will make of that.

"Or if it will even survive."

18

Asi sank his face into his hands at the table as I filled my people in. Coleman, Asi and Mary were gathered around the kitchen table. Kristal was leaning against the kitchen island with a beer in her hand.

"Patel was good people," Asi said slowly. "India is almost as bad as Germany or Ireland for being a mixing point of supernaturals. Everything from deva and asura born there, to imported fae, vampires and kami. Efreeti from the Middle East, jianshi from China…there would have been a lot more supernatural bloodshed over the centuries without her. We needed that neutral person without ties to the rest who was powerful enough to enforce her arbitrations."

"And now she's gone and the world is getting much scarier," Mary said. "It's been over three hundred years since a Magus was killed, Jason. The Masked Lords just took a scary step up in their actions… and it was a *test*."

"They've killed a Power before. They killed *four* of the High Court before," I reminded her. "They're branching out, but it's not really a step *up*, per se."

"Except that no one challenges the Magi," Coleman told me. "It's one thing to challenge the High Court, who have a thousand other distractions to keep them occupied. The Magi have no such distractions. No courts, no responsibilities. If they decide to turn their powers to hunting someone down, there is nothing holding them back."

"It seems the Masked Lords aren't worried." I sighed. "It also seems they've recruited back to strength. As it was explained to me, their ritual required twenty-one participants of roughly the power of a Fae Lord, and only half of them escaped the war in Ireland."

"They can only have so many true Lords among their number," Coleman said. "There aren't that many Lord-level Fae in the world— maybe two hundred. *Maybe*."

"So, roughly a tenth of all Fae Lords have broken their fealty to the High Court," I concluded. "At least. Anyone get the feeling there's something *wrong* with our damn system?"

"I wasn't going to say it," Mary said sweetly. "On the other hand, one of my Clan Alphas tried to wreck the city a year ago, so...we're not much better, I guess."

"And they're hiding themselves from the Wizards. That takes a lot of power in and of itself, and they can only offload so much of that onto the Masks."

"I think that has to be their weakness," Asi finally said. "If they're shielding themselves always, that drains a lot of power. They have to have some safe zone, some place they can hide."

"That doesn't help us much," I told him.

"Except you told us *Asi* was to replace another weapon," he noted. "Why? Did they lose that weapon?"

Coleman chuckled.

"No. The fourth Power they killed last time was Calebrant, the Lord of the Wild Hunt. Jason's father.

"*Esras* was already linked to the Horned King and the line of Lugh. Calebrant's last action was to make that link stronger. He bound the weapon to his bloodline so only his kin would ever be able to wield it."

"Which is a list that currently consists of myself and Ankaris," I told Asi. "They have *Esras*, but they can't use it without capturing one of us. Or, I suppose, literally getting their hands on a large quantity of our blood."

"That explains why we were supposed to deliver your entire body," he noted. "I'm not certain that gives us anything useful, though."

Mary was looking thoughtful, then snapped her fingers.

"Wouldn't that be a sympathetic link?" she asked.

I stared at her.

"I'm not sure I follow, but please, go on," I told her. No one else in the room seemed to know what she meant either, but I knew better then to dismiss Mary's brain. She was probably the smartest person in that room.

She flushed slightly.

"I don't have any power as you guys judge these things, but I read a bunch of fantasy and used to play D&D," she admitted. "In those fantasies, if you have a sympathetic link—a piece of an object or a person—you can use it to scry even if the target is concealed somehow.

"If you're bound to the spear to such an extent that no one can wield it, surely we can follow that bond, can't we?"

I looked at Coleman.

"Damh? You're the most familiar with hunting with fae magic."

"We don't use anything like that," he admitted. "But...it might work. There's even more ways to bar our tracking magic than there are to block a Wizard's Sight." He shook his head. "Hell, a cold iron nail in your shoe is enough to thwart us if you know what you're doing."

"We could try it," I suggested. "We have, what, three Hunters with the Gift of Tracking?"

"Including me," Coleman agreed. "Let me see."

He rose and walked over to me, putting his hand on my shoulder. I felt a warm tingle of power run through his hand as he focused his gift, trying to trace the link between myself and the spear my father had bound.

Coleman stood there and the rest of us were silent for at least thirty seconds, then shook his head.

"That is a *very* clever idea, Ms. Tenerim," he told Mary. "It's something I'm going to have to experiment with in general; we've never thought of trying to acquire things that belong to the target for tracking. We usually just, well, start where they were and follow them from there."

"Did you get anything?" I asked.

"I can tell the link is there with my Gift," he said. "I can feel it, but I can't trace it. Part of it is that I don't have any practice doing this. As I work with this method of Tracking, I think I might be able to do more, but part of it is also that the other end *is* shielded."

"You know what the answer is, then," Asi pointed out. "If a Hunter cannot Track it, but the concept works… you need a Power, my lord. Preferably a Wizard—and if the Wizards are as furious with the Masked Lords as you say…"

"Then MacDonald may well help us," I agreed. "And if he isn't willing to help us for that, he still owes me a boon for saving his life."

I took Mary's hand and squeezed.

"He'll help," I told her. "And you may have just given the key to finding these bastards."

"That's good," she replied. "Because for a moment there, I thought I was embarrassing myself for nothing!"

———

THE GUARDS AT THE "SIDE ENTRANCE" to MacDonald's Tower were different this time. Lan Tu's brother, Skavrosh, was in command. He shared his sister's height but wore a crisp business suit and black veil —and was carrying a meticulously maintained AK-47.

He was the only goblin there today, though, and his two fellow guards were both dog shifters from Clan Fontaine.

I recognized them both and was surprised to see them. Clan Fontaine's Alpha had betrayed the Wizard and the city's Covenants, joining a conspiracy to kill off MacDonald in exchange for the promise of being made Speaker.

Only part of the Clan had actually been involved in that, I supposed, but the presence of Fontaine shifters among MacDonald's security staff suggested the Magus was more forgiving than I was.

"Lord Kilkenny," Skavrosh greeted me, with a small bow. He kept his eyes on me as he bowed, and his finger was right next to the trigger guard of his rifle. His job was to keep MacDonald safe. There would be no risks taken here.

"I need to speak with Magus MacDonald," I told the guards. "It is urgent."

"The Magus is in conference," Skavrosh told me, his black eyes unreadable above his veil. "But you can go upstairs and wait. The constructs will bring you coffee so long as you don't leave the waiting area."

And if I left the waiting area, well, my best guess was that MacDonald had at least as many armed retainers in the Tower as I had at the house.

"I can wait," I confirmed. "But this is important."

"I trust you on that," he told me. "That's why I'm letting you wait for him instead of telling you to come back later, eh?"

————

DESPITE THE GROWING collection of random supernaturals in his employ, MacDonald still kept his secretarial tasks and general house-keeping in the hands of magical constructs. No mortal would have been able to tell that the collection of near-androgynous blonde women running the Tower weren't real humans unless they saw enough of them together to realize that they were all *very* similar.

I had more than enough exposure to pick them out by now; plus, my own gifts allowed me to sense the presence of the invisible constructs also in MacDonald's recently renovated waiting room. I knew that the two "decorative" cabinets in the room contained an extensive array of weapons tailored to fight almost any supernatural in existence.

It was a sign of trust that there were no living guards in the room, though. There were faster and deadlier supernaturals out there than me, but my gifts were certainly capable of tearing open those cabinets and allowing me to steal weapons from them before the constructs could react.

Instead, I took a seat in one of the comfortable chairs as a construct wordlessly brought me a coffee. With only me in the room, there was no pretense that the magical creation had actually bothered with the coffee machine. She handed me a steaming Starbucks latte—or at least a perfect duplicate of one, since this cup had almost certainly never passed within the walls of a chain coffee store.

"Thank you."

The construct bobbed her head at me and I chuckled. The creatures weren't alive or sentient by any measure…but they *were* more than mere extensions of MacDonald's will, too, more capable of exceeding their programming than many thought.

Treating them like people never hurt.

"How long is the conference expected to last?" I asked the construct. They were sufficiently connected to MacDonald to have that information, even if the Magus was the only one who knew.

"He is uncertain," she replied. "The Magi discuss the death of one of their own. This will take some time." She paused. "He suggests you get comfortable, Lord Kilkenny. We will bring you supper."

I sighed and nodded.

"I appreciate it," I told the construct. "I will wait for the Magus."

19

I WASN'T ENTIRELY sure if the constructs had any skills that MacDonald didn't. If that was the case, then the Magus was an incredible cook along with his many other talents. I'd been fed lesser meals at five-star restaurants.

The good food and coffee helped while away the time as I waited for his conference to be finished, but I was still in the Wizard's waiting room for over an hour before one of the constructs appeared out of nowhere.

"MacDonald is available now. He's waiting for you in his office," the magical creature told me.

"Thank you."

The construct set out to lead the way and I followed with a hidden sigh. I did know my way around the Tower now, but the constructs were...rather literal in interpreting their instructions.

This one had been told to bring me, so it was going to bring me.

MacDonald was sitting at his desk when I entered the room, his head in his hands and a coffee cup happily filling itself next to him. The cup finished filling and he grabbed it as I took a seat across him, and he took a long swallow.

"Kilkenny," he greeted me. "I apologize for the wait, but my brothers and sisters are...concerned. I was supposed to meet Oberis for supper three hours ago. Hopefully, he'll forgive me."

MacDonald and Oberis were lovers, a situation that avoided conflict of interest only by careful actions on MacDonald's part. I was pretty sure the Seelie Lord would forgive the Wizard missing a dinner, given everything going on.

"It's been a bad few weeks for us all," I agreed. "I take it your fellow Mages have had no luck tracing the Masked Lords?"

He grimaced.

"We think of ourselves as near-omnipotent and -omniscient, gods among men who wield powers even few supernaturals can even begin to imagine," he said bitterly. "We are neither used to nor graceful about being thwarted.

"And you are correct. The Masked Lords chose to challenge us because they knew they could hide from us. There will be consequences for this in the end; we do not forget easily...but they have eluded us for now."

"That's what I expected, even if I hoped for better luck," I admitted.

"Then why are you here, Kilkenny?" MacDonald asked. "I have neither the patience nor the time for idle chatter tonight. You waited an hour to see me, and there are demands on your time as well."

"We think we know how to find the Masked Lords," I told him. "It didn't work with the tracking abilities available to the Wild Hunt, but our tests suggested the idea was solid. We just didn't have the practice and power to break through their defenses."

He lowered his coffee cup back to his desk and studied me levelly.

"The massed power of the Mages has been bent to this task," he pointed out. "What do you think we did not try? Did not attempt? Why do you think we failed but your help can make us succeed?"

"Because I am linked to *Esras*," I reminded him. "By blood and magic, that spear is connected to me—and I imagine it is kept close to their chest. Before, we didn't want to find the spear. We wanted them to come to us.

"Now, though, finding the spear will bring us to them and we can unleash the vengeance they've earned upon them."

He studied me in silence.

"You know that you can wield *Esras* yourself, right?" he said. "If we bring you to the spear, you become a wild card in this game. A potential threat."

"I can't imagine the spear will make that much of a difference to me," I replied. "It's just a weapon, after all."

MacDonald chuckled.

"So is the gift I gave you," he pointed out. "But you are correct. We may be able to track the spear through you. We were so focused on hunting the Masked Lords themselves, we did not consider seeking their prizes. Potentially, we could also seek *Asi* through your new Vassal...but that is almost certainly shielded against this kind of magic.

"*Esras*, however, is now useless to them. We shall have to see."

He rose from his chair in a single forceful motion.

"Come with me," he instructed.

"Magus?"

"This is my office, Jason Kilkenny. It is not my Working space."

––––––––

I FOLLOWED the Wizard through his Tower. Most of the spaces I'd seen in the building, outside of MacDonald's own bedroom, were super-modern. The Tower was one of the newest, most modern buildings in downtown Calgary.

MacDonald's ownership of it was obscured through more trusts, pension funds, nonprofits and numbered companies than I could follow, but he owned it in its entirety. He lived and worked in the top half-dozen floors, and the company whose name was on the building had the rest.

Passing through the chrome and glass, however, we eventually reached a section of wall that looked like it had been removed from a medieval castle. Glass, steel and plaster gave way to barely-worked stone and a large metal door.

The door was doubly anachronistic. The wall looked like it came from the sixth century, the door looked like it belonged in the twelfth at the latest...and its locking system looked like it belonged in the twenty-fifth century.

Multiple tiers of passive and active maglocks secured the door, and the key seemed to be an entire array of complex high-tech readers. My rough guess was that opening the door required a retinal print, a palm print, and a DNA sample.

Except the man who'd installed it was a Wizard. Somewhere in all of that array of readers was probably a very simple switch that couldn't be seen from the outside, because MacDonald simply looked at the door and all of the locks calmly opened.

"Feel privileged, Lord Kilkenny," he told me as he led the way in. "Less than a dozen living non-Mages have seen my Working chamber." He chuckled. "Honestly, I'd be surprised if there are a hundred living non-Mages who have seen any Mage's Working chamber."

The crudely worked stone of the wall gave way into smooth stone quickly. The entire chamber had been carved into a single cave, and I could tell that we were no longer in an office tower in Calgary.

Or we were, but no one had lifted a fifty-meter-wide boulder up to the top of the tower. This space was as attached to the real world as Oberis's Court or the extra rooms in the basement of my house.

The sanctum had been moved over the years, but my guess was that it was attached to the wall that we'd passed through. It had probably once been a real cave, but that had been centuries ago at least.

Lines of orichalcum inlay swirled across the space in symbols that were as far beyond me as rockets were beyond the cave-dwellers who'd invented fire. I could feel the Power pulsing in this place, but I could barely even begin to comprehend what MacDonald would need this for, let alone how it worked.

"Take a seat in the center, Lord Kilkenny," MacDonald ordered. Candles were materializing from thin air, already lit as he placed them around the room with a gesture. "Once you're ready, we will begin."

He paused thoughtfully as he placed another ten candles.

"I must warn you. This will almost certainly hurt."

———

BY THE TIME I had taken a seat in the center of the chamber, there had to be at least a hundred candles lighting up the room. There were no chairs or cushions, leaving me sitting cross-legged in the blank spot that all of the orichalcum lines seemed to lead to.

"Good," MacDonald said briskly as he made one more circuit of the room, checking candles and the lines of the runes. I couldn't see what he was doing half of the time, but it looked like he was laying out other objects as well.

All of this was significantly more effort than I was used to seeing put into magic—and not quite what I was expecting from seeing a Power work. This was more than a simple tracking spell.

"Are you ready?" he finally asked.

"As I can be. What should I expect?" I asked.

"That depends on how strongly our masked friends have secured the spear," MacDonald admitted. "This might be very quick and simple, rendering all of this preparation unnecessary."

"Or?"

"Or it could be long, complicated and painful," he told me. He passed me an orichalcum bowl and a silver-bladed knife. "I need some of your blood in the bowl, then place it at the convergence of the lines."

I'd been expecting something similar. Not that it made cutting my hand to bleed into the bowl any more fun. I healed faster than humans, but not nearly as fast as many supernaturals.

It took a few seconds for the cut to clot over, by which time I'd hopefully dripped enough into the bowl. Wincing against the pull of the clot, I put the bowl where MacDonald had indicated and then leaned back.

"Now. Wait."

Power filled the room. MacDonald was often an unassuming man, and it was easy to forget you stood in the presence of the one of closest things available to a god.

Suddenly, I wasn't in a room with a man. I shared the chamber with a Presence, an entity older and more unknowable than anything a mortal would ever meet. This wasn't the first time I'd been around a Power in full form, however, and I swallowed the urge to scream and run.

His magic wrapped around the room. Candles flared brighter and orichalcum lines glittered like the rising sun. The energy spiraled through the Working chamber...and then struck me.

The blood in the bowl in front of me started to hiss and steam, and a moment later, heat flashed through my body as my own blood warmed under the magic.

For the first few seconds, it was merely uncomfortable. It rapidly progressed to burning throughout my entire body, my entire circulatory system heated far beyond what a human or inhuman body was designed to stand.

And *still* power flowed through me and the runes grew brighter. Unconsciously, I flung my hand out into the air. The clot broke under the heat and the gesture, and more blood splattered out and *stopped* in midair.

A spinning circle formed of my own blood took shape, a glowing portal into another place, but it showed nothing. Just an iron wall.

"Hold," MacDonald barked. "Do not let it go."

I'd thought I'd been burning up before. Now *fire* flashed through my body as the Magus focused all of the incredible might of a Power of the world on me. The Working chamber amplified his strength, and his magic hammered into me again.

And again.

And again.

I coughed hard and realized I was spitting up blood. *Steaming* blood that spattered across the spinning disk in front of me.

The iron wall shattered. Whatever shield had barred our way failed in the face of the strength of the link my father had forged and the power MacDonald was pouring down that link.

I could see *Esras*.

It was...surprisingly plain. A shaft of dark brown ash held an old iron spearhead, a wide leaf shape with a smaller cross-blade in the center. There was no rust or marking on the blade, though, and it seemed to glow with a soft golden light.

The view pulled back slightly, revealing that the spear sat in a display case surrounded by bulletproof glass. Even my untrained eye could pick out the alarms and laser tripwires around it, and MacDonald pulled the vision back farther.

It was inside a vault of some kind. It wasn't the only item in the vault, but it clearly held pride of place. I barely had time to register that the vault contained anything else, though, before the Magus kept drawing the view back.

There was a reason for that. *Esras* had distracted me momentarily, but fire continued to burn through my veins and I realized that I was reaching the limits of my endurance. If we didn't actually *locate* the spear, the spell might well kill me.

I only had the tiniest glimpses after that as the pain swept through me, but the view kept drawing back until it was a bird's-eye view of some kind of structure

Then the spell ended...and I collapsed forward into a pool of my own blood.

20

I WOKE up in an unfamiliar bed with someone washing my face.

"Be calm, be calm," Lan Tu's familiar accented voice said as I started to move. "You're recovering, but rest."

I exhaled and let her finish washing the caked blood off my face before I opened my eyes. The room looked much like I expected: the kind of medical suite assembled by people with money and no desire to visit a hospital.

Lan Tu quickly went over most of my vitals before pronouncing me fit to get up.

"I thought you'd heal faster," she admitted. "You've been down for hours. My *trùm* advised Mary and your people; I am to inform him now you're up."

"Thank you, Lan Tu," I said. "Do you know if Mary is coming here?"

"My *trùm* asked her to wait until he'd spoken to you," she told me. "I have passed on what I have seen; she knows you are well."

"Well, huh?" I asked with an arched eyebrow at the blood-soaked cloth in the goblin's hand.

"You are now," she replied. "My *trùm* is quite upset at your injuries. If I leave to get him, will you please stay in the bed and rest? You're still healing."

"Go ahead," I told her.

I let myself sink into the cushions on the bed as she disappeared. It might *look* like a hospital bed, but I'd never been in a hospital that spent this much on the mattresses and pillows. Even with the oxygen monitor on my finger and the IV drip, I was possibly more comfortable there than at home.

It was only a few minutes at most before MacDonald returned, the graying Wizard checking my vitals himself before coming over to the bed.

"You're fine," he told me gruffly. "Lan Tu is just used to treating shifters and goblins, both of which heal faster than you do. You'd have needed a blood transfusion were you actually mortal."

"Great. Did it work?" I asked.

"The effects on you were worse than I anticipated," he admitted. "I apologize for that. I have rarely, if ever, encountered anti-scrying defenses of that strength. Without your blood-link to the weapon and my power, we would never have penetrated it."

"But we did?"

"We did," MacDonald confirmed. "I suspect they may have neglected the defenses around it as well, now that they have focused on *Asi* as their new tool." He shook his head. "It is possible that they had assembled sufficient power to protect the spear from even a blood-link-based scrying by a Magus. I cannot emphasize how paranoid and powerful your enemy is, Lord Kilkenny."

"They killed a Wizard, Mage MacDonald," I reminded him. "I'm not surprised. But you know where *Esras* is?"

"I do," he confirmed. "And that brings me back to how paranoid your enemy is...and how well informed."

"Sir?"

"You understand that there are Covenants that bind the Magi that we would not share with others, yes?" he asked. "Realize that those Covenants are old, and certain promises and commitments in them were made for reasons that have been forgotten by any mortal."

That didn't sound good.

"Magus?" I said questioningly.

He sighed.

"There are places we are sworn to never go," he told me. "Scattered around Europe, Asia and Africa, in the main. Cities, counties, small countries..." He shook his head. "Rome. The entire island of Malta. Places home to Powers we did not desire to challenge. Some of those Powers are no more. Others remain but are long retreated from even the Powers' eyes."

"And they're hiding in one of those places?"

"Malta," he confirmed. "A renovated old fort of the Order of St. John. The...creature whose territory we promised not to violate remains on the island, in the temple at Ġgantija."

I didn't even know what that *was*.

"What kind of creature?"

"What mortals once called gods. She has gone by many names, but she was worshipped by the Stone Age dwellers of Malta first, so when the world changed, she returned there." MacDonald shook his head.

"If they are on the islands of Malta, she knows they're there and they have paid sufficient tribute to go unbothered. She doesn't care about even supernatural politics. But..."

"But if you were to attempt to intervene there?" I asked.

"My brothers and sisters would prevent me if they could. We do not know the limits of her power or her willingness to invoke chaos. A Power on her islands would be a challenge she could not ignore."

I sighed.

"And if I were to go? With, say, an army of asura and Hunters?"

"She would barely notice you unless you decided to remain," he admitted. "She won't defend them, regardless of how much tribute they've paid, but she won't permit a Power to enter her islands unchallenged."

I exhaled.

"So, you can't help us," I said.

"I cannot. I can tell you where they are and where within the fortress they have hidden *Esras*, but I cannot enter the islands of Theia's domain."

"All right." I nodded grimly. "Then it looks like it's a good thing I picked up Raja Asi and his friends. Every gun and sword is going to be helpful for this."

"Step carefully, Jason Kilkenny," MacDonald warned. "Even though Theia should not intervene, she is old and capricious. And remember, the Masked Lords must be expecting an attack.

"What they have done cannot go unanswered."

21

"Malta."

Mabona sounded angry. Her projection just looked tired. The video of Ankaris was much the same, and the people gathered in my own conference room weren't much better.

Mary was sitting next to me, managing to not quite hover. Coleman and Asi were doing their best to out-loom each other.

Oberis, Robert and Talus were also linked in by videoconference.

"I'm guessing that the High Court is bound by much the same restriction as the Magi?" I asked. Her tone would line up with that.

"We have no official treaty with the Titaness," Mabona told me. "But Theia will not permit a Power on her islands, and she is powerful enough to enforce that." My Queen winced. "Even among Powers, there is a gradation of who is stronger, and it most often goes with age."

"The Titaness is over seventy-five hundred years old," Ankaris concluded. "Even the Wild Hunt generally avoids her territory." He shook his head. "We should have guessed. Malta has always been a place for supernaturals who are not Powers to hide.

"So long as her tribute is paid, she does not care who is on her island other than the Powers."

"Will she protect them if we go after them?" I asked.

"I don't know," Ankaris admitted. "We have generally erred on the side of not interfering in her space."

"We have no choice now. If I take a team of asura and Hunters into Malta to retrieve *Esras*, am I going to be fighting a Titan?" I demanded.

"We don't know," Mabona repeated. "I don't believe she cares. A quick in-and-out operation should be safe."

"You said she requires tribute to stay on her island?" Mary asked.

"Yes. Silver or platinum, usually." Ankaris shook his head. "Theia is probably sitting on one of the world's largest stockpiles of those two metals."

"So, why don't we simply pay her tribute when we arrive, *then* move against the Masked Lords?" my girlfriend asked.

The meeting was silent for several long seconds, then Asi laughed aloud.

"We need to keep this one, my lord," he told me. "She's smarter than the rest of us put together!"

"You may be right," Ankaris allowed slowly. "Theia *might* choose to intervene if she sees our actions as...well, rude. But if you pay her appropriate honor and tribute, she should stand by and allow you to move against the Masked Lords."

"All right," I said, squeezing Mary's hand. "And what is the appropriate tribute for a strike team of thirty-odd asura and Greater Fae?"

"About fifteen tons of silver or a quarter of that in platinum," Mabona said instantly. "The favor of one of the oldest Powers alive does not come cheaply."

I winced.

"Okay...can someone lend me that?" I asked plaintively. "I don't think my bank account stretches that far."

"It will be arranged," Mabona told me. "Give me twenty-four hours." She managed to smirk despite the bags under her eyes.

"You'll need the practice in long-distance Betweening, anyway."

I sighed and nodded. She wasn't wrong. I hadn't actually left Calgary since learning to walk Between. The trip to Malta would be entirely outside my experience.

As THE MEETING BROKE UP, Mary and I retreated to the master suite of the house. Given the number of people living in the building now, that suite was our only actual private place in the entire ten-thousand-square-foot-and-expanding structure.

"I barely feel like I belong in these conversations," she admitted as she leaned against me. "I'm literally in a meeting with two frigging *Powers*, Jason."

"And you're the one who saw the solution," I pointed out. "As Raja said, it feels like you're smarter than the rest of us most days."

"That's because I'm a wildcat shifter and even *you* are a Fae Noble," Mary reminded me. "Neither of us is used to being able to just bull through things on sheer power, but I *still* can't—and there are starting to be a lot of situations that *you* can."

I hadn't even thought of that. I still thought of myself as "just a changeling" around half of the time, but she was right. I was also starting to regard a lot of things as surmountable problems that changeling me would have run away screaming from.

Not least a Masked Lord fortress inside the territory of what was potentially the *only* living Titan. My confidence there had more to do with the allies I was going to bring with me, but I was at least confident that I could *survive* being in the middle of the fight we were planning.

Even a year earlier, that wouldn't have been true.

I nodded and wrapped my arms around her.

"I can't say I haven't changed," I admitted. "My past is the same, but I keep getting dragged into this shit. And then we found out who my father was and everything that came with that."

"I know." She rested her head against my shoulder. "It's just weird, you know? I started dating a changeling, someone on roughly the same level of supernatural-ness as me. Now...now I'm dating a *Fae Noble*."

"It's still me," I told her, despite the chill running down my spine. "I'm not going anywhere. Unless..." I swallowed hard. "Unless you want me to."

"No," she said instantly. "*Mine.*"

I laughed at the fierceness of her tone and leaned into her myself.

"Good. I'm not planning on changing anything with us, even if *my* life keeps changing underneath me."

"I'm coming with you to Malta," she told me. It wasn't a request, and I nodded. "I'll bring Barry and his team, but I'm going to be with you in Malta. To watch your back, if nothing else."

"Good," I said. "Love…I have grounds to trust Coleman and Asi, but…" I shook my head.

"Damh Coleman has other allegiances. The asura…Powers be, I barely know anything about them except that they've sworn me Fealty. Having people with me that I know, that I can trust without question…"

I kissed her head.

"That's worth more than I can explain, I think. It's going to be dangerous and I wouldn't *ask* you to come," I admitted. "But I'm selfish enough to admit I'm grateful that you want to."

"Good boy," Mary told me with a chuckle. "So, this paying-tribute business. Any idea how that works?"

"Right now? I'm assuming we show up in Malta and borrow a Brink's truck," I said with a chuckle of my own. "This is entirely outside my experience."

"Mine, too," she agreed. "It's going to be interesting."

22

"YOU NEED to be familiar with where you're going, or at least the overall geography," Coleman told me as we stood in the middle of nothingness. "Where you are Between corresponds to the 'real' world, but how closely is variable. A variable you can control.

"At this level"—he gestured around at the vague clouds of gray around us—"the ratio is high. Every step you take here crosses multiple kilometers in the world. It's easy to get lost."

"That's understating things," I admitted. I couldn't pick out *any* landmarks or identifiers around me.

"It's a question of practice," he told me. "Look there." He pointed.

I followed his pointing hand. There was something there…something shrunk into insignificance versus its real-world presence.

"Is that the Rockies?" I asked.

"Exactly," he confirmed. "Almost nothing humanity has ever built is large enough to register this deep into the Between. You can go deeper…but few can do that and come *back*," he admitted. "Our beacons that we leave in the real world only reach this deep. If you go deeper, there are no landmarks. No links to the world. No beacons."

"So, how do we find our way?" I asked.

"We stay at this level and navigate by mountains, lakes and continents," he told me with a grin. "Even this deep, the trip to Malta will take almost two hours. We'll go over a map of the Mediterranean before we leave, make sure everyone knows what terrain we're covering."

"What about water?" I asked.

"Doesn't matter here," he said with a shake of his head. "You're not standing on the ground, Kilkenny. The only thing supporting you is your will. The only thing allowing you to breathe is your Gift."

"And we're bringing an entire group with us?"

"It's not as easy as I'd like," Coleman told me. "There's a reason we normally only have one Companion per Hunter. Including you and me, however, we only have ten Hunters. I'm guessing we're bringing more than twenty people."

"As many as we can," I replied. "If we could bring everyone, I would. That's a dozen shifters and twenty-plus asura."

"We can't," Coleman said bluntly. "If we had more Hunters, maybe. I'm *told* that twenty-seven Hunters—three cubed, of course—can create a safe pocket in Between and use that to transport larger groups. I've never seen it done."

"What can we do?" I asked.

"With a bit of work and practice, two passengers per Hunter," he told me. "My Hunters and Companions, you and I, and twelve others."

He sighed.

"I know it's not what you'd prefer—it's not what *I'd* prefer—but its all we can carry with only ten fae who can walk Between."

————

"YOU'RE ADORABLE," Raja Venkat Asi told me and Coleman an hour later when we broached the subject. "Forgetful, blind, arrogant...but adorable."

"Excuse me?" Coleman demanded.

"Kilkenny appears to be trying to forget that we were once his enemies," Asi pointed out.

...that was probably more correct than I was willing to admit. The less I thought about the fact that I'd fought the Asi Warriors before their survivors had entered my service, the less mental dissonance I had to deal with.

"*He* is forgetful," Asi concluded. "*You* are arrogant. You presume, Hunter, that the otherworld is restricted solely to you? That no other can follow you there or survive there?"

The Hunter troop Captain winced.

"That has generally been my experience," he admitted.

"But you chased me Between when you were hunting me, didn't you?" I asked. I'd forgotten the gold portals and the men who'd followed me into the trap we'd originally laid for the Masked Lords.

"We have less flexibility in our access than you Hunters do, but yes, three of our number—including myself—can enter the Between under their own power. All of my asura can *survive* Between."

He shrugged.

"If you can walk us across the barrier and guide us through the depths of the otherworld where even I would not normally dare to walk, then we do not require your Hunters to carry us."

"Then we can carry the shifters along with our Companions," I told Coleman. "I'm not going to complain about bringing fifty guns instead of thirty."

For me, the Between was chilly, with cold, crisp air. For someone without my Gift, it was a frozen vacuum. I was more than a little surprised that the asura could all survive there—and I had to wonder if that was because they had the same tolerances as a Hunter or if they simply didn't actually need to breathe.

"Let's get ready for the jump," I instructed. "We're waiting on Mabona to arrange the tribute, and once that's set up, we'll make our final plans."

Eighteen fae. Ten shifters. Twenty-two asura.

I really hoped the Masked Lords had relied on secrecy for their main defense.

23

MALTA WASN'T ACTUALLY *HOT*, per se, when we arrived. It just felt that way after almost two full hours of traveling Between, a place that even for a Hunter got colder over time.

There was no one in my little army who wasn't shivering as we emerged into the winter sunshine of the Mediterranean. The asura got the worst of it, still used to warmer climes than the rest of us and less inured to the ravages of the Between than Asi had suggested.

"Are your people okay?" I asked him and he held up a hand, his entire body continuing to shiver in the sunshine.

A long exhalation later and he looked over his team.

"We'll be fine," he told me. "I...have never taken this long a journey through the otherworld. I underestimated how bad it would be."

My actual Wild Hunters and Companions were fine, but they'd known what they were getting into. If nothing else, they'd all made the journey from Ireland to Calgary via Between.

Mary and her shifters looked about as bad off as I felt. We'd been Between before, but a trip of this length was something new for all of us.

"You can't warn someone what a long journey in the deep Between is like," Coleman told me. "I tried. But mere heavy clothing and winter preparation doesn't stack against the kind of bone-deep chill the Between brings."

"It's something else," I agreed. "Where are we?"

"North coast of the island of Gozo," Coleman replied. "Four or five kilometers from the Ġgantija complex where we'll find Theia."

"The fortress is on Malta itself, isn't it?" Mary asked. "How are we getting there?"

"Mabona sent one of her Vassals ahead from Ireland to prepare the way," I told her. "She should be meeting us shortly with a couple of rented vehicles, but we weren't going to sneak weapons through airport security in multiple countries."

Even most of the Hunters were visibly armed. The Companions, the shifters and the asura were all carrying guns and blades.

Of the ten Hunters there, only four of us could actually create Between storage spaces. A troop like Coleman's would make sure they had at least one so that they could store *all* of the troops' weapons.

I'd half-expected to be attacked on emerging from Between.

"Where are we meeting her?" Coleman asked.

I pulled out a phone and checked the GPS.

"At the nearest highway," I answered. "About, oh, ten minutes' walk that way."

"After all of that, we still need to walk?" Mary demanded.

"We couldn't have fifty people appear out of nowhere on the side of the highway," I said. "That ends up attracting attention we can't afford."

"And from there?" Coleman asked.

"From there, Mary and I go visit a god," I admitted. "One of the trucks Ana is bringing is full of platinum and silver. That's for the Titaness, to buy her permission for us to attack the Masked Lords."

"What happens if she refuses us?" Mary asked softly.

"Hope that doesn't happen," I told her. "Theia is quite capable of sending us all back to Calgary with a wave of her hand...but from what everyone is saying, I doubt that she's likely to feel that charitable."

To GET anything resembling secrecy on the crowded islands, we'd appeared in the middle of a farmer's field. From there, we carefully picked our way over to the Triq ix-Xagħra highway, where Ana Ormon was supposed to be waiting for us.

Fortunately, my Queen seemed to pick capable Vassals. We reached the highway to find a trio of trucks waiting for us. Two were semi trucks, as large as they got on this island, I guessed. The third was an armored transport vehicle.

A blonde woman with gray streaked through her hair was waiting for us with a big grin on her face. She waved when she saw me and crossed to the fence.

"How was your trip?" Orman asked cheerfully. I knew her apparent age was an affectation, but the Fae Noble radiated grandmotherly charm in a way I'd rarely met.

"Cold but swift," I replied. "Our rides?" I gestured at the trucks.

"Both are fitted out to carry people," she said. "The spells on them will fool most scanners and everything except a visual search." She shrugged. "They're usually used for smuggling migrants, but it's amazing how little money it took to rent them and their drivers for a few days."

"I'm guessing the spells are ours?" I asked.

"My glamors, yeah," Orman confirmed. "I didn't *tell* the drivers I'd added anything to their trucks, either." She shrugged. "The shielding will last a few weeks after we're done. Might get a few poor bastards deeper into the EU before they get in trouble, who knows?"

"You've got the tribute truck?"

"The armored van." Orman glanced back to check on it, then returned her attention to me. "I'm driving that one, but I wouldn't mind an extra in the back. Ten tons of silver and two of platinum... we're only hauling only a hundred million euros or so in precious metals."

"Mary and I are riding with you to Ġgantija," I told her, then turned back to my people. "Coleman, we need a Hunter to ride shotgun in the tribute van."

"All right." Coleman gestured for Riley to join me. "Drive safe, sir. We'll see you at the ferry?"

"Assuming everything goes according to plan, yeah." I shook my head. "Try not to draw any more attention than you need to. We need to honor the Titaness, but we also need to make sure that the Masked Lords don't see us coming."

24

ORMAN TOOK the truck along the highway and up onto a plateau. At the north end of the natural rise was a collection of stacked rocks marked off by ropes and tourist trails.

"There's the temples," she told me. "World Heritage Site, tourist attraction, the works."

"I'm guessing that Theia isn't living in them anymore, then?"

"Yes and no," the Fae Noble said. "There was an access to her complex in there, but it was buried in the collapse after she left Gozo and the temples stopped being maintained.

"She moved *back* after everything went wrong for the Titans in the Olympus area and hasn't left since. Her home isn't the temples, Kilkenny."

"It's the entire plateau," I concluded aloud. "How do we get in?"

"We take a side road down to the edge of the plateau and then commit suicide," she said cheerfully.

"We what?" I demanded.

Orman laughed.

"The road ends next to a cliff. We make the proper ablutions, then drive through the cliff."

GLYNN STEWART

Illusions, glamors and false realities. Welcome to the world of the supernatural.

"All right. You know the right words? I'm guessing it's more complicated than 'speak friend and enter,'" I noted.

"I do and they are." She shook her head. "Took some research. She still has some followers here, but they're *very* used to keeping their heads down after a few centuries of being ruled by Christians and Brits."

"Does she know we're coming?" I asked.

"She knows *I'm* coming," Orman replied. "Or, at least, I'm assuming the locals I got the key phrases from told her I was on my way. I don't think she knows I'm bringing friends—and I don't think anyone would have warned the Masked Lords about one random fae looking for a warm exile."

"Happens often enough, does it?"

"Our records suggest there's about a dozen fae across the islands Theia claims as her own," she told me. "I'm guessing there's more, if the Masked Lords have been using the place as a safe haven, but that's what we know about."

"So, she's expecting one exile paying a tribute of a few kilos of platinum…and she's getting an army." I shook my head. "I'm sure that's going to go over well."

"You have a better idea?" she asked.

"Nope," I conceded. "Our 'better idea' was making sure that she knew we were here and paid tribute so we weren't operating without her permission. Surprise means everybody gets surprised."

"Worrying isn't going to help anyone," Mary interjected. "Let's go pay up."

———

DRIVING through the wall was probably one of the two or three most terrifying voluntary experiences I'd ever undergone. Ana Orman hit the accelerator after completing the small ritual, gunning the engine toward the cliff so none of us had a chance for second thoughts.

Fortunately, we'd done everything right and the armored van

142

flashed through the solid-seeming stone wall without even slowing down—and Orman immediately slammed the brakes as we entered a large tunnel.

The tunnel was big enough for the truck but it wasn't particularly *long*. We came to a screeching halt at the entrance to a well-lit cave that had been set up with a modern loading dock.

Half a dozen burly young men were scattered around the room. None of them were visibly armed, but I could feel the power radiating from them even inside the armored van.

I didn't recognize what type of supernatural they were, but I could tell that these were Theia's protectors...and only a fool would go up against them unprepared.

One of them, a strapping blond man who towered well over six feet tall, stepped up to the side of the truck and spoke in fluid Maltese.

Orman's response was sufficiently halting to earn her a grin and a laugh.

"I speak English, miss," he told her with a faint French accent. "You are expected, yes?"

"I am Ana Orman. I have tribute for the Titaness."

"I see." He stepped back and studied the van. "We were expecting you alone, with a personal tribute. This seems somewhat more...substantial."

"That is conversation for my companion and the Titaness," Orman said, with a gesture toward me. "It must be kept secret."

He nodded, but he also stepped closer to the van again. He gave the very clear impression that he both could and would stop the vehicle moving if he didn't give permission for us to go somewhere.

"Your business with Omm may be private, but I can not permit a stranger to enter her presence," he told us. "Introduce yourselves."

Orman started to object but I waved her off.

"I am Jason Kilkenny, Noble of the Wild Hunt and Vassal of Queen Mabona of the Fae High Court," I said. "In the back of the truck is Riley Moriarty, Hunter of the Wild Hunt."

"I am Mary Tenerim, aide to the Speaker of Calgary's Shifter Clans," Mary introduced herself. "I am here as an ally to the Fae Courts."

Our greeter inclined his head to us both.

"That wasn't so hard, was it?" he asked. "Leave the truck here. Does Mr. Moriarty need to come with you?"

"He is here to protect the tribute until it is turned over," I explained. "Only the three of us need to meet with Theia."

"Very well." He stepped back. "I am Spiro Michelakis, grandson of the Titaness Theia. If you offer harm to my grandmother, I will destroy you utterly."

There was no threat in his voice or body language. It was simply a statement of fact.

"Our presence here needs to remain—"

"A secret, yes," he finished for Orman. "That is for Omm to decide, not me. I will not betray you until she has decided. Until then, you are safe here unless you violate her hospitality."

That was a better offer than I'd been expecting, if I was honest.

"Thank you, Spiro Michelakis," I told him as I stepped out of the van. "Shall we, then?"

———

MICHELAKIS LED us deeper into the underground complex, an anachronistic confusion of architectural styles from over five millennia. The very modern loading dock gave way to an underground entrance plaza that looked directly out of an old Greek city-state, a magical false sun lighting up brilliant white marble columns and brightly painted statues.

For all of the size of the plaza, it was entirely empty. The half dozen guardians in the loading area were the only people we'd seen in the caverns so far. The place was creepily silent, feeling more like a tomb than an actual living space.

I noticed the size of the doors as Michelakis led us across the plaza. All of them were easily twice the height of what I'd expect in North America, let alone on an island in the Mediterranean. I was expecting old buildings with tiny doors, but the archways and doors were at least four or five meters high.

Titan wasn't just a name, it seemed. Myths of giants and gods were running through my mind as Michelakis opened a set of immense double doors and led us into the throne room.

Two more of the epically muscled young men were waiting on the inside of the doors, but they were the only occupants of the immense room other than the woman on the throne.

My thought that the complex felt like a tomb came rushing back to me as I looked at Theia the Wide-shining, Titaness Mother of the Sun and Moon.

It was hard to tell with her seated, but she was at least three meters tall. Even sitting, she towered over both myself and her grandson—and neither of us were short men.

She wore a dress of golden fabric that glittered in the light of another magical false sun and Power rippled away from her in waves…and yet.

And yet. For all of her size and power, her skin was sunken in on itself. There were still streaks of gold in her hair, but most of it had faded to a scraggly dirty gray. Theia was *old*, beyond the dreams and understanding of even many supernaturals.

She barely moved as we entered, her head slowly turning to focus on us.

This complex wasn't Theia's home. It was the tomb for a creature who would *never* die.

"So." Her voice was tired and scratchy, but it filled the throne room easily. "The son of Calebrant comes before me. You edge far too close to my prohibition on Powers on my islands, young Kilkenny.

"Speak swiftly or be undone!"

Well, that wasn't quite the response I had been expecting, but I could work with it. I moved forward several steps and bowed deeply.

"Great Lady Theia," I greeted her. "I am no Power. Not even close. I am merely a Noble of the Wild Hunt, here on the business of the High Court. We did not wish to enter your territory without notice or tribute, so here I am."

"The High Court has no business in my islands," she snapped. "Why are you here?"

There was no way anything except honesty was going to work

here. It was unwise to lie to a Power, and for all her age, I suspected that Theia was the most powerful entity I'd ever shared a room with.

"A rogue faction of Fae Lords has raised their banners against the High Court," I told her. "They are regrown from the remnants of the faction that killed my father and several other Powers of the High Court.

"Now they have stolen the sword *Asi* from the asura who guarded it, and used its power to murder the Magus Sandhya Patel. They have eluded pursuit by asura, fae and wizard alike, but we have learned they have a fortress here."

"And I am expected to care why? They are not Powers; they have not broken my strictures. If they are here, they have paid their tribute and have not bothered me."

"We do not expect you to care," I replied. "As you say, they have met your rules. But they are murderers and criminals in the larger world, and we seek your leave to bring them to justice.

"Rather than attempt to hit and run without speaking to you, I would have your permission to operate in your territory. We have brought the traditional tribute to become resident here, though we will only be here for a few days, weeks at most."

She grunted, leaning on her hand and studying me.

"Spiro?" she snapped.

"They have brought silver and platinum," he said instantly. "Ten tons and two. A generous tribute."

"My own counsel I will keep on that, child," Theia told him, silencing any further commentary from the young quarter-god. She focused her gaze on me like an angry laser.

"I am not inclined to authorize violence on my islands, son of Calebrant," she said. "Such attracts mortal eyes and other troubles. Twelve tons of silver and platinum. How many warriors do you bring to me?"

"Ten Hunters and eight Companions of the Wild hunt, twelve shifters and twenty asura," I counted off. "Plus Ana Orman, a Noble Vassal of the Queen of the Fae."

"Such unhesitating honesty is refreshing," Theia told me. "Except you brought an army to my islands, son of Calebrant. And what will you do if I deny you?"

I shrugged.

"I suspect that your denial will result in us finding ourselves in Italy at the very least," I admitted. "I have no doubt in your ability to find my people and remove us all from your island if you wish."

The coughing sound that followed had me momentarily concerned for the old Titaness's health—and then I realized she was *laughing*.

"You have spirit, child," she told me. "I do not promise my protection to those who pay me tribute. And in all honesty, if I did, the actions of these Masked Lords would invalidate that promise.

"Your tribute is accepted, son of Calebrant. You have one week to do what you must and get you and your little army out of Malta. Your welcome will last no longer. Am I understood?"

I bowed again.

"I understand completely, Great Lady. I thank you—"

We were no longer in the throne room. The three of us were standing on the side of the highway, with Riley a couple of feet away from us. A cold wind swept in off of the ocean and I exhaled a long breath.

"Orman?"

"Kilkenny?"

"Call Coleman. Let's make sure the trucks pick us up on their way to the ferry." I smiled.

"We have permission—which means we have work to do."

25

THE TRUCKS WERE ROUGHLY what I'd expected when Orman had told me
they were normally used for smuggling migrants. They might be set
up for people, but it was a very crude and uncomfortable arrangement.

There were no seats or even air conditioning units in the back of the
trucks. A collection of blankets and cushions of varying quality
covered the floor, and there was a water cooler strapped to the wall
with a collection of plastic cups.

I suspected that the container had been significantly dirtier before
we'd stuffed twenty-plus supernaturals into it. Telekinesis and other
powers made short work of most dirt. They couldn't make the
padding any less distressed, but they could at least make it *clean*.

The trucks rolled onto the ferry without any major issues. They
were presumably weighed along the way, but if any inspection was
supposed to take place, it had instead collided with a wad of currency.

"Ferry takes forty-five minutes," Orman warned me. "About thirty
minutes before we leave and thirty before we can offload at the other
end." She shook her head. "That's two hours without being able to
even crack the seal."

"That sounds...unpleasant," Mary said. "Can we do anything
about it?"

"We already are," I told her. "That's why we're not baking in here." Mary shook her head.

"We're not?" my girlfriend asked, brushing sweat away from her hair. "I feel bad for anyone stuffed in here without our advantages."

"People die in these trucks," Orman said quietly. "But it's one way to sneak into the EU that isn't being watched as closely as some others, and it's safer than staying where they are."

Air continued to circulate around us, driven by the various supernaturals in the truck, as Mary and I leaned against one wall.

"The meeting with Theia was weird," Mary admitted after several minutes of silence. "Was that what we were expecting?"

"It went better than I was expecting," I confessed. "I wasn't expecting her to be so...old, I guess."

"She's probably one of the oldest living sentient beings in the world," Coleman told me. "Best guess is that she predates the ruins at Ġgantija...which are dated to about four thousand BCE."

"So, somewhere over six thousand years old," Mary calculated. "I didn't think even Powers lived that long."

"Powers don't die of old age," I pointed out. "I didn't think they actually *aged* at all. They just tend to die before they get past about two thousand."

"Politics," Coleman concluded. "We know the Puck is the oldest living fae, but they're not telling anyone how old they are." He snorted. "Or anything *else* about themselves, for that matter."

"I think Theia just...gave up," I said slowly. "She has the power to change her form if she wants. If she looks like that, she no longer cares." I shivered. "That complex feels like a tomb, not a home."

"So, she's what, sitting there waiting to die?" Mary asked. "But... she won't?"

"That's about what I read off her," I agreed. "Someday, I think she'll wake up again. Someone will push her limits or hurt one of her descendants." I shook my head. "I wouldn't want to *be* that someone. She needs a wakeup call, but her waking up will shake the pillars of the earth."

"And until then?" my lover said softly, squeezing my hand.

"She will sit in her tomb and wait to see whether or not she can die

—and the rest of the world will leave her alone, because she's old and powerful and we aren't going to dare to judge her!"

————

FOR ALL THAT it felt like we spent forever in the back of the trucks, Malta wasn't a very big island, and we reached the private estate that housed the Masked Lords' base less than three hours after Theia teleported our delegation to meet the trucks.

The hired drivers off-loaded us in silence and disappeared without a word, carefully not noticing what direction we headed off in ourselves. A few minutes after we were alone, we were settled on our stomachs on top of a hill, surveying the property.

A tall fence surrounded the entire area, with a gate and guardhouse on the driveway leading to the highway. The same fence continued down across the beach into the water, providing a secured private beach.

I didn't know if Malta's laws allowed that, but the estate looked like it belonged to the kind of people who could buy exceptions.

There was a twentieth-century mansion roughly in the middle of the site, a sprawling post-modernist extravaganza in glass, steel and concrete. I could see motion inside the building, so it was definitely occupied, but I doubted it was the center of the Lords' operation there.

"The mansion is too obvious," Coleman said aloud, echoing my thoughts.

"MacDonald's vision said it was in a vault under a ruined fortress," I reminded him, and pointed at the ruins. "Something like that."

The ruins were at the north end of the beach but still well within the fenced perimeter. *Ruins* was doing the structure a disservice, in truth. It was a surprisingly intact late–Middle Ages fort. Someone had renovated it to host cannon at one point, and someone else had bombarded the upper levels to rubble to get rid of said cannon.

The original occupiers had clearly written it off, as most of that debris was still there and the fortress *looked* wrecked. Except…

"Looks like the ground floor and probably the second floor are basically intact," I pointed out. "If you were being careful, you could easily keep it looking like a ruin to anyone passing by, even to visitors to the house, while renovating the interior to be a working building."

"Layer in the Gift of Force, and excavating an underground structure linked to it would be easy," Coleman agreed. "And without the Wizard's vision, I would have ignored it…even if I was moving against the house."

"We need more information," Asi pointed out, the big Indian supernatural dropping to the ground next to us and looking out toward the sea. "I'd rather not have a squad of Nobles from the house hit us from behind while we're attacking the bunker."

"We'll get more information," I promised. "I brought the best scouts in the world, Raja Asi." I waved Mary over to me. "I didn't bring the shifters to keep my girlfriend involved and safe, gentlemen. I brought the shifters because *nobody* scouts like they do."

"Jason?" Mary asked as she arrived, gripping my shoulder as she squatted next to us.

"I need you and your people to scout the target," I told her. "We need to know how many bad guys are in the house. If you can locate an access to the fortress—or better yet, straight to the bunker or even the vault—that would be great.

"What I'd love, though I trust MacDonald enough not to need it, is confirmation of just who is here," I concluded. "We're about to commit an act of terror by mortal standards, which is *going* to attract attention. The more certain we are that this is the right place, the better."

"We'll see what we can find," my lover replied. "Trust me, no one gets too concerned about random wildlife."

———

COYOTES, wolves and lynxes might not be native to Malta, but feral dogs and cats were. You had to be looking closely to realize that the canine shifters weren't dogs, and Mary's ability to simply disappear when she chose still astonished me.

Ten minutes after I'd asked them to scout the property, all of our shifters had vanished and the rest of us settled in to wait.

There wasn't much in terms of visible activity. A few people in the glass sections of the house. A pair of guards at the gate. A two-guard patrol wandering the property.

The guards were all fae. Gentry to a one, in fact, which made them a significant threat.

On the other hand, all of the guns my people were carrying were loaded with cold iron. We'd come loaded for fae, which meant Gentry were less of a challenge than they otherwise would be.

Without cold iron rounds, after all, Gentry were slightly tougher to kill than modern tanks.

Through the scope of my rifle, I watched the fortress. There was no activity for a while, but eventually I spotted two women stepping through what *looked* like a solid wall of rubble.

"Coleman, flag the rubble on the northwest corner," I murmured. "Two people just walked right through it."

I turned my scope to look over the women and inhaled sharply. The one on the right was a Noble I didn't know, a gray-haired middle-aged fae radiating calm power. The one on the *left*, however, I knew.

Maria Chernenkov was a Pouka noble, a shapeshifting fae with a need to eat human flesh. She didn't, however, need to be a sadistic murderer. That she did for fun.

She'd also been the wife of the Fae Lord Andrell, who *had* been a Masked Lord. She'd been part of the sequence of events that had led to my learning what the Masked Lords were—and she was definitely one of their operatives.

"Chernenkov is here," I said aloud. "I guess we know we're in the right place."

"Huh. I figured she'd been trying to work out how to get into Calgary and kill you," Coleman muttered back. "You *did* stick a cold iron spike through her shadow."

As a Pouka noble, Chernenkov was the closest thing to truly invulnerable I'd ever encountered. Her essence lived in her shadow and could only be injured by cold iron.

I'd rammed a cold iron railroad spike through her shadow when we'd last met. From what I understood of the Pouka nobles, it was almost certainly *still there*. And she was one-third less immortal than she'd been before she met me.

"Yeah," I agreed, hesitating as I studied the woman who'd repeatedly tried to kill me. "I don't think that's a coincidence."

"You think it's a trap?" my Hunter troop captain asked.

"I think it may as well be," I admitted. "They had to know that, sooner or later, we'd send me or Ankaris for the spear. They had to be expecting an attack.

"Whether they're ready for us to be here *today* is a different story, but they'll have this place as secure as they can with whatever resources aren't tied up using *Asi* to murder gods."

Raja Asi hissed on the other side of me.

"Someday, Lord Kilkenny, I will have my revenge for that," he said grimly.

"Right now, I'm counting on the fact that they won't have allowed for *you*," I told the asura. "Let's wait for Mary to get back. I think no matter how ready we or they are, this is going to get messy."

———

THE SHIFTERS GOT BACK JUST before nightfall. Nearly four hours of scouting left them looking exhausted and hungry, but we'd carefully established a camp in the lee of the hill, hidden from both the road and the estate.

I'm not going to pretend the food we had waiting for Mary and the others was *good*, but it was there and waiting when they rejoined us.

We let them tear into it, then once Mary and Barry were leaning back in folding chairs with steaming cups of coffee, I arched an eyebrow at them.

"Well?"

"The place is a fortress," Barry said bluntly. "And not just the old Hospitaller fort, either. The building might have been built with regular glass, but its been replaced since. Bulletproof and then reinforced with magic."

"I figured. What about the bunker?" I asked.

"Looks like the main access is through the old fortress, which has at least some intact structure inside," Mary told me. "There's power and heat in there at least. I'd guess a modern guard barracks."

"There doesn't appear to be a direct access from the house," Barry pointed out. "Smell suggests there's an access by the garage; I'm guessing there's actually an elevator inside there, since the garage doesn't look big enough for more than half a dozen cars."

I nodded. Turning the garage into an access for an underground parking garage would make sense if you were trying to hide your vehicles.

"There's a helipad out near the beach," the werewolf continued. "Well hidden from anywhere people might be, but it looks like they bring in supplies and people by air. Helicopters, probably floatplanes as well."

"There certainly aren't any *boats* at the pier," Mary agreed. "About a dozen people, all fae, in the above section of the fortress."

"Roughly the same in the house," Barry told us. "But who can say what's in the bunker?"

"I also picked up a familiar scent near the fortress," my girlfriend said. "Chernenkov."

"I saw her," I said quietly. "Her and a noble I didn't know. Damh— do we have cold iron spikes of any kind?"

The Hunter nodded slowly.

"We do. Not many, though. I think we've got half a dozen or so stored Between."

"It'll have to do," I told him. "Bullets only disable her. Even if we manage to destroy the body, she'll just find a nearby horse and resurrect herself through it."

"Right," Barry said. "That explains it."

"Explains what?"

"I was wondering why what looked like a fae court fortress had a stable. Half a dozen horses were being taken out for a ride by a grouchy-looking hag. If Chernenkov is here, then…"

"Then they've made sure she'd got an easy route back if things go sideways." I shook my head. Those poor horses. A Pouka Noble's emergency resurrection involved basically tearing their way out of the unlucky equine.

"So, what do we do?" Coleman asked.

"If we hit the bunker, people are going to swarm from the house and the fortress," I said. "We could try and sneak in through the garage, but I'm not expecting this to go quietly."

"We can probably hit everything," Asi suggested. "Send my asura at the fortress, the Hunters at the house, and use the shifters to clean up anyone who runs.

"Then, while Chernenkov and her friends are distracted, you and a few of our best go in through the garage. We're here for the spear, aren't we? Do we really need to wipe them all out, my lord?"

"No. But we do need to break this base," I told Asi. "When this is over, the Masked Lords need to know they have no sanctuaries, no hidden bases. I like your idea, but we need to make sure no one gets away.

"I prefer prisoners to corpses, but we can't let the Masked Lords keep a secret base here."

And, well, much as I should have been able to rely on Asi's fealty, I wasn't leaving any part of the mission *entirely* up to his asura.

26

WE WAITED until nearly midnight before we kicked off the operation. None of us were particularly impeded by darkness. Our opponents weren't impaired by darkness either, but they were used to Malta's clock.

For us, adjusted to *Calgary*'s, it was early afternoon and we were all perfectly awake.

The first act was up to the Hunters. As everyone else snuck toward the fence, they moved into the guardhouse. By the time we reached the gate, it was wide open and Coleman was busy turning off what lights the property did have.

Two unconscious Gentry were restrained in cold iron manacles in the small building. They weren't going to be a threat.

"There's a second security room in the house," the troop captain told me. "I can kill all of their feeds, but as soon as I do that, they'll know there's a problem."

"They'll know there's a problem if they see us, too," I reminded him. I turned to the others. "Ready?"

Riley would lead the assault on the house. Asi would lead the assault on the fortress himself, with a Hunter and two Companions replacing three of his asura to spread the forces out. Mary and Barry would lead the sweep teams.

I, Coleman, Orman and two asura Asi had handpicked would make the attack on the garage. Riley and Coleman were the only ones with the spikes to take down the Pouka if she got involved.

Most likely, she was going to come for me as soon as she knew I was there—and that would be *fast* once the rocket went up.

"We can't sneak past cameras and motion sensors, Jason," Mary told me. "We'll take down the roaming patrol and be ready for runners, but we will be seen."

"I know. Riley, Asi?"

Both nodded and Asi removed his suit jacket. He tossed the formal garment into the guardhouse and stretched, rippling golden muscles in a way that made every male in his vicinity either wince in envy or struggle not to drool. I carefully did *not* pay attention to the women's reactions.

It was more than a little unfair that the cold-blooded assassin was probably the single most attractive male for at least a few hundred kilometers in any given direction.

"It's time for a down payment to be taken in blood," he told us. "I will not fail you, my lord."

"We know the drill," Riley added drily. "The Hunt has done this before. Give us five to convince them to get stuck in, then the garage should be clear."

"Remember, we *know* there are two Masked Nobles here," I reminded them all. "Only a handful of us can face one of those. If there's a *Lord* here..." I shivered. "Ping me, Asi and Coleman, and *run*. The three of us can take a Masked Lord together."

I saw Coleman's concealed wince at that. Raja Asi, Coleman and I would all qualify as Nobles as the Wild Hunt classed these things. Together...we could *probably* take a Fae Lord.

Probably.

I'd done it on my own once, after all.

———

EVERYONE ELSE WENT FIRST, leaving my small strike team standing by the guardhouse, waiting.

Gunfire started at the house first, almost certainly a team ordered out when the security room reported their cameras going down. The ruckus at the fort didn't even start with gunfire. I wasn't sure *who* had brought the grenade launcher, but the staccato explosions of multiple grenades made for a noticeable opening salvo.

Given that the only people with access to invisible storage spaces were the Hunters, I was pretty sure the grenade launches were from one of my people.

I couldn't tell the difference between the various rifles being fired, though the rapid sequence of gunshots told me that the defenders were also carrying assault rifles of some kind or another. Different sounds underlay the gunfire and grenade explosions after a moment, as the defenders realized they were facing supernaturals and started unleashing the full extent of their abilities.

"Now, I think," I said conversationally as the distinctive screech of a banshee's war cry cut through the gunfire. "If Jessica has started screaming, she's going to have *everyone's* attention."

Jessica Colombia was one of my Hunters' Companions, basically a living support weapon in this context. She could calibrate her voice from "normal conversation" to "sonic weapon that could shred a tank."

The scream I could hear was probably closer to the latter. Someone had almost certainly just died in a *very* noticeable fashion.

"After you, Kilkenny," Coleman told me as he drew his arms from Between. The silver-hilted sword went at his waist, the Steyr in his hands with a sling over his shoulder.

I drew my own weapons. I'd left the sword Between, but I had my own rifle and the whipstock MacDonald had forged for me.

A leather pouch at Coleman's waist held the three cold iron spikes we were carrying for Chernenkov. This would have been a rough enough night without the Pouka noble being there.

Finding the garage was easy, at least. The driveway went in a straight line there from the guardhouse, passing within a few meters of the house at one point.

Even the bulletproof glass of the structure had been shattered at this point, but my people weren't even trying to push into the building. They were keeping up a barrage of fire to pin down anyone in the building and neutralize anyone who came out.

Passing by the fight, we reached the garage. It was completely empty...and also lacking in the elevator we'd been expecting. No people. No cars. No access downward. It wasn't even really a garage, just an empty shell.

"That's not right," I said aloud. "The shifters said they smelled an access to the underground here."

"It might be outside? Or hidden?" Coleman asked.

"No, it's here," I replied, stepping into the building and looking around. "Probably half-concealed with tech and cleverness and half-wrapped in glamor. We don't have time for this."

"Suggestions?" my subordinate asked.

"Back me up," I ordered. "It's time for us to make ourselves a door."

27

ECHOING gunfire reminded us that we didn't have a lot of time. It was entirely possible that we could take the facility via the not-quite-frontal assaults going on at the other two entrances, but the faster I got my hands on *Esras,* the better off we were.

I drew the whip and Coleman drew his sword as we faced each other across two meters of bare concrete. There was almost certainly some mechanism that opened the floor or otherwise provided access… but we didn't have time to find it.

I called faerie fire, green-white flames flickering out from the wooden whipstock and driving deep into the floor. Coleman stabbed his sword into the ground, flame and force flashing out sideways from the strike.

My Gift of Fire normally summoned just that: fire. I *could,* however, use it as an extension of my senses. Right now, I sent seeking tendrils of superheated flame into the concrete. Dirt and stone alike shattered under the heat as the two of us drove down into the ground, seeking the tunnel I figured had to be beneath us.

After the first two feet, I was starting to worry…and then we broke through a foot later. There was a full meter of concrete and dirt between where we were standing right now and the underground tunnel leading to the true heart of the fortress.

That was no match for the power Coleman and I brought to bear. Fire and force swept out from each of us in laser-straight lines. For a moment, the space between us was framed in glowing-red melted concrete.

Then we both latched onto the chunk of earth with our Gifts and *pulled*. Four cubic meters of earth, concrete and steel lifted out of the ground, and we threw it to the side. We could see light spilling up from below, and I grinned at the open hole leading deep into the ground.

"Well, that worked," I said aloud. "With me, people."

Of the five of us in that garage, I was the squishiest by far. Coleman and the asura could easily jump down the fifteen feet without injuring themselves. I would probably break something.

Or I could use the Gift of Force to control my descent, basically flying down to the ground as my subordinates jumped past me. I was the first into the hole and the last onto the floor of the tunnel beneath us.

"Well, that answers that question," Coleman told me as I touched down, pointing toward the end of the tunnel. "The actual elevator is *in front* of the garage."

"Sneaky buggers," I agreed. "All right, let's get to moving. Somewhere down here is the vault MacDonald saw."

"I don't suppose you know where?" the Hunter asked.

I started to shake my head, then stopped. There was *something* tugging at my brain, a direction? A calling? Not quite a presence, not quite a memory, but…

"I think I might," I admitted. "Of course, there's only one way down this tunnel, so it's easy so far."

———

THE TUNNEL WAS INTENDED as a vehicle entrance, not one for people on foot. It wasn't particularly well lit and it was surprisingly long, but it was also unguarded right now.

After about fifty meters, it gave way to an underground parking lot. Ramps led down to what looked like another four levels below us as well, and there were about a dozen stalls per level. It was an impressive display, ranging from near-junkers that would attract no attention at all to luxury sedans to…

To, well, armored personnel carriers. Those were too big to make it down the ramps to the lower levels, so the two green armored vehicles were on the top level, looming over the regular cars around them.

"Coleman, can we make sure those APCs never go anywhere again?" I asked.

"I think so." The Hunter walked over to the large vehicles, studied them for a moment, and then used a blade of Force to slash their tracks into pieces.

"They'll drive again," he admitted. "If someone puts a few days of work into repairing them."

"Somehow, that makes me feel a lot better," I told him. Surveying the rest of the underground structure, I finally spotted a pair of heavy double doors that looked like they led deeper into the complex.

"That way." I pointed.

My little strike team fell in around me as we moved toward the doors, but I paused as we neared them. The tugging I was feeling, toward the spear, didn't go through those doors.

It went *down*.

"Let's hold off on those," I said. "*Esras* is…" I closed my eyes and let my hand follow the tug. "That way."

I opened my eyes and looked at my own pointing hand.

"I'm guessing on the bottom floor," I concluded. "There may not be a door on the bottom, but we can make one if we need to—and they won't be expecting us to cut through a wall."

"You're the boss," Coleman agreed.

"My lord," one of the asura interjected, pointing at the nearest vehicles—a pickup truck and an SUV that looked like a three-quarters-scale version of my Escalade. "If we want to avoid being attacked from behind, we should hotwire these and blockade the door."

That was a good idea.

"Do it," I ordered. "That'll buy us time if we need it."

Orman joined the two asura in getting into the vehicles. We weren't being subtle or gentle—the driver's-side doors were completely removed, tossed aside like tissue paper as my people forced the cars to start and drove them into the doors.

There was a crunching sound as the pickup hammered into the doors—and a worse one when Orman rammed the SUV into it from the other side. The pickup was crushed into the heavy security doors, covering their entire width with its crushed bulk.

The SUV wasn't in much better shape, but both of my people were out without injury.

"All right, folks. Down four floors and through a wall, I think."

———

DESCENDING DOWN THE RAMPS, I took a few seconds to touch base with Mary by phone. She was basically running the aboveground operation, playing backup as the shifters made sure the two main assault forces had the support they needed.

It was a good thing our phones passed through gnomish hands before they reached ours. They had far fewer difficulties with signal than the regular version.

"How are we doing?" I asked.

"The house is a wreck and the shooting has stopped there," she told me. "We haven't run into the Noble or Chernenkov yet, so they have to have been in the fortress. That's proving a much tougher problem."

"How bad?"

"Bad," she admitted. "We haven't lost anyone yet, but Asi isn't making any progress. They've reinforced the old walls with magic and rebar, and there's only one way in. That situation is *not* under control, but no one is trying to run yet, either."

"We're going for *Esras* first," I told her. "Once you've IDed Chernenkov or the Noble, let me know. If everything goes *right*, I'll be able to hit them below while you've got them distracted."

"Be careful."

"As much as I can be," I said. "I don't want to lose anyone I don't have to."

There was a pause, and then Mary swore.

"Love?"

"Chernenkov just jumped Asi," she told me quickly. "*Move*, Jason. He can hold her, but I don't know if he can beat her."

I was the only one around who had fought Chernenkov to a stand-still, and I had to agree with Mary. Raja Asi could fight Chernenkov. He could hold her off while Riley tried to get at her with the iron spikes, but he couldn't kill her.

And since we knew Chernenkov had friends...

"We're moving. I'll be in touch."

I put my phone away and looked at the others.

"It's getting heated upstairs," I told them. "We need to move faster."

————

THE ONLY THING really slowing us down was the desire to not run directly into an ambush. Since we now knew that the worst-case scenario for an ambush was upstairs fighting an asura warlord, we could go faster.

Even the physically weakest supernaturals—a category that still included me if I couldn't use the Gift of Force to augment my actions—still had the fitness and endurance of an Olympic-level athlete.

We'd been heading down the ramps at a brisk walk, and now we started running. I couldn't let the people upstairs die for our distraction, especially not if I could turn the tide of the entire battle if I got my hands on *Esras*.

I wasn't entirely sure how that would work, but everyone around me clearly believed it to be the case. For some reason, if the Spear of Lugh ended up in my hands, that was the end of this fight.

It was no surprise, really, that the lowest level of the parking garage didn't have an access into the base. It had a stairwell we'd missed in our hurry upstairs that linked it to the higher levels, and that was it.

"Where's the spear?" Coleman asked.

"There," I pointed. "Not far, either. Maybe twenty meters. Without knowing where the interior stairwells are, I'd say the other side of that wall is probably the vault entrance."

"Can you step Between?" Orman said.

"Not without being sure where the open space is," Coleman replied before I could. "Hole-cutting time. Kilkenny?"

"With me."

We raised our weapons again, our power fueled by concern for our friends as we unleashed it on the innocent stone and concrete in our path.

A meter of stone gave way. Then another. Then *another*. We punched through four meters of concrete-covered island bedrock before we hit open air again. Debris filled the hole we'd made and spilled out into the garage behind us and the lobby ahead of us.

"Go!" I snapped. Coleman stepped Between ahead of us and I led the others across the debris field.

Gunfire echoed in the hall as we burst out into open air again. Coleman had dodged their fire, but he was engaged with a half-dozen Unseelie Gentry carrying ugly-looking bullpup assault rifles.

"*Take them*," I barked, and my people obeyed. Gunfire echoed in the enclosed space and swords flashed as my asura charged.

The Gentry had reacted quickly to the wall being wrecked and a Hunter appearing amidst them but hadn't been expecting *more*. Two went down in a hail of cold iron bullets. Coleman cut a third in half with his sword as they turned to face the new threat.

Force fueled my leap across the room, turning a light jump into a vault that brought me down in front of them. My whip flashed out, fire hammering the closest Gentry's gun to wreckage as he tried to defend himself with it.

The whip destroyed his gun and then took him down a moment later.

The fifth unexpectedly sprouted a cold iron dagger in the middle of his forehead. Thrown by supernatural muscles and guided by Force, Orman's dagger would have missed only if he'd reacted.

The last Gentry knew a bad deal when she saw one and tossed her gun to the ground, holding her hands in the air.

"Fuck this," she said flatly. "I claim the Hunt's Mercy!"

Technically, very technically, the Wild Hunt were a kind of police. "Hunt's Mercy" meant she was claiming the ancient right to be tried before a court. It might or might not save the Gentry's life in the end—Fae Lords were *not* known for gentle sentences—but she would live through today.

"Understood," I told her. "Orman, bind her. Coleman, take a look at that vault door."

The door at the other end of the room was exactly what I'd expected: the massive triple-locked doors of a major bank. I could *feel* that the spear was on the other side—and from this close, I could tell that *Esras* was merely the most powerful artifact in the vault.

"I rather think not," a calm voice told us in a perfect British Received Pronunciation accent. A graying Fae stepped out of the stairwell and shot our prisoner in the head without slowing his step. An iron mask concealed his features as he faced us calmly.

"I'm not going to give you my name," they continued, tossing aside the gun and producing a gnomish warblade—cold iron blade, protected hilt, enchanted to the nines—from thin air. "Today, I am merely your executioner."

We'd known the fortress was home to two Noble members of the Masked Lords.

We'd assumed that meant that there *wasn't* a true Fae Lord.

We'd been wrong.

28

THE MASKED LORD gestured with the warblade and it duplicated in the air, a dozen floating blades appearing out of thin air. The new blades were things of Glamor and Force but no less lethal for all of that.

"You know what you have to do," Coleman told me as he pulled his rifle up on its sling. "*Go.*"

Gunfire echoed in the hall as my companions opened fire on the Masked Lord. This wasn't a fight they could win. Two asura and two Greater Fae against a *Fae Lord*?

The addition of my own powers might change the result, but I knew what Coleman meant and I dodged Between as three glamorblades flashed at my head.

From Between, I couldn't follow the fight. I could only hope that Coleman and the others were at least staying alive as I attempted to do something almost as dangerous as it was bloody stupid: navigate through the Between, *underground*, to a place I'd never been. Navigating to somewhere I'd never been was safe enough in general, except it had a margin of error.

If that margin put me outside my target, that wasn't a big deal. Except if I was outside my target underground, I could easily end up trapped, unable to escape.

Today, however, I had a beacon. *Esras* sang to me across the boundary between worlds, and I crossed to it with unexpected ease. I had enough sense of the real world to be sure that I emerged into empty space next to it, and I *stepped*.

The vault was chilly and the air felt vaguely dry. There was a sterile air to the place, as if every factor from temperature to air mix to pressure had been carefully accounted for and controlled.

It looked like a museum. The vault was a thirty-meter-on-a-side square with a five-meter-high roof, and it was filled with glass display cases positioned around neatly laid-out aisles.

The display cases contained what I'd expected. Row upon row of weapons: swords, spears, daggers, bows, even rifles and handguns. Every one of them a work of art, the result of weeks or months or *years* of work by expert fae craftsmen.

Every one of them an artifact of power, forged to destroy the enemies of the fae—and stored here to be used against the enemies of the Masked Lords.

The outer walls were lined with safety deposit boxes as well. I didn't feel power radiating from them, which suggested that they were filled with more normal contents: gems, gold, bearer bonds and other instruments of wealth.

This was probably the most secure secret vault the Masked Lords owned, and they'd stockpiled weapons and wealth there to fuel their campaign—and if everything went according to plan, it was all going to end up being mine.

At that moment, however, my eye finally settled on one thing. In the center of the room, there was a display case on a raised pedestal, one I recognized from MacDonald's vision. Alarms and tripwires surrounded the bulletproof glass case. Even being allowed in this vault did not mean you were trusted enough to approach *Esras*.

The wide iron spearhead glittered to my eyes as I stepped onto the dais. I didn't care about the alarms and ignored them as they started going off. None of the tripwires appeared to be attached to lethal devices, but the bulletproof case itself was locked and sealed in cold iron.

It wasn't a foolproof barrier, even against fae, but it would slow most fae down long enough for the alarms to do their work. Unfortunately for the designers, the people responsible for answering those alarms were currently occupied.

Unfortunately for me, if I didn't get the case open quickly, the people doing that occupying were going to end up dead.

The wizard-forged whipstock was in my hand before I even realized I'd reached for it. Green-white flame answered my call, MacDonald's gift vastly augmenting my own power as I poured heat into the locks.

The cold-forged iron frustrated my power for a moment, but the orichalcum runes on the wooden stock flared brighter and the lock *exploded*. Superheated liquid iron smashed into my shields…and while cold iron might have cut through, it was no longer cold-forged iron at that point.

A gesture flung aside the now-loose lid of the display case, and I hung the whip from my belt as I reached for the spear with trembling hands.

I swear *Esras* leapt into my grip, jumping the last half-inch out of its case to slot neatly into my fingers. The ash wood was cool against my skin but fit perfectly, my fingers wrapping around the wooden haft as if I'd done it a thousand times.

Something woke up. I wasn't sure if it was in me or in the spear, but a new warmth flooded my body as I instinctively settled into a combat stance I'd never learned.

I didn't have time for testing or experimentation. With the spear in my hand, I turned back to the vault door and leveled the weapon.

"If you're half as powerful as everyone tells me you are, let's see about this door," I whispered…and channeled faerie fire.

With MacDonald's gift, my originally green fire had acquired a white core of even further superheated flame. The Wizard's power had augmented my own but also changed its character.

With *Esras*, my fire was still faerie fire. It was still mine, a sparkling green color…except now it faded to a pale green so light, it was almost invisible. It wasn't the white core of the orichalcum-fueled extra energy I'd unleashed before.

This was my own faerie fire turned up beyond eleven. Green or not, the line of fire I unleashed on the door could have rivaled the corona of the sun for heat as I misjudged the power of the spear.

The vault door shattered. A few moments before, I'd exploded a lock that weighed a few hundred grams.

This time, I exploded a vault door that weighed over three *tons*. I managed to bring my Gift of Force to bear quickly enough to contain the explosion and channel it, focusing it into a line of superheated debris that went flying directly at the Masked Lord.

He managed to shield himself, somehow, but was thrown backward regardless. The Mask slipped from his face, cracked in half from the force of the blow, and he tossed it aside as he rose to face me.

My subordinates were alive. Coleman and one of the asura were even still up and facing him, though Orman and the other asura were now unconscious against a wall.

The Lord ignored them now, focusing on me as I walked through the wreckage of the door with the spear in my hand.

"Well. It seems that answers the question of whether one of Calebrant's blood could wield the spear without problems," he said calmly. Even without the mask, I didn't recognize him. Without it, I could tell he was a Seelie Lord, but that was all.

"Chernenkov said you would be coming. She's going to be grumpy she missed you."

The warblade flashed back into his hand and he bowed mockingly.

"Jason Kilkenny, I presume?" He smirked. "I am Lord Everard Rose. I don't think that toy is going to make much difference for you, I'm afraid...and I *do* know that if I kill you while you carry it, the blood bond is broken."

He was probably right. I certainly didn't know enough about blood bonds and ancient magical weapons to say one way or another.

I grinned anyway, pointing the spear at him as I returned the slight bow. If my bow was any less mocking than his, it wasn't due to a lack of effort.

"There is one key criterion to that, Lord Rose," I reminded him. "You're going to have to kill me...and you are *not* the first Masked Lord I've faced."

Rose laughed—and flung a dozen glamor-blades at my face from nowhere.

I blocked with Force...and misestimated the augmenting power of the spear. My intended focused shield turned into a wall of brute force that smashed furniture to splinters and sent Rose flying backward.

His own Gifts flared to life, slowing his flight and pulling him back to the ground. He looked more than a little surprised, but that didn't stop him from retaliating.

Rose charged forward, glamor-blades flickering into existence around him as he moved. Glamor-forged duplicates of the Fae Lord appeared as well, one man becoming an entire squadron as he lunged for me.

I gripped *Esras* and dove sideways, channeling force to bring myself out of the path of his strike. More force shielded my subordinates, protecting them as Lord Rose's power filled the room with death.

It washed over all of us and shattered against the wreckage of the vault door...and then it was my turn.

I kept up the shield over Coleman and the others and channeled fire down the spear, flinging sparks of pale-green faerie fire across the room like stardust.

That...was new. Both parts. I couldn't usually multitask like that, and that kind of area strike was beyond my power. Even MacDonald's whip only made what I'd always done more powerful. This was something else.

Rose managed to deflect most of the sparks away, but several struck home. The smell of burning flesh filled the lobby as my power seared his flesh and he swore at me.

He straightened behind his shield, facing me with his sword drawn.

"I know when I'm beat, kid," he said flatly. "It's been fun, but we're—"

Coleman appeared from Between beside the Fae Lord like an avenging angel, his sword flashing around in a brutally powerful strike. The Hunter was no match for a Fae Lord...but he didn't need to be.

The cold iron sword took off Rose's head in one swing, and the Masked Lord crumpled in silence.

I exhaled, meeting my subordinate's gaze.

"Thanks," I said. "I don't think I could have stopped him running."

"We didn't have the time for our usual grandstanding," Coleman replied. "Asi's still dueling two nobles on his own upstairs and *that*"—he pointed at the spear—"is his only hope.

"So, let's go."

29

As we moved up through the interior of the Masked Lords' bunker, it rapidly became clear that they'd thrown everyone at trying to hold off our attack. They were more desperate than my conversation with Mary implied.

Rose hadn't been in the basement to fight me. He'd been in the basement to grab the key artifacts from the vault and *run*. The Lords had already written off this base.

We'd left the conscious asura to hold the vault and watch over Orman and the others, in case someone else tried to finish what Rose had gone down to do. I didn't necessarily need the contents of that vault, but I certainly didn't want them in the hands of the Masked Lords.

I wondered if the people still fighting on the surface knew they'd been written off yet.

They certainly weren't expecting us to attack from behind. The main floor was well set up for this, with firing positions concealed by both mundane and magical stealth and only one access point. A dozen mixed fae were holding those positions, mostly engaging with gunfire.

An occasional fire bolt or similar use of power was showing up as well, but this was the kind of situation mortal humans had invented automatic weapons for, and there were few improvements on them.

I sent fire careening along the room. Green sparks of faerie flame hammered into them from behind, and Coleman opened fire with his assault rifle. Half of them went down, wounded or dying, before the rest realized they were under attack…and threw down their weapons.

It was over in seconds.

"Coleman, bind them," I ordered. "I need to get outside."

I could hear the staccato sound of gunfire combined with the *hiss-crack* of power through the firing slits. We'd neutralized the defenders, but that wasn't doing my people any good while two Nobles were tearing through their ranks.

Leaving the surrendering fae to the Hunter, I stepped Between and emerged in the middle of a hellzone. The fields surrounding the house were *burning*, a rapidly spreading grass fire that was threatening *everyone*.

In the middle of it, laughing as he dueled with two women, was Raja Venkat Asi.

Bloody red lines marked his golden flesh as he danced around the fae with a massive sword in his hand. Chernenkov was half-trans-formed, long claws flashing out from her hands as she attacked. Her companion was a more traditional Fae Noble, a classical beauty in modern body armor and wielding a glowing white sword.

Riley had started making his move in the moments before I arrived. He stepped Between with a cold iron spike in his hand, materializing behind Chernenkov and driving for her shadow with the weapon.

She backhanded him with a hand full of claws, sending the redhaired Irishman flying with blood spraying from his chest.

I was there before he hit the ground, *Esras* flashing through the air to block her as she tried to finish the job. Sixty kilos of enraged half-demon-horse, half-fae-woman slammed into the wooden haft of the spear and crashed to a halt.

"No further, Chernenkov," I told her. "It's me you want. Think you can do better this time?"

THERE WAS a banshee in the area, and Chernenkov's scream when she saw me was still the loudest sound in my ears. She spun around the spear's haft and flung herself at me.

My free hand met her in midair, a gauntlet of pure force wrapped around my fist as I hit her. She flew backward, hitting the ground next to her companion and rising instantly.

"I've no reason to run now, boy," she hissed. "You won't be as lucky."

Unfortunately, it looked like my arrival had been a near-fatal distraction for Asi. The Masked Noble had run him through while I was saving Riley, and the asura stumbled backward.

Then I realized that he *still* had her sword in him, and suspected it hadn't been as accidental as it looked. The cold iron couldn't kill the asura—at least, no more so than a regular sword rammed through his gut—but the same wound would be almost instantly fatal to me.

He'd taken the blow to remove the most dangerous weapon from the fight. Clever bastard.

Of course, that left me facing two Fae Nobles, one of whom looked on the edge of going berserk and another who just looked furious.

Power *flared* along the length of the spear as I met Chernenkov's gaze.

I smiled.

She charged.

Esras met her halfway, the ancient spear blade slamming into her chest with sickening ease. Fire and force flashed around the spear shaft as I flung her to the ground, then I threw out a hand.

The cold iron spike Riley had tried to attack her with was on the ground. It resisted my magic for a moment, then came rushing into my left hand as I used my right to pin the Pouka Noble to the ground with the ancient spear.

I slammed it into her shadow before she transformed away. Her body *rippled* around the blade, claws slashing toward my face only to recoil as the cold iron stabbed into her shade, her true spirit.

She screamed again, recoiling away from me. I tried to follow, only to find a glamor-clad warrior barring my way.

Asi had stolen the fae noble's sword, but she clearly had the full

Gift of Glamor. The arms and armor of a fairy-tale knight covered her now, and she blocked the spearhead with her shield.

The glamor-forged shield flung my strike aside, but it flickered as *Esras's* energy interfered with the magic. I dodged backward as she stabbed at me. She nicked me, drawing blood through my enchanted Kevlar regardless.

I brought the spear around as she charged again. She was faster than me, but I was fast *enough*. *Esras* flickered from block to block, and her glamor-blade sputtered as it was interrupted again and again.

I focused my energy and *pushed* against her glamor. For a fraction of a second, her entire glamor collapsed. No sword. No shield. No armor.

I struck. Pale-green flame encased the spearhead as I lunged, and I hammered the tip of the ancient spear into her chest. The faerie fire exploded out as I pierced her heart, and a burnt husk collapsed to the ground.

But the Noble had bought Chernenkov time to regroup. She'd taken on a new form now, one I'd never seen before. She'd gained several feet in height and looked even more like a twisted, nightmarish cross between horse and human than ever before.

Ten feet tall, she towered over me and fire encased her as her claws extended. It seemed that the Pouka Noble still had some tricks left for me.

"For my love!" she bellowed, her voice echoing across the field as she attacked.

Whatever *Esras* was giving me, it wasn't making me any faster. I went flying as deadly sharp and brutally strong claws smashed into my armor.

Only the fact that I went flying saved me from being sliced open from stem to stern, and Maria Chernenkov wasn't giving up. She was on me before I stopped moving, leaping at me as I used telekinesis to bring myself to a safe landing.

I rolled sideways, barely managing to maintain my grip on the spear, as her claws drove into the dirt. A second strike slipped across my shoulder, leaving a burning line where she cut my flesh...and then a sharp-edged hoof slammed into my stomach.

I stumbled and another hoof took out my legs. Claws hammered into my shoulder, pinning me to the ground.

"My lord!" Riley bellowed, the Hunter bursting out of Between with a cold iron spike in each hand.

Chernenkov paused for a fatal second and a burst of gunfire hammered into her chest. She might have me pinned to the ground, but that meant *she* wasn't moving.

I grabbed her arm, *keeping* her claws in me as Mary stepped closer. Her rifle barked again, more cold iron bullets smashing into the Pouka…and while Chernenkov was focusing on my lover, Riley dove in and slammed both spikes into her shadow.

I didn't know if Chernenkov had managed to get the spike I'd left in her shadow out in the months since we'd last met, but with three cold iron spikes hammered into her tonight, it didn't matter. She was done.

She screamed—and my free hand brought *Esras* up from the ground in a sharp stabbing motion my muscles remembered even though I'd never learned it. Fire flared around the spearhead once more, and the Pouka tried to get away.

It was over in seconds, and I slowly pushed her away as I slowly rose to my feet, using one of the most ancient and powerful artifacts in the world as a walking stick.

"Mary," I greeted her as she stepped over to me.

"Jason." She looked down at the twisted corpse at our feet, then very calmly shot Maria Chernenkov in the head three more times.

"She's dead, right?"

"I think so," I admitted. "Is the rest over?"

"Everybody's either surrendered or dead," Mary confirmed. "We control the estate now. At least until the police show up."

Right. Cops. That was a headache I had forgotten about in the chaos.

30

THE GRASS FIRE gave us some cover, I realized as I looked out over the wreckage of the estate.

"We need to clean up as much as we can as fast as we can," I told Riley and Mary. "Get our wounded and prisoners into the fort and double down on whatever sneakiness they've got in place there."

The house was already a wreck, and I shook my head at it.

"Make sure the house gets more wrecked and toss any bodies you can into the fire," I continued. "The rest we'll need to move into the fort with us while we clean out the vault."

"What about the tunnel?" Riley asked. "How obvious is the access from the garage?"

I winced.

"We cut a giant hole," I admitted. "We need to bring the garage down on top of it, make sure it's got enough debris over it that the locals aren't going to realize the tunnel is there for a few days."

I was continuing to lean on the spear as I gave my orders...and then I realized I didn't hurt anymore. Looking down at where Chernenkov had dug her claws into me, I whistled silently.

The wound was gone, with only the cuts in my armor above it to show I'd ever been injured.

"*Esras* appears to accelerate my healing," I said quietly. "I'll start moving the wounded if you two get started on making sure that fire spreads far enough to cover our tracks…and *not* far enough to threaten any innocents, am I clear?"

"We've got it," Mary told me. She kissed me fiercely, then disappeared back into the night.

Riley merely saluted before doing the same. I left the pair of them and walked over to where Asi was carefully removing the sword from his stomach.

"Need a hand?" I asked.

He snorted.

"I've had worse, but I wouldn't mind getting the chunk of metal out of me, if you would be so kind, yes," he told me.

The sword had been wielded by a fae. The blade was cold iron but the hilt wasn't. As I grabbed it, I couldn't help but admire it—sharkskin-wrapped titanium. Decorative, practical…and heavy enough to help balance the unavoidably crudely forged blade.

Asi exhaled sharply as the blade came clear with a gush of blood. He'd already acquired a length of thick cloth from somewhere that he wrapped around his midsection with the ease of practice, binding the wound tightly to keep the blood under control.

"Yeah. That hurt." He coughed.

"Where's your sword?" I asked him, studying the blade he'd neatly removed from my fight before it could threaten me. It was svirfneblin-forged hand-hammered cold iron. The hilt was utterly modern, the blade frankly crude. A ring of orichalcum runes were inlaid around the base of the blade, a difficult task for the Unseelie fae who'd forged the weapon.

It was an impressive weapon.

"Somewhere in the damn field," Asi admitted. "If we're in a rush, I don't think I'm getting that one back. Let the fire have it; that'll bury it."

"Take this one," I told him, flipping the sword around *Esras's* haft to offer it to him hilt first. With only thin gloves between my hands and the cold iron, holding the blade *itched*.

He arched an eyebrow at me.

"You'd trust me at your back with a cold iron blade?" he asked softly.

"Given that you let yourself get *stabbed* with this particular one to help protect me, I'm going with yes...Raja."

It was the first time I'd called him by just his first name, and the meaning of that—and of my offering him a sword that could easily kill me—wasn't lost on Raja.

He took the blade and saluted carefully.

"I swore Fealty," he said slowly. "It's...good to have done so to a man who understands."

———

WE WEREN'T AS PRACTICED in cleanup as we probably should have been. The Wild Hunt would normally off-load that task to the local fae court, but there *was* no local fae court in the Titaness's territory.

Mary and her team were more experienced at this than the rest of us, and it showed. By the time the sirens started to close in, both of the modern buildings were aflame and the grass fire was spreading around.

We'd done what we could to clear away weapons and cartridge casings, but the fire was a gift. Anything that we'd missed would be charred into unrecognizability. Questions might be asked...but they wouldn't be asked today, as we moved deeper into the Masked Lords' underground bunker.

"I don't think the gunfire actually attracted attention," Mary said as we reconvened. "So far, it's looking like all we've got are fire trucks. That won't last, especially not when they start pulling bodies from the house, but it'll buy us time."

"We'll need to make good use of that time," I told my senior subordinates. "This was more than just a storage house. A Masked Lord? A vault of weapons and funds? This was a major staging point.

"There's a good chance they either wrecked their computers or they're secured enough to keep us out, but paper records aren't so easily wiped," I continued. "We need to sweep this entire facility.

"At the same time, Damh, I want you and the Hunters to go

through the vault. That thing is stuffed full of weapons, gold, gems…a thousand different things of value, and I want it all."

I grinned at him.

"We're probably going to need to install our own vault at the house in Calgary to hold it all, but I *want* it. And more importantly, I want the Masked Lords to *not* have it."

"We can manage that," Damh Coleman confirmed. "We'll fill up a couple of our Between storage spaces; that should more than suffice."

"What about the prisoners?" Raja asked. "I presume that, given the general weak stomachs of Westerners, you're not planning on shooting them in the back and stacking them in the vault for their friends to find later?"

I physically winced at his not-quite-suggestion. I was coming to realize I could *trust* Raja, but I had to remember that he didn't think like me. I'd taken a thousand-year-old warlord into my service. He was far more willing to embrace massacre than the rest of us.

"We need what they know," I replied. "We'll interrogate them. In fact…" I grinned again, and this time, I felt truly evil. "I suspect they know *your* reputation well enough that you'll make a fantastic bad cop. Orman, think you can play good cop?"

The Vassal who'd done our pre-attack preparation grunted. She was recovering rapidly, but Rose had done a number on her ribs and she had a concussion that would have been life-threatening if she was human.

"I don't know if I can do 'good,'" she told us. "I can do grumpy-but-less-homicidal-than-Asi, though."

"That will probably be more than sufficient," Raja replied with a chuckle. "We'll interrogate the prisoners. What happens to them after?"

"We don't have enough people or resources to take them anywhere separately," I admitted. "So, they're coming to Calgary with us initially. After that, I'll call Ankaris, and the main Wild Hunt will take them off my hands."

They weren't likely to enjoy that. The Mercy of the Hunt wasn't known for, well, being merciful.

"How badly did we get hurt?" I finally asked. I'd led my people into a pretty nasty fight. Raja's people were basically irreplaceable, and I wasn't particularly certain what the wait time for replacement Wild Hunt personnel was, either.

"We lost two of the Companions," Damh told me. "It could have been a lot worse. Most of our people are wounded, but they'll be healed up in a day or two. Faster if we can meet up with a Healer or a doctor somewhere."

"And your people got beat up covering mine," Mary said. "They didn't have much in terms of silver, so we've got a few light wounds, nothing much. Everything else is already healed."

"Three of my asura will fight no more," Raja said quietly. "Many of the others will be longer healing than the shifters or the fae. We are difficult to injure, but we do not heal as you do."

"We should be able to borrow a Healer from the Wild Hunt, and there are doctors in Calgary we can call on," I told him. "We'll see your people treated. All of our dead will be brought back to Calgary and from there sent to…wherever they should be buried."

That was a new one to me. I'd been involved in operations where people had died before, but those had always been under someone else's authority. When people had died in Lord Oberis's service, he'd been the one responsible in the end.

There was no getting away from this one, though. The five dead supernaturals had died under my command.

That was going to take some absorbing.

31

Our cellphones weren't truly running on the mundane wireless networks. I didn't pretend to understand the half-technological, half-mystical background to what was going on. I just knew that my cellphone would work anywhere in the world, call any number, mundane or supernatural.

Despite all of that, we didn't get signal Between. As we stepped out of that strange nothingness into the woods outside my house, our prisoners corralled amidst us, every one of the Hunters' cellphones went off in sync.

Not the asuras' phones. Not the shifters' phones. Not even Orman's phone.

But my phone and the phone of every single member of the Wild Hunt was buzzing frantically. I pulled mine out and looked at the screen.

It was an emergency recall notice, calling every troop of the Wild Hunt back to Tír fo Thuinn. That partially underwater ancient fortress served as the home base of the Hunt, far from prying mortal eyes.

"Sir?" Coleman asked desperately, looking around at his exhausted troops and the prisoners. "We have to go."

"I know," I agreed instantly. "So do I. Raja!"

The asura was by my side instantly. Wounded or not, he remained an imposingly powerful presence.

"See to the prisoners and the interrogations," I ordered. "I'll make a call and get you backup, but the Hunt is being recalled."

"The Hunt?" he asked. "As in the entire Wild Hunt?"

"Looks like," I agreed. "Tír fo Thuinn is under attack. We may have moved against the Masked Lords, but they were moving against us while we were distracted."

Raja reeled off a string of curses I didn't understand, probably in at least two languages.

"We should go with you," he said.

"I need you to watch the prisoners and the house," I replied. "The Hunt must ride to the Horned King's call, but I cannot abandon my other responsibilities. I need you to take care of them."

He was wounded, besides. Raja was unquestionably my most powerful ally and subordinate, but he'd taken a blade to the guts. He would be fine…in a day or two. Right now, he was injured.

"Please, Raja," I said quietly. "If nothing else, I need you to guard Mary."

That, it seemed, was enough of a straw. He nodded jerkily and walked away, barking orders to his asura.

"I'm not staying here," Mary told me once he was out of reach. "Wherever you go, I go, Jason."

I wrapped her in my arms.

"This isn't about keeping you safe," I told her. "This part isn't your fight. I've never been to one of the old Irish fortresses and I don't know what I'm walking into. I trust Ankaris and Coleman…and that's it.

"Remember that Andrell came from Ireland and was sent by the High Court. This should be safe ground, but the last time we fought the Masked Lords, half the High Court died—in Ireland."

She was silent.

"Plus, if you don't stay here, Raja *will* insist on coming and he won't survive another battle, my love," I said softly. "He'll drive himself to death trying to avenge his people, but we still need him. This won't be the end of it."

"All right." Mary shook her head, then kissed me. "Then you better get moving, mister, before I change my mind."

"One phone call, then we're gone," I promised.

———

I CALLED OBERIS. It was probably telling as to how our relationship had changed over the last year that I had his direct cellphone number—and he picked it up instantly.

There had been a time I had to go through his aide. Of course, said aide had hated my guts *and* been betraying Oberis, so that hadn't ended well for anyone.

"Kilkenny," he greeted me. "You're alive, so I'm guessing your expedition went well."

"As well as it could have," I told him. "I have the spear."

That hung on the line in silence for several seconds.

"That's good," he replied. "Terrifying, frankly, but good. Is everything under control?"

I had to swallow a laugh. Everything was most definitely *not* under control.

"I have wounded, dead, prisoners and a storage room full of stuff we pulled from a Masked Lords vault," I said. "And Ankaris has just called the entire Wild Hunt to Tír fo Thuinn.

"I need your help."

That was a dangerous admission among the fae. We weren't nearly as bad about twisty contracts as we'd once been...but traditions died hard, and debts and boons were a tricky ground. I was offering Oberis a blank check for a boon and we both knew it—and I now held one of the most powerful magical artifacts in the world.

Of course, Oberis owed *me* in turn—and knew there was only so much he could ask so long as I swore fealty to the Queen of the Fae.

And I trusted him.

"What do you need?" he asked instantly. "I'm guessing you're not taking a plane to Ireland."

"Not a chance in hell," I agreed. "I have about ten minutes before every Hunter in Calgary is jumping Between to our home base, but I can't leave my prisoners unguarded, and my asura are in rough shape. I need hands, my lord. Anyone you can spare." I paused. "That you trust."

"That's the risky one right now, isn't it?" Oberis said quietly. "Can your people hold down the fort at your house for a bit? Talus isn't in town, but I can shake some trees and round up some goblins and Gentry under Robert if I have an hour or two."

"I think we can do that. I'm leaving Mary in charge, so she'll probably shake up some shifters as well. I need to be gone, my lord, so…"

"Your house will be here when you get back," Oberis promised. "I swear it thrice, upon my honor, upon my blood, upon my power. Neither your people nor your valuables will come to harm."

"Thank you. I owe you," I told him, acknowledging the debt.

"No, you don't," he replied, refusing the debt in turn. "I don't think we can even consider ourselves even, Jason. You killed an Unseelie Lord for me." I could *hear* him shake his head.

"We are *far* from even, Jason Kilkenny. Ride hard, Hunter. I do not know what awaits you in Tír fo Thuinn…but I fear the worst."

"So do I."

32

Tír fo Thuinn was technically an island. It was also about thirty meters below sea level, originally built well before what humanity regarded as "recorded history." Part of the area historians called Doggerland, it had been one of the first hill forts built in the area.

When the waters had drowned Doggerland, the fae who lived in Tír fo Thuinn had protected it, first with magic and then with massive earth embankments.

And then, later, as the waters rose and humans started traveling the waters between England and the mainland in numbers, it had been protected with magic again. Spells and constructs woven around the sunken fortress discouraged mortals from coming anywhere near it.

Though no one would ever have consciously realized it, Tír fo Thuinn was a small blank spot in the maps and shipping lanes that no one ever sailed through or even flew over. It was the oldest of the old forts, the most ancient site of the fae and the home of the Wild Hunt since before there had even *been* a High Court.

It absolutely should not have had a trio of green amphibious assault boats jammed into the tops of the embarkments, their machine guns providing covering fire for an organized retreat.

That, however, was the scene we emerged from Between to find. Tír fo Thuinn's outer fortifications were a wreck, shattered by explosives of some kind, and bodies were scattered across the field.

The Wild Hunt's reputation and authority were far out of scale with our actual numbers. If even a quarter of the dead I could see from my position on the wreckage of the fort's walls were ours, the Hunt had been shattered.

"Coleman, Riley," I barked. "Find cover and set up fields of fire with the Companions. Keep those bastards moving! I need the rest of the Hunters with me."

It was bad. The core fortress was on fire. It was mostly stone and earth, so that wouldn't last long...but it was still a bad sign.

My subordinates scattered into the wreckage of the first layer of fortifications, a mixed earth-and-brick berm. There wasn't much *left* of the broad low wall, but there was enough for us to take cover and open fire at the attackers.

What was most terrifying in some ways was that only a handful of the attackers were fae. Even from there, a good hundred feet from the closest enemy, I could tell that most of them were mortal.

They were mostly black men, almost certainly mercenaries recruited from the aftermath of the various brush wars in Africa. As peace infected a continent, a certain type of soldier found themselves in desperate need of employment—and the Masked Lords had found themselves in need of gun hands.

We added our fire to that of the remaining defenders, helping scatter the remaining attackers back to their boats—but the sounds of more gunfire farther into the fortress attracted my attention, and I looked at the six Hunters I'd just sliced off the rest of my team.

"With me, people," I told them quietly. "To the sound of the guns."

They didn't say anything aloud, but they followed me into the Between a moment later as I raced deeper into the ancient fortress of the Wild Hunt.

———

WE CAME out of the void into fire—of both kinds. The building was on fire around us and gunfire filled the halls.

A loose defensive line blocked access deeper into the fortress, a dozen Hunters and Companions holding the position as they traded fire with their attackers. Those attackers were all fae this deep, Gentry and Greater Fae who lashed the defenders with gunfire and magic alike.

I stepped out of Between, dodged a burst of gunfire, and took half a second to assess the situation. We were just inside the entrance to the great hall, and the defensive position was in front of the doors leading inward from the hall.

The attackers were in the middle of the hall, using pillars and ancient tables as cover. The sheer mass and age of the furniture in the room meant that it had absorbed years of energy from the supernaturals around it.

It was still merely wood…but it was tough old wood and it withstood bullets handily. On the other hand, I was now *behind* those attacking fae.

Even if I hadn't known how to take advantage of that, *Esras* did. The spear thrust forward with barely any conscious thought on my part, and fire lashed out again. Two hags went down before they even knew they were under attack as the lance of heat cut through them, and then the Hunters I'd brought with me opened fire.

Everyone in this mess was using cold iron rounds. Anything but the most cursory of wounds would be fatal, so I wove power in front of my people to keep them safe. We advanced into the attackers' rear.

I expected them to surrender, to be honest. That mistake cost me a bullet to the shoulder as one of the Gentry returned fire. My armor held and the Gentry died, fire flashing out from my hands in near-instinctive response.

Then it was over. A dozen Greater Fae and Gentry, beings with life expectancies measured in centuries, were dead on the ground—and they weren't the only ones in the hall.

I crossed to the barricade.

"What the hell is going on here?" I asked. "Is the fortress secure?"

The leader of the hastily assembled defenders doffed her helmet and gave me a rough salute.

"No one's made it past since we got here," she told me. "But we didn't get here in time. I know at least some made it deeper in, and I have no contact with anyone. Our radios and phones are being jammed, and everyone's been under too much pressure to try anything else."

She sighed.

"Ironically, stepping Between inside the fortress is a mess at the best of times. Whoever these people are, they've also done a number on the beacons we use to help with that. Ankaris is deeper in; I haven't heard from him…and radios or no radios, I should have."

I didn't know the woman, but she was clearly a senior Hunter. That meant the odds were roughly fifty-fifty on whether she was a Vassal of Ankaris or not…and if she was, then she would be able to talk to him regardless.

"His Vassal?" I asked.

"Amandine Delacroix," she introduced herself in an exhausted tone. "Vassal of the Horned King, Third Guardian of Tír fo Thuinn. I don't even know where the other Guardians are!"

"Can you locate Ankaris, Guardian?" I asked. "The forces outside are falling back to their boats; my own Companions are assisting in the defense. We need to find your liege."

She closed her eyes, focusing…and then snapped them open again in horror.

"He's in the main annex," she told me. "He's wounded. *Badly.*"

"Show me the way."

———

As we rushed through the wreckage of one of my people's oldest forts, it became clear to me that we had been too late. If we'd come directly there from Malta, we would have been in time, but we hadn't received the alert then.

I didn't know how long the alert had languished in the wireless ether before we'd returned to the regular world and received it, but it had been too long. Even the ten minutes it had taken us to make arrangements for our prisoners and resupply wouldn't have made a difference.

The Masked Lords had hit Tír fo Thuinn hard with a mixed force of mortals and supernaturals, all fully equipped with cold iron arms and knowledge of their enemy. The violation of the Covenants of Silence inherent in that was going to have wide and long-lasting consequences, but they clearly didn't care.

Bodies were scattered through the halls. Unsurprisingly, most of them were the Masks' mortal mercenaries, but there were plenty of fae —both in Hunter gear and not.

If half of the Wild Hunt had survived the day, I'd be surprised. The main security and paramilitary force of the fae had been gutted.

From what I could tell, the spearhead of the Masked Lords' attack had never even been slowed down. They'd lost mercenaries and companions along the way, but they'd kept going toward their objective: the main annex.

I could *feel* the power in the place, too. A hauntingly familiar but different feel. *Asi* had been here. The Masked Lords spearhead had been their ritual team.

Their god-killers.

If the great hall was the entryway to Tír fo Thuinn and the primary eating space, the main annex was the throne room. I didn't know the layout of the fortress, but I knew that it would be where Ankaris would hold court.

And very clearly, the attackers *had* known the layout of the fortress. Delacroix led me through a set of large double doors and then stopped dead in her tracks.

I stepped past her and studied the space. The main annex had been a beautiful space. The ancient stones had been worn smooth by thousands of years' worth of feet, with statues and tapestries added over time to smooth whatever harsh edges remained.

Murals covered the walls, depicting scenes lost to even fae myth. Even the furniture was artifacts of another time. A single piece from this room would have made any human archeologist's career—or fortune, if they were willing to sell it.

And it had been smashed to pieces. Ankaris was not a Power, but he *was* a member of the High Court, filled with the energy and strength of his role and bearing artifacts easily as powerful as the spear I carried.

He had fought with all of his power, but the Masked Lords had come with *Asi* and a spell written to kill gods. I could feel the tear where they'd entered Between when they were done...but their bloody work had been done before they left.

A raised stone dais led up to an ancient throne, both carved from the island's living stone. Ankaris was sprawled across the lower steps, his emerald armor cracked and burned. The horned helm of the Horned King was in his lap, his head bare and showing that his armor had survived better than he had.

"My lord!"

I'd crossed the room to him before I even saw someone was kneeling next to him. The green-armored woman with the massive two-handed sword was unfamiliar to me, but she was cradling Ankaris's hand.

"It's too late," she told me softly. "They...they broke his *soul*. He's dying."

I knelt by my cousin and took his other hand in mine.

"Ankaris, can you hear me?" I asked.

"Jason," he croaked. "Good. I needed...someone. Someone to stand witness."

"We can save you," I told him. I wasn't sure how, but I suspected if anything could...it would be *Esras*.

"No, you can't," he told me with a cough. "My energy...my power is fleeing me. I don't even know why I'm not dead yet...the spell should have killed me instantly. But it gives us time."

"What do you need?" I asked. I didn't truly know Ankaris, not well. We were cousins and he'd declared me a Noble of his Hunt, but we'd only had six months to learn about each other.

"Stand witness," he told me firmly. "Pull me up."

I helped him sit up, then held him up as he coughed blood. Fae blood looked much the same as human blood normally...but right now, Ankaris's blood was *black*.

He gripped the helm in his hands and gestured the woman to him.

"Grainne." He indicated her. "First Guardian of Tír fo Thuinn. My second. My strong right hand."

He coughed up more blood.

"Bend your head, Grainne Silverstar," he told her. "It'll be for the last time, I promise."

She knelt beside us and bent her head. Without further ceremony, Ankaris shoved the green helmet with its ancient antlers onto her head.

"I declare you my heir, the new Horned King," he said weakly. "Witness this, Jason Calebrantson!"

"I witness," I said quietly. "With eyes and ears and heart, I stand witness. Thrice it is witnessed...and it is done."

"So...it had to be," Ankaris coughed. "I'm sorry, Jason...in the end, I guess I wasn't very good fam..."

And in mid-word, Ankaris the Horned King died.

33

Dawn rose over the North Sea with a chilly wind that managed to cut down into the artificial bowl that housed Tír fo Thuinn. It had been a busy and heart-wrenching night.

Bodies were lined up on the grass outside the fortress. Hunters and Companions alike were covered in white sheets as we prepared to commit them to the catacombs beneath the ancient fortress.

A massive pyre burned in the northwest corner of the island, the Masked Lords' soldiers and mercenaries given the most cursory of rites before we cleared their bodies away.

Damh Coleman was kneeling in the weakly growing light, looking out over the field of bodies, when I joined him.

"Damh," I greeted him, making sure he knew I was there. I was tired—everyone there was—but it was more for him.

He gestured at the dead.

"I knew every one of them," he said quietly. "The Hunt was never very large, Jason. A few dozen troop captains reporting to fourteen Nobles and three Guardians. I didn't just know my fellow officers. I knew every Hunter and most of the Companions."

"I figured," I told him. "I only really knew Ankaris. Which was bad enough. I'm sorry."

I shook my head and laid my hand on his shoulder.

"Our troop?" I asked.

"Fine," he said with a shake of his own head. "Everyone's fine. We came to the end of the party, when the Masked Lords had already left and their minions were retreating. Too late to make a difference."

"We couldn't stay in Malta," I reminded him. "The Titaness's patience was limited, as was our ability to avoid the local police. We had to leave...and once we were Between, there was nothing we could do to change what happened here."

"I know." He sighed. "I don't know if the Hunt will recover from this. Half or more of us are dead on this field, Jason. We are *broken*."

And with the Hunt, much of High Court's power. The Masked Lords had spent money and blood like water on this attack, and it had won half their war for them in a single swoop.

"Master Kilkenny," someone called. I turned to see one of the walking wounded—a Companion who'd taken a cold iron round in an extremity and lived—walking toward me.

"What is it?" I asked.

"King Grainne has called a meeting of the Nobles and captains," she told me. "To see where we go from here, I guess. In thirty minutes in the great hall."

"We'll be there," I promised. "Nowhere else to be right now."

The courier nodded and continued on, looking for the other survivors of the Hunt's command structure.

"You going to be okay, Damh?" I asked.

"Ask me in a week. I don't know yet," he admitted. "Once we've got them laid to rest in the catacombs and we know more about what we're going to do, I might know."

"What about Ankaris?"

"He goes in the catacombs, too. The deepest levels, the ones only magic keeps dry." Damh snorted. "Next to your father, now that I think about it."

———

I HADN'T REALLY HAD time to register much of Grainne Silverstar before, what with my cousin and commanding officer dying in front of me. Now, as the last survivors of the Hunt's officers gathered in the great hall, I took a moment to assess the new Horned King.

She was a tall woman even for a fae, towering at least six inches over six feet. She had copper-red hair cropped short against her scalp in what might have been called a pixie cut on a less intimidating woman.

Her shoulders were broad and heavily muscled, a clear result of the massive two-handed sword she now had strapped to her back. She'd shed the green armor of the previous night in favor of a dark green suit, and she looked over her new subordinates with hollow eyes.

Including myself, there were four remaining Nobles of the Wild Hunt. With Silverstar's promotion, Delacroix was the last remaining Guardian. Fourteen troop captains, including Damh Coleman, sat with us.

Twenty fae, all Hunters.

"How many?" Silverstar finally asked, looking at us. "How many are left?"

Quiet numbers came from each of the troop captains, reporting how many of their Hunters and Companions survived. It was a sobering picture. The remaining troops had absorbed the survivors who'd reported to dead troop captains, but Coleman's troop—already short people from the fight in Malta—was the most intact.

A troop was supposed to be sixteen fae, plus the troop captain themselves. All told, including everyone in this room, the remaining Wild Hunt was under two hundred people.

"Recruiting doesn't really help us much," Silverstar said bluntly. "There aren't very many Hunters outside our ranks to begin with. Even if we could somehow draft them all, that would only allow us to assemble another troop at most.

"The Wild Hunt is going to be a weaker force than we have been, but that is the world we now live in," she continued. "I am attempting to make contact with the rest of the High Court, but I have had no luck. I believe I would know if they were dead, but they are not responding to any form of communication available to me.

"We now have no choice but to prepare for war." She sighed. "In fact, I see no choice but to abandon Tír fo Thuinn, at least for now. Our sanctuary has become a target. I now have the power to seal the defenses so no one except the Horned King can open them. Our home and our honored dead will be *safe*, but we must turn our focus to the outside world."

No one looked happy with that, but she wasn't wrong. With only a fraction of our original strength, if we were to fulfill our duty and protect the High Court, we had to leave the fortress.

"I need you all to speak with the Vassals among us," she ordered. "Their links to their lieges will be our best tool for tracing the people we are supposed to protect. Something has gone wrong, beyond what we can see, and I fear for the safety of the entire High Court."

She made a dismissive gesture.

"Get to it," she snapped. "Kilkenny, remain. We need to speak in private."

———

COLEMAN HESITATED as the rest left, but I gestured for him to follow. Whatever Silverstar had to say, I didn't have much choice but to listen. Even if the woman had just held a "meeting" that had consisted of her snapping orders at everyone.

After a minute, we were alone in the great hall and I found myself looking up at the new Horned King, one of the largest women I'd ever met.

Fae titles were odd to someone who'd grown up in the mortal world. It didn't matter what gender the Horned King was. They were always the Horned King. Same with the Queen of the Fae, the Ladies of the seasons and the rest.

The Puck was, from what Mabona had told me, a shapeshifter who refused to let anyone hang a gender on them. Or, well, anything else.

"Ankaris is dead," Silverstar said calmly. "Remember that, Kilkenny."

That was...not what I'd been expecting.

"I don't think I'm likely to forget," I replied slowly.

"I am not Ankaris," she continued. "I am not blinded by some strange concept of familial loyalty or hanging on to the last scraps of a favorite uncle's legacy. Your place here is from his weakness, not mine."

Ah. Okay, that I could follow, I suppose. I was a Noble of the Wild Hunt by Ankaris's word, but I remained a changeling, a quarter-human. That didn't sit well with many fae.

Apparently, the new Horned King was one of those fae.

"Perhaps," I allowed. "But my place is what it is now, isn't it? And we have a job to do."

"And no time for the trials and tribulations needed to remove you or replace you," she admitted. "But we have at least one issue we can clear up."

She held out her hand.

"Give me the spear."

I hesitated.

"I'm sorry, what?" I asked.

"I warned you once," she snapped. "I am *not* Ankaris. Do *not* defy me or I will strike you down. The Spear of Lugh is not yours. It belongs in the hands of the heir of Lugh, the Horned King. It is part of *my* regalia, not yours to claim by your father's mistake or your weak blood link.

"Give. Me. The. Spear."

Her power flared out around her, a green-tinted shadow seeming to fill the immense room as she glared at me and ground out her command.

Even so, for a moment I was tempted to defy her. It was in Silverstar's power to command me, yes, but I *also* answered to the Queen. As Mabona's Vassal, I could defy the new Horned King.

It would probably see me expelled from the Wild Hunt, but she could not *kill* me without angering Mabona. And Silverstar, like Ankaris before her, was not a full Power.

Mabona was.

That would trigger *another* civil war, one we could ill afford as the

Masked Lords hammered on our gates. I slowly nodded, lifting *Esras* from the ground and offering it to her.

The moment she yanked the spear from my grip, I knew it wouldn't work. The blood bond between myself and the weapon remained, even as it was in her hand. Its power didn't answer to her.

Even as she held it with both hands and focused her energy on it, I knew the spear wasn't going to change its mind.

"What have you done?" she demanded.

"Nothing," I told her. "The blood bond remains."

"Then remove it," Silverstar ordered.

"I can't," I admitted. "Calebrant forged it. I can't undo the work of a *Power*, King Silverstar. I can hand you the spear, but I can't make it so someone who isn't of Calebrant's blood can wield it."

"And if I lock the spear in the armory here with the rest of the artifacts that go unused and seal the fortress behind me, what will you do?" she asked.

"Nothing," I told her. I wasn't sure what her game was, but I knew I wasn't going to *argue* with her. "You're right. The spear belongs to the Horned King. If you wish me to wield in your service, I will. If you wish to lock it away forever so it can't be used against the High Court again, that is your right."

She shifted her grip on the spear, and I was reminded that there *was* one way to break the blood bond. If she killed me with *Esras*, that would definitely release the spear so she could wield it.

For a few seconds, it looked like she was considering that as an option, then she swore.

"Fine." She hurled the spear at me.

Esras itself told me where to move and I sidestepped easily, catching the spear from the air with the Gift of Force and bringing it back to my hand. I bowed to the Horned King.

"I am sworn to the service of the Hunt and the Horned King. I will follow where you lead."

"I don't want you anywhere *near* me," she snarled. "Get out of my fortress, Kilkenny. I can't strip you of your status, but I will not pretend that you are worthy to fight with my Hunt. Go back to your pathetic house in your pathetic city. The true Hunt will end this war, don't worry."

There...wasn't much I could say to that. With a stiff bow, I withdrew from the great hall of Tír fo Thuinn.

34

I ENDED up wandering the halls of the ancient fortress in a daze until I found myself at the entrance to the catacombs. They were normally sealed with a pair of iron gates, but those were open as we were slowly moving our dead into their permanent resting places.

Runes arced over the doorway, starting at the floor on the left and running all the way to the floor on the other side. The script was ancient, the language even older. The runes pre-dated the flood that had drowned Doggerland.

I couldn't read them but I knew roughly what they said: Here lie our honored dead. Let them rest and never be forgotten.

In a moment of sudden decision, I stepped through the archway and into the tunnels. Strangely, I knew where to go. I wasn't sure if that was *Esras*...or me.

Whatever the strange sense of direction came from, it allowed me to make my way through dark corridors with ease. The catacombs were carved from bedrock that should resist the water outside for a million years—and had been reinforced with magic regardless.

At some point recently, strings of dim LED lights had been laid throughout the underground part of the complex. They weren't bright, but they required almost no power and were more than enough for fae to see by.

The sconces that had once held torches were empty now, but they grew scarcer as I descended deep under the ancient fae fortress into the heart of the earth.

At the bottom, at least twenty meters deeper than the island itself, I suddenly stepped into an open space with no electric lights. I paused on the edge next to the last flight of evenly carved steps and let my eyes adjust.

There was still light in there. Not the LED of mortal artifice, but ancient sparks of power. An entire wall was natural crystal. Once, it had drawn light down from the surface, but now that light had to pass through water to even reach the crystal formation.

It was enough. After a moment, I could see that much of the crystal formation had been carved by fae hands and powers over the years. A row of statues of forbidding-looking men and women occupied half of the crystal wall, each wearing the same antlered helm.

The murky light from that crystal wall scattered gently across the barrow mounds that filled the cavern. Neat rows of mounds laid over the centuries—the *millennia*.

This was where dead gods were laid to rest. A rough cairn had been begun at the end of the row closest to the entrance. Stones had been brought from the surface to form the dome, and once Ankaris was laid to rest, dirt would be laid over that frame.

A new statue would eventually be added to the crystal wall, and another statue would sit at the front of the burial mound. Every mound here had a statue in front of it. Magic sustained them against time, and yet, the oldest statues were still indistinct.

The one next to what would be Ankaris's grave mound was perfectly intact, though. Magic had carved the stone into a perfect image of the man buried beneath the grave behind it.

A man I had never met and yet whose influence continued to shape my life.

There were no names on these statues or graves. No one would come down there who didn't know who the Horned Kings had been.

Even I, who had come to the world of the fae as an adult, could recite the names of all forty-three fae in this cavern.

But I was there to see one.

I was here to see Calebrant. My father.

———

THE ADVANTAGE of using magic to carve stone was that the artist could truly mirror the reality in a way that few could do with a chisel. Looking at the plain statue in the underground cavern, I could see myself in my father's face.

He'd been taller than I was, with even longer hair than my own shoulder length. The statue had captured its waves perfectly as it hung halfway down his back, loose even under the horned helmet.

He almost certainly hadn't worn it like that in battle, but even magic allowed some artistic license.

"I feel like I should have brought something," I told the statue. "Some token, but I didn't even know I'd be coming here. I guess my feet knew where I wanted to go, even if I didn't."

My father's statue was unsurprisingly silent.

"I appear to have pissed off your latest replacement just by existing," I said quietly. "Not much I can do about it. She's the Horned King. I'm...just your son." I snorted. "Not that I even knew I was that until this year.

"And here I am, talking to your statue, because I never met you when you were alive." I sat on the ground, cross-legged with *Esras* across my lap.

"But you're the reason I have this spear. The reason I have the Gifts and power I have. I feel like I should know more about you than I do."

I didn't get the impression that many people had known Calebrant well at all. Mabona, maybe. Probably my mother.

"I wish Mom had lived long enough to be able to tell me about you," I said. "Doesn't feel right that I only know you secondhand, and not through her."

My father didn't talk back. Statues were great listeners, I supposed.

I felt more than a little crazy sitting on the cold stone floor next to my father's grave, talking to him.

"I wish I'd met you," I finally told the statue. "Everyone seems to think I'm going to finish what you started. Save the High Court, defeat the Masked Lords. All I've got is a magic spear and a sarcasm problem."

That wasn't true. I realized that even as I said it, and I actually found myself smiling.

"And friends," I told him. "And allies. I'll miss Ankaris, but he's not the only person I can rely on. If Silverstar wants to send me away, that's her right. I have my own home and my own army now.

"And I have *Esras*." I shook my head and ran my fingers down the old wood. "So, I guess I'm not even really feeling sorry for myself down here. I just needed to talk to someone...and we never had a chance, did we?"

I used the spear to lever myself to my feet.

"You screwed my life up pretty good, you know," I said to the statue. "But I don't think that was your intent. Hell of inheritance you left me. I guess it's time to get to work using it, isn't it?"

Because if I didn't stop the Masked Lords, sooner or later, someone was going to be burying me in the catacombs above.

35

Damh Coleman was leaning against the wall next to the catacombs when I came up, saluting crisply as I met his gaze.

"I figured you'd find your way down there," he told me. "How's your father?"

"Dead longer than I've been alive?" I asked. "I'm running low on time, Damh. Silverstar kicked me out; I'm heading home pretty quickly."

"Then we're heading with you," Damh replied without hesitation. "I haven't received orders to the contrary, and last I checked, my troop reported to you."

"Do you really want to put yourself on the wrong side of the new Horned King?" I said. "She doesn't strike me as the type to forgive and forget."

"She'll learn," my friend said. "If she thinks she can run the Wild Hunt like a mortal army, she's going to learn a few hard lessons. We're soldiers, yes, but we're also *Hunters*. We have our own honor and our own rules."

He shook his head.

"If you're heading back to Calgary, we're with you." He glanced at

Esras. "I half-thought she was going to try to make you give up the spear when she asked you to stay."

"That's exactly what she did," I admitted. "The spear had its own ideas. The blood bond isn't broken. With Ankaris gone, *Esras* only answers to me."

"Makes sense in a way," Damh mused as he fell in beside me. "The Spear of Lugh answering only to the blood of Lugh."

I stopped in my tracks. That couldn't *possibly* be right.

"What did you say?"

"Wait, you didn't know?" Damh asked.

"The blood of Lugh?" I echoed back at him.

"Your father was his descendant. Not in direct line, but the only one known. You're the last living child of the bloodline of the first Horned King."

"What about Ankaris?" I asked.

"He was, too. He was your cousin, after all. But they're both gone now, which leaves you."

"Me." The descendant of Lugh. That was…a terrifying thought. But also…

"I guess it doesn't matter. I have *Esras*, but Grainne Silverstar is the Horned King, the heir of Lugh's power." I shook my head. It wasn't like I was planning on having kids, either. One of the "advantages" of dating Mary was that most supernaturals weren't cross-fertile.

We could all have children with humans, but few of us could have children together.

"It's why Ankaris declared you Noble," Damh admitted. "That and the fact that while your Gifts were limited, they were powerful enough to meet our standards. You are your father's son, Jason Kilkenny. I'll follow you."

"I hope it doesn't get you in more trouble than you can afford," I said.

"You underestimate how much trouble I can afford," he replied with a chuckle. "I'm a troop captain of the Wild Hunt."

Before I could attempt to convince him otherwise, a single gunshot suddenly cracked across the fortress.

I met Damh's gaze.

"What the hell?" I demanded.

"I don't know," he admitted. "It was that way."

We did the only thing we could. We ran toward the gunshot.

———

FOR A FEW TERRIBLE MINUTES, I thought the Masked Lords had come back. The lack of follow-up gunfire suggested otherwise, though, but I still had no idea what was going on when Damh and I charged out into the main assembly field of Tír fo Thuinn.

The scene in front of us didn't help me establish what was going on. Most of the surviving Hunters and Companions were gathered on that field, split into at least four groups.

The largest was gathered around Silverstar. From the looks of it, she was the one who'd fired into the air to try and get everyone's attention...but there were a *lot* of guns around and they were not being aimed particularly safely.

"I have given my commands," she barked. "I am the Horned King. You *will* obey."

"We can't just leave our dead to rot!" someone replied. I didn't recognize the speaker. Unlike Damh, I didn't know everyone there, not even in passing.

"We have a higher duty," Silverstar told them. "And regardless, these are *my* commands. We will abandon Tír fo Thuinn. I will seal it against all enemies and we will seek out the rest of the High Court.

"Only once we have gathered the High Court together again can we hunt down the Masked Lords and have our revenge."

That...was a *terrible* idea. Concentrating the High Court would put all of the Fae Powers in one place. In theory, that was a lot of magical might...but in practice, I had the sinking feeling that it would only provide the Masked Lords with an easy target.

It wasn't my place to argue with Grainne Silverstar, though. Quite the opposite, I wasn't even supposed to be there anymore!

"We are not leaving our dead!"

"Fine." Silverstar moved with a grace and speed none of us could match. Her gun snapped around and she fired. This time, she wasn't aiming for the sky, and the Companion who'd objected fell backward.

She'd shot him in the head with a cold iron bullet.

"*I am the Horned King,*" she bellowed. "Obey me or I will strike you down!"

A few skittered over to join the group clustered around her, but all she seemed to be achieving was pushing the groups arguing against her together.

"Is this treason, then?" she demanded. "Mutiny in the Hunt? Ankaris chose me as his successor. Delacroix, would you defy him?"

The only other remaining Guardian looked terrified to be called upon, but she swallowed and stepped to the front of the chaotic mess that was roughly a third of the remaining Wild Hunt.

"We have a sacred duty," Delacroix said loudly. "We swore an oath to guard Tír fo Thuinn for all eternity. To bury our dead in its halls. To guard the High Court... Abandoning Tír fo Thuinn to *force* the High Court out of hiding betrays those oaths."

"We have no choice," Silverstar declared. "Tír fo Thuinn is vulnerable. Scattered, the High Court is more so. A solitary Power cannot stand against the Masked Lords' new weapon. We must gather the Court and face our enemies as one."

"Then we call the Court and bury our dead while we wait to hear," Delacroix replied. "It is not *our* place to command the Powers of the fae!"

"But it is our place to defend them," the Horned King proclaimed. "If you will not help me do so, then you are a traitor and a waste of my time!"

That...was enough. I slammed *Esras* against the stones as I strode forward, channeling power into a shield that shouldered aside Silverstar's strike at Delacroix. Flickering glamor-blades shattered against the stone as I moved to stand between the now very clear two factions.

"Horned King or no, you do not hold the right of life and death over the Hunt," I told Silverstar. "You, too, are bound by sacred oaths, Grainne Silverstar."

"You have no place here, *Kilkenny*. Be gone."

I sighed.

"You know my name," I told her. "But let's get it out, shall we?"

I funneled power into my voice.

"I am Jason Alexander Odysseus Kilkenny Calebrantson," I bellowed. "I bear *Esras*, the Spear of Lugh. I am the son of the Horned King, a Noble of the Wild Hunt, and I will *not* see our sacred trusts betrayed."

The assembly yard was silent.

"You challenge me?" Silverstar demanded.

As a Noble of the Wild Hunt, I theoretically could challenge her for the antlered helm. I didn't *want* the damned job. I just wasn't willing to let her kill anyone else today.

"No. You are the Horned King," I told her. "But I will not permit you to shed the blood of Hunters and Companions upon these, our most ancient grounds. Whether you will it or not, I am a Noble of the Wild Hunt and I call on you to respect our oaths and our honor."

There were...seventy, maybe eighty Hunters and Companions behind me. A somewhat larger group in front of me, gathered around the Horned King.

"You defy the Horned King," she ground out. "I will spare your lives, but you are all mutineers and traitors. You are all barred from Tír fo Thuinn. If you would hide behind Calebrant's *brat*, then go with *him*.

"But any of you who remain on this ground in ten minutes will die by the hand of their King!"

———

THE FIELDS of Tír fo Thuinn were silent as Silverstar finished her pronouncement.

It was the last thing the fae who'd defied her wanted. They wanted to stay there and bury their dead...but it was within her authority to exile us from the ancient fortress. If the Horned King expelled us, we were expelled. Banned.

She wasn't, quite, expelling us from the Hunt itself. But she was exiling us from Tír fo Thuinn.

"Delacroix," I said quietly as I stepped back into the crowd. "You with me? You might still be able to—"

"I'm with you," she cut me off.

I turned, intentionally showing Silverstar my back. It was a risk, but it was one I had to take as I looked over the half-dozen troops' worth of Hunters and Companions who'd defied the Horned King and suddenly become my responsibility.

"Follow me Between," I told them. "It seems we are no longer welcome here."

I took one last look around the fortress where my father was buried and inhaled a breath of air. That air was tainted with blood and smoke, the sickening smell of burnt flesh mixed with the faint taste of cordite from the previous day's gunfire.

I met Silverstar's glare and bowed, slightly.

"It is your right," I told her. "But I promise you: I will honor my oaths. I ask that you do the same."

"Get out of my sight," she snapped.

I stepped Between, walking calmly away from Tír fo Thuinn. I felt Damh behind me. And Delacroix. And the Hunters I knew from Damh's troop...and then others. More.

More, in fact, than had been openly defying Silverstar. The Hunters and Companions she'd exiled had followed me...and so had others. At least half the Hunt was Between with me as I walked through another world to cross the waters of the North Sea.

We couldn't make the entire journey like this, not without knowing who was following whom and where we were going. I targeted an abandoned set of Scottish moors and emerged once again.

A chill breeze cut across the hilltops and I surveyed the area. We were being watched by some vaguely curious sheep and that was, thankfully, it.

Dozens spilled out of Between behind me. One moment, the moor was an empty, windswept hill, dully lit by the gray morning sun of a Scottish winter.

The next, it was full of fae, many still in shock at what had just happened. The hillside was very quiet as I looked out over what had suddenly become *my* people and realized that I was suddenly the leader of *half of the Wild Hunt.*

"Delacroix..." I trailed off. She'd followed me into this. I figured I could—that I *should*—use her first name. "Amandine. Damh. Find what we've got for officers, troop captains, Nobles. Hell, people the others will respect and follow.

"We need to get organized before this turns into a mob."

I didn't know what getting organized entailed—or what a mob entailed, for that matter. But I knew that Amandine and Damh did.

And part of me suspected that if I *didn't* get my rogue Hunt organized, the High Court was going to be in serious danger.

36

It took twenty minutes for us to establish who should even be *in* a council of war. Thankfully, it didn't take much longer to gather the officers to actually have said council.

Amandine and I were the only Nobles, but we had ten troop captains, including Damh. I looked around at their stressed faces and knew that the situation was still far from under control.

"How many of the Hunt followed us out here?" I asked gently.

"Including ourselves"—Amandine gestured around—"one hundred and six."

"So, we're going to have ten troops of ten," I said firmly. "I'm assuming you all have at least some people from your own troops, correct?"

The captains nodded. I knew Damh had everybody, for example. Most of the troop captains had brought at least three or four of their troop with them. It looked like I actually had more of the Hunt's midranking officers than the Horned King did.

"Pull people you know from the stragglers into your troops," I told them. "We'll probably need to reallocate people once we've got everyone organized, but that can wait until our next stop. Right now, we need to make sure that everybody out here knows who to look to for instructions."

"Where do we go from here?" one of the captains asked.

I looked over at her.

"I'm sorry, captain, I don't know everyone's names," I admitted. "You are?"

"Siobhan MacNeil," she introduced herself. "Our new King seems to have gone mad, but that doesn't tell us where we go next!"

"The best thing we can do in the long term is wait for Silverstar to regain her balance," I told them. "We don't defy her and we continue to do our duty. I'm uninclined to try and force the Court to gather, but I will be making contact with Mabona once we're all safe. We'll move against the Masked Lords once we're ready, try and bring this damn civil war to an end."

"Where is safe?" another captain asked. I glanced over at him and he shrugged. "Archie Pittaluga, my lord."

I couldn't object to the "my lord." Not here, not now. Not when I'd just somehow ended up in charge of half the Wild Hunt.

"Once we've got everyone organized, we'll step Between to my own home base in Calgary," I told them. "I have the space there to put up everyone, though it'll be a tight squeeze for a day or so as I arrange additional housing.

"That will give us a base of operations as we try to sort out what the hell is going on. As I see it, we have three objectives now."

I waited to see if anyone objected to me simply dragging them all to my house. No one did, so I nodded to them and continued with the objectives.

"First, we need to protect the High Court. That means we need to make contact with at least one of the Powers so they know they can reach us and we know if they're in danger. I'm a Vassal of Mabona, so that's the easiest task. I'll need you to identify if anyone else's Vassals ended up in our collection here.

"Secondly"—I counted visibly on my fingers—"we need to neutralize the Masked Lords. They had a major base in Malta which has now been destroyed, but it won't have been their only facility. If nothing else, they are Fae Lords, which means they have courts and resources of their own that they can access openly.

"We need to identify them and move against them. We remain the Wild Hunt, with the authority to prosecute and arrest even Fae Lords. We will find the Masks and we will end this civil war."

"And Silverstar?" Pittaluga asked carefully.

"That's our third objective," I told him. "While preserving the High Court and ending this damn civil war are higher-priority, we must also keep our eyes open for opportunities to fix this schism in the Hunt. Grainne Silverstar is the Horned King. We were, I feel, correct to defy her—and definitely correct to refuse to allow her to randomly execute officers of the Hunt.

"But we must make peace with her, sooner or later. She is the Horned King," I repeated.

"Makes sense to me," Pittaluga said. "But I think we've got one problem that'll bite us in the ass if we don't do something about it."

"Which is?" I asked.

"Chain of command," he told me. "You're in charge, but that's only because we put you in charge. Someone can argue, could push back, could change their minds."

He shook his head.

"Only one solution I see."

The rest of the fae around me clearly understood what Archie Pittaluga was going for. *I* didn't...not until they knelt.

Pittaluga knelt first, bowing his head as he spoke words as ancient as the fae themselves, if translated through a dozen languages along the way.

"I swear you Fealty, Lord Calebrantson. My sword is yours. My life is yours. My will is yours. Twice and thrice I swear you Fealty, obedience and honor unto death."

Even Damh Coleman had never sworn me Fealty. I'd been placed in command of him and, like most nobles of the Hunt, I'd relied on the chain of command.

Now he swore Fealty with the rest and I could *feel* the ancient two-way bond of our people settling into my soul as eleven Hunters pledged me their lives and swords.

"Thrice sworn, I cannot thrice deny," I told them. "I accept your oaths, your lives and swords. I swear I will honor your trust and serve our shared sacred oath."

And if I didn't...it wouldn't matter. Fealty was almost impossible to break. Their lives were mine now.

Damn.

37

RETURNING to the house in Calgary was almost comedic. Mary and Raja were out of the building to greet me almost immediately—and were both shocked to silence at the continuing parade of Hunters and Companions pouring out of the Between.

"Raja, please tell me that we have that new space in the basement set up as a barracks," I said plaintively. "And that we have at least one more of those prefabs. I brought some friends home, as you can see."

Mary shook her head and kissed me before my subordinate could respond.

"We've moved Raja's people into the basement, yes," she told me. "We've only got the one prefab building, but I bet Eric can conjure another couple from his stores if you ask."

"Then I guess I'd better find my phone again," I admitted. "There's a hundred and six people coming, if you're trying to count," I told them. "They're...uh...mine?"

"Did Ankaris assign you new support?" Raja asked. "I can see the logic."

"No." I sighed. "Ankaris is dead. The Masked Lords killed him. His successor and I had a difference of opinion."

"You're going to have to tell me later," Mary interjected. "It looks like I need to go play administrator and find people beds. You owe me," she said warningly, then kissed me and strode off to take charge.

"The Horned King is dead," Raja echoed. "And a hundred of his people are here. You had an interesting few days in Europe, I see. I can feel the links of Vassalage, you know."

That would have been a non sequitur, but I knew why he was saying it.

"All of the troop captains and the Guardian," I confirmed. "Roughly half of the Wild Hunt has sworn me Fealty. I'm not quite sure what to do with that."

The asura turned to study the surprisingly organized crowd on our front lawn.

"'Half,'" he repeated. "There are only a hundred fae here, Lord Kilkenny. The Hunt should be hundreds."

"They're dead, Raja," I told him. "The Masked Lords stormed Tír fo Thuinn. They killed Ankaris and shattered the Hunt. The new King then managed to cause a schism in the Hunt." I gestured around.

"These are the ones who followed me, who weren't willing to accept the King having the power of life and death over his Hunters."

Raja arched an eyebrow at me.

"He doesn't?" he asked.

"No. There are long, *long* traditions around the authority the Horned King has, but randomly executing people who talk back is not on the list," I told him. "But Grainne Silverstar is the Horned King... and half of her Hunt has sworn Fealty to me."

Raja chuckled.

"I believe you were warned that you would gather a court to you," he reminded me. "I don't think anyone expected you to steal the Wild Hunt."

"Behave, Raja," I said under my breath. "These people have seen their friends, brothers, commanders, massacred. You of all people..."

"I know," he allowed, with a small nod. "I understand. The Masked Lords are assembling quite an account that needs to be balanced."

"The spear will help." I hefted the weapon, feeling its wood warm in my hands. "Beyond that...I need to know my enemy, Raja, and I'm getting really frustrated with being one step behind."

"I am yours to command, my lord," he told me. "But I don't know fae politics. My involvement in them has always been rather...specifically targeted."

"I need to talk to my Queen."

I'd tried phoning her before we'd left Scotland, but no one had answered. Now that I had my wayward and heavily-armed sheep somewhere we were safe, it was time to start trying more...energetic methods of communication.

————

I TRIED the phone again first. It was worth a shot, after all.

This time, it didn't even go unanswered. I went straight to a voice mailbox. One that was full. I wasn't entirely surprised by that, at least.

To my knowledge, Mabona used cellphones like many people's parents: she made and answered calls on it and that was it. She wasn't necessarily *behind* on technology—fae lived too long to truly get set in their ways—but I knew she didn't check her voicemail.

The next step was conferencing software via the Fae-Net. I had contacts for both Mabona and her chief of staff, the Vassal responsible for coordinating her schedule. I didn't have Win Jernigan's phone number, but I could reach her by email and videoconference.

Except today. The software calmly told me that neither was available. My messages hung in limbo and I checked a different screen.

Unlike many mortal websites, Fae-Net sites and software were built for fae, and we were two things at the best of times: utterly melodramatic and rigidly hierarchical. There was no way that I could see, for example, when Mabona had last been on the conferencing software.

I *could*, however, see when Win Jernigan had last logged on.

I looked at the GMT timestamp for a long time, at least twenty or thirty seconds, while I did mental math.

It could *not* be coincidence that the woman responsible for handling the correspondence and scheduling of the Queen of the Fae had gone offline less than fifteen minutes after Ankaris had been attacked.

It had to be, though, didn't it? Nothing that had happened to

Ankaris, even in his fortified home base, should have affected Mabona, wherever she was hiding.

Something was very wrong.

I closed my eyes and focused on a spot inside of myself that I usually tried to ignore. I was *mostly* comfortable with the various aspects of being a Vassal at this point, but the direct link between my soul and Mabona was still creepy to me.

I had once been warned that if I tried to ignore one of my Liege's commands, I would find myself still acting in pursuit of it unconsciously. The link between Vassal and Liege was a deep one, and one I now knew both sides of.

Through that link, Mabona could know if I was injured. Where I was. What I was doing.

The return link wasn't as powerful. It required focus and I usually tuned it out. Right now, I was realizing that might have been a critical mistake.

Testing the link was nerve-wracking. It was still there; I confirmed that quickly. I was reasonably sure I'd have known if Mabona was dead, but I was starting to think I might have missed anything less than that.

Once I'd established it still existed, I sent a mental query, the equivalent along this channel of a knock.

Nothing. No response.

Mabona was *there*, but she wasn't responding to my attempts to communicate.

Unthinkingly, I picked up *Esras* from where I'd laid the spear down, and placed it across my lap. With my hands on it and calling on the ancient weapon's energy, I reached down the link again.

This level of intrusiveness was, for lack of a better word, rude. If I'd tried to do this while Mabona was conscious and aware, I'd get yelled at at the very least.

I forced the connection open from my side, linking my mind to my Queen's more closely than we'd ever done before. I could *feel* her wounds, the bone-deep exhaustion that had dragged her into unconsciousness.

She was in a coma. Not a deep one, I didn't think, but I wasn't a doctor or a Healer. She hadn't been physically injured, though. It was a mental wound, one that had struck at her essence.

At her Power. The link to the greater reality that underpinned everything, the link that made her the next thing to a god walking the earth...and also her link to the rest of the High Court.

"Powers that are," I whispered.

The Masked Lords had used Ankaris's link to the rest of the High Court to attack them through him. That was why he hadn't died instantly. They hadn't even *been* attacking him, not really. They'd been using him as a conduit, and the process had eventually killed him.

There was a touch of awareness to Mabona's mind, the sleeping goddess whose edges I was probing. A tiny portion of her presence touched me, an injured owner reaching out to pet the dog who was watching over them in their infirmity.

That wasn't exactly a reassuring metaphor.

There was a *need* to that awareness, too. There was warmth and recognition in it; she knew I was there, but there was a calling.

My Queen needed me...but she'd distorted the link when she'd gone into hiding. I'd managed to make a connection with her, but I couldn't *find* her. I doubted I was the only Vassal getting her vague message, her sleeping cry for our help.

But only the Vassals already with her knew where she was. I had no way of locating her. I wasn't strong enough to pierce the veils of a Power...

Esras warmed under my fingers in response to that thought, and I chuckled.

"Just how aware of what's going on around you *are* you?" I wondered aloud. The closest thing to a response I got was a sense of puppylike eagerness to help.

I shook my head and called even more deeply on the weapon's power. I focused my strength along a link that wasn't designed to hold that much energy, trying to shine a light through a veil that was meant to frustrate exactly what I was trying to do.

The veil resisted me. My push scattered the sleeping awareness I'd touched. For a moment, I struggled against the sleeping power of a god.

Then the half-dreaming awareness I'd connected with returned. The fragment of Mabona that was aware didn't control her power. It couldn't turn off the veil...but it could help me pierce it.

A god's mind fought itself to help me make the connection I needed to. I didn't think it was going to be enough, and then it was. A tiny gap opened in the veil Mabona had woven to protect herself, and I had a full connection with her for the first time since she'd gone into hiding.

I knew where she was. I knew she was injured, defenseless.

For all that I had become, for all that I had learned of my father and all the fealties that had been sworn to me, I remained a Vassal of the Queen of the Fae.

And that meant there was only one thing I could do.

38

MARY WAS WAITING for me when I stepped out of the darkened conference room. She'd pulled up a chair, but it didn't look like she'd been there very long—if for no other reason than because she was leaning on a pillow but was still awake.

"I know that look," she told me as she straightened. "You were looking for Mabona?"

"She's in a coma," I replied. "I know that...and where she is. That's all. I don't think she's currently in danger, but..."

"But if your Queen is injured and unconscious, she's in danger. What do you need, love?"

"How are we doing with the horde?" I asked her. "Thank you for taking that on."

"Eric is on his way. He says he's got another pair of those prefab army barracks in his Between storage, so that will give us enough space. I borrowed a bunch of pickups from the Clan and have sent people all over town shopping for beds, so we'll have somewhere for folk to sleep by nightfall."

My sense of time was completely thrown at this point. I'd jumped time zones forward and backward twice in the last five days.

"What time is it?" I asked.

"Fourish," she replied. "You look shattered, Jason. Are you planning on going out yourself?"

"She's nearby," I said. "In the mountains, I think. She's shrouded the world around her—I can't localize her tightly and without a beacon I can't walk Between to her.

"I need a car, a map, and someone more familiar with the mountains than me."

"You've got me, so that'll cover the last one," Mary said with a chuckle. "I think we've got maps somewhere, and your Escalade is in the garage." She studied me. "You're not driving it, though."

That was a very firm executive decision, and I looked up at her.

"You look shattered, Jason," she repeated. "I'm not going to try and tie you to the bed or anything like that—tempting as that idea is on a few levels—but you are damn well not driving a car.

"We'll find your location on the map, grab a couple of somebodies to ride shotgun, and then *you* can navigate while *I* drive."

I exhaled a long sigh. I knew when not to argue with my girlfriend...and she was right.

"You're right." I repeated the sentiment aloud. "Let's find that map, then we'll grab Raja and one of your wolves. I want the Hunters to sleep. It's been a rough few days for them."

"And we may end up calling them up into the mountains?" Mary suggested.

"Exactly. I don't know what's going on, but having a hundred-plus people who can make it to wherever through the Between on short notice...that's a reassuring backup."

"All right." She led me through the house to a filing cabinet and pulled out a map of the area around the city, laying it out on a table. "We're here." She tapped the map.

"Then..." I studied the map for a few seconds, poking at the feeling in my head. "Can I get a pencil?" I asked absently.

Mary had one in my hand almost before I'd finished speaking. If I survived the next few days, it was going to be because I'd managed to fall in love with the right wildcat shifter when I'd arrived in the city.

I drew a long line on the map, starting at where Mary had indicated we were. It cut northwest at a sharp angle and into the mountains, well north of the resort communities I was vaguely aware of.

"Along this line," I told her. "Around…a hundred miles. Plus or minus ten or twenty."

I'd learned the strange mix of metric and imperial units the Canadians used, but for something this instinctive, I went back to what I'd grown up with.

"A hundred and sixty kilometers or so." She studied the map. "That puts us around the Sawback and Vermilion ranges. There's not much out there, but we might be able to swing around on the back roads."

"Let's plug the best we can into the GPS and go hunting," I replied. "I'm guessing a private hunting lodge or something similar. It'll have power, but probably satellite internet and phones. Might not even be on the map."

"The road should be," Mary told me. "We'll find her, Jason."

And if we found her, I could throw up a beacon my people could use to navigate Between to us.

———

ERIC AND RAJA were standing by the front entrance as we came up from the main area on the bottom floor. The two couldn't have been more of a study in contrast, the perpetually shirtless asura warlord towering over the heavily dressed and bearded gnome.

Eric was also the only person of my close acquaintance who was of roughly the same age as the old asura. The Keeper had been many things before he settled down in the service of the fae as a whole.

"You're heading out," Eric greeted me. It wasn't a question.

"I think I've located Mabona," I told him. "We can't take everyone out there, not without attracting more attention than we can afford, and her defenses will prevent us traveling there Between without a beacon to guide the exact way."

"Are you up for this, Kilkenny?" the gnome asked, studying my face.

"Mary's driving," I admitted. "I might sleep, at least until we hit the mountains."

"Good call. I assume you're not going alone?"

I chuckled.

"Is everyone going to mother me while I try and run this army I suddenly acquired?" I asked.

"Training new Nobles and Lords is literally part of my job, Jason," Eric pointed out. "And so is keeping you alive."

"If you've found the Queen, I'm coming with you."

I looked up to see Kristal stepping through the door. Kristal Sayer and the rest of the nymphs assigned to guard me had been summoned to other duties before I'd left Calgary. And yet here she was.

"You didn't go anywhere, I see," I noted.

"We were supposed to be met at the London airport with orders and tickets," she told me. "No one showed. We hung around in Heathrow for a day, then I decided we may as well come back here."

She snorted.

"I hope someone is still going to be paying off my credit card. Emergency flights are not cheap."

"We'll take care of it if we can't get back in touch with the Queen's support structure," Mary promised. I glanced at her in surprise and she laughed.

"No one updated Jason on exactly what we pulled out of that hole in Malta, did they?" she asked.

"I meant to include that in my request for an actual salary," Raja said with a grin. "Bearer bonds, stock certificates, diamonds, gems of other types, gold, silver, platinum… Most of the paper is old but still valid."

"How valid?" I asked carefully.

"I spoke with Shelly on your behalf already," Eric told me. "Getting everything transferred into a corporation in your name will be complex but straightforward enough. You can afford to pay your people's credit card bills, Jason."

"And then a couple hundred million," Mary finished. "You have the resources to run your own court now, my love. And the Masked Lords *don't* have that money, which I think all of us regard as a win."

"Fair enough," I said with a soft chuckle of awe. "All right, Kristal, Raja, you're riding in the back with Barry and the heavy firepower. Bring some heavy firepower."

I offered Eric my hand.

"Can I ask you to keep an eye on things until Damh and Amandine are awake?" I asked the old Keeper. "They've had even rougher days than I have. I saw the Hunt shattered. They saw their friends massacred."

"I'll keep the place safe," he promised. "Go find our Queen, Jason."

39

Despite my promises to the contrary, I'd intended to stay awake the entire trip. So, of course, the next thing I knew after us leaving Calgary's city lights was Mary shaking me awake while Raja filled up the SUV's gas tank.

"We're in the mountains now," she told me. "Filling up in Canmore before we go into the park."

I shook myself and rubbed my eyes.

"How long was I out?"

"An hour or so. Traffic was pretty light and you needed the sleep," Mary said. "Plus, if there were any problems, Raja *is* propping his feet on a machine gun."

There was a blanket thrown over the M60 in his row, but she wasn't exaggerating. The middle row had an M60 and Kristal's boxy submachine gun. The back row had a blanket tossed over an assortment of other weapons, including several large swords.

Apparently, the big curved sword Raja favored was called a tulwar, for example.

My own weapons were in their usual spot Between, including *Esras*. I figured that traffic cops might question why someone had a six-foot-long spear in the passenger seat of an SUV.

I was starting to get more and more of a sense of what the spear thought of things, too. It hadn't been happy to be stuffed Between. It was only really "happy" when it was in physical contact with me.

Perhaps most interesting was that, so far as I could tell, the ancient spear didn't even like violence. The blood bond my father had forged, however, meant that it could only truly be its "full self" while I was holding it.

"How far does the GPS say we have left?" I asked Mary.

"About another hour, at which point we're turning off onto roads the GPS doesn't have programmed into it," she said. "How do you feel about navigating by map?"

"Grumpy and uncomfortable." I poked at the glove compartment. "It's in here, right?"

"Yeah. They don't actually want random tourists on the roads we're about to go on, so even the maps aren't great." Mary leaned her head against me for a few seconds. "I hope you know where we're going, love."

"I think so," I confirmed. I still had the link I'd forced open to Mabona. We were getting closer.

Unfortunately, it didn't seem like she was getting any more awake.

———

It was late enough when we reached the entry to the park that the gate attendant gave us a rather harder looking-over than I was expecting. It was a good thing we'd concealed the weapons, as I was pretty certain that Canadian park rangers, especially, would disapprove of us bringing heavy weapons into the park.

Mary, of course, just spun a happy burbling story about going in for dinner and staying at one of the hotels in Banff. I wouldn't have known enough about what was normal to tell a believable story—though, to be fair, I didn't get the impression we needed much of a story.

Once we were through the gates, we followed the highway about halfway to the tourist trap masquerading as a town we were supposedly heading to. At that point, Mary turned us off onto a side road that curled its way around a mountain next to the main road.

Ten minutes later, she slowed the SUV down as we pulled up next to a road that was barely better than a dirt trail.

"Here's where the GPS gives up," she told me. "Got that map out?"

I did, in fact, and had been using my own phone to pick out exactly where we were. The paper map, at least, had the dirt side roads on it. It was far from perfect, but it at least gave us an idea of where we were.

As for where we were going, well…that was up to me now.

"Down that road," I said with a sigh. "We're still at least fifteen miles away. Deep into the back country, I'm guessing."

"Looks like. All right, everyone, hold on. This is going to be bumpy."

She was thankfully exaggerating. One of the advantages of the very large, very expensive vehicle that Eric had acquired for me was that the shocks were in perfect condition.

It was still a rough ride, but it wasn't so bad as to count as *bumpy*.

"I imagine the Queen traveled here Between, right?" Kristal asked from the back seat. "This seems rather…beneath her dignity."

I chuckled.

"Kristal, it's beneath *our* dignity, let alone Mabona's," I told her. "But it's also somewhere almost no one is going to look."

We came up to a turn-off on the dirt road, an even *more* decrepit-looking lane, and I pointed.

"That way, Mary. We're getting closer."

She turned us up the road and we drove deeper and deeper into areas no tourist was supposed to see.

Somehow, I was unsurprised as the road actually started to *improve* in quality as we went on. We passed several gated roads with discreet signs. Past the gates, neatly maintained gravel lanes passed back into the hills.

Some were probably private lodges. Most were almost certainly park properties.

"This turn," I finally pointed out. I checked the map as I did so and exhaled slowly. "This is the last one. Nothing leaves this road. Goes up deeper until it hits a lake."

Studying the map more closely, I saw the icon on it.

"Looks like there's a park building on the lake itself; I'm guessing some kind of research facility. I think she's closer than that, though."

I could see Mabona hiding out in a coopted mountain research shack, but I couldn't see her spending weeks or months there—and she'd gone to ground almost ten weeks before. Somewhere between there and the end of the road, there was another private lodge, one that belonged to the Queen of the Fae.

———

ANY QUESTION of whether we'd found the right place was answered about ten seconds after we opened the gate. Mary was starting to move the Escalade forward again and a sniper round slammed into the windshield.

The SUV had started as an expensive, heavily built vehicle. Then I'd left it in Eric's hands repeatedly over the last few months. The windshield might *look* normal, but tanks would have blushed in envy at its damage resistance.

Which was a damn good thing at that moment, because the bullet had been aimed directly at Mary.

"Drive!" I barked. "The car is armored; it can take the fire. Go!"

She slammed on the accelerator as a second round hit in the *exact* same spot. Even the enchanted windshield cracked slightly under that impact, and I swallowed a curse.

I hadn't really needed the confirmation that our sniper was supernatural, but that kind of accuracy was just that. I wouldn't want to rely on *my* ability to hit a target that small twice at any range, but it was also the best way to punch through the defenses of something like the Escalade.

Mary twisted the wheel, sending the SUV skidding sideways as a third round smashed into the frame of the window. She hadn't managed to force a miss, but she'd avoided the third hit on the same spot that *would* have broken the windshield.

"That's an antimateriel rifle," Raja said calmly from the back. "NATO heavy rounds. What is the windshield *made* of?"

238

"Glass and the magic of one grumpy old gnome," I told him as a *fourth* round smashed into the car.

We were moving forward fast enough now that the bullet hit one of the side panels and bounced off. The glass on the Escalade was tough. The panels were almost unbreakable.

Two more bullets struck home before the sniper stopped shooting. For a second, I thought we were home free—and then the car echoed with a loud crash as Raja rolled down his window and fired *something* out of the side of the vehicle.

He hit the rocket he was aiming for over a hundred feet clear of the car, the armor-piercing explosive detonating in midair. The asura paused, hummed thoughtfully, and then fired a second shot from the massive pistol he'd produced from somewhere.

A second rocket exploded and Raja continued to study the forest.

"I think we're clear now," he announced.

"Rockets?" I asked.

"It's what I would have done," he told me. "AMRs are fantastic, but if they fail, you need something heavier." He tapped his ear. "Distinctive sound, too. Once I had the window open, I could hear them coming."

"Thank you," I said, then looked over at Mary. "Mabona's along the road, up the mountain. Let's go see how she's doing."

For some reason, I doubted the sniper was *her* security...which suggested at least part of the answer.

40

THE DRIVEWAY WOUND its way about a mile out from the rough back road we'd been following. I could feel us getting closer to Mabona with every moment, but it was still a relief to emerge from the trees and find the ski lodge waiting for us.

The lodge was a trio of chalet-style buildings arranged around a paved parking lot. Single-story wings connected the three buildings to allow for travel without leaving the buildings in storms or bitter cold.

They also allowed the lodge to function as a three-sided fort, and a row of SUVs of similar bulk to my Escalade had been lined up to form the fourth wall.

A wall that was being watched. A warning shot kicked up dirt in front of us as we slowed towards the wall, very clearly intended to miss.

"Stop here," I told Mary. "I don't blame them for being paranoid. Leave this to me."

We stopped the SUV and there was no more gunfire. I got out of the vehicle and slowly approached the impromptu barricade, my hands in the air.

"Hello, the house," I shouted. "I'm Jason Kilkenny. Unless I've managed to *spectacularly* end up in the wrong place, you know me."

There was no response for several seconds, and then a familiarly lithe form jumped up on the hood of one of the SUVs. Standing a few inches over six feet tall and moving with inhuman grace, there was no question the guardian was fae.

The Steyr rifle in his hands and the silver-hilted sword slung over his shoulder marked him as a Hunter—which was what allowed me to recognize him.

"Kilkenny," he greeted me as he stood in front of the barricade. "You'll understand we're a bit nervous."

"Oisin, son of Liam," I replied. "You know me. Not just by name, by face."

Oisin and his sister were Vassals of the Queen, and Mabona had sent them to help me out during the chaos of my arrival in Calgary and the conspiracy I'd wandered into the middle of.

He didn't come any closer and the gun didn't waver.

"I've met Jason Kilkenny, yes," he allowed. "But faces can be forged—and voices, too."

I sighed and called *Esras* to me. The butt of the spear slammed into the snow-covered gravel and I met Oisin's gaze flatly.

"I am Jason Alexander Odysseus Kilkenny Calebrantson," I told him loudly. "I am the bearer of *Esras*, a Noble of the Wild Hunt, a Vassal of the Queen of the Fae—a sworn defender of the High Court and your ally. I have weathered storms and gunfire to reach your door, and I seek the counsel of the Queen we both owe Fealty. Will you deny me?"

He was a Hunter. I could lie about what I was claiming to be, but to lie about my true name with *Esras* in my hands would be *hard*—and a Hunter would have seen right through it.

"No," he said slowly, then laughed and slung his rifle. "You'll forgive me, I hope, my brother. We are under siege in what was supposed to be our safehouse. No one should have been able to find us."

"Most people aren't Vassals who bear ancient arms," I told him as we clasped forearms. "I managed to pierce Mabona's defenses and find her, but not well enough to bring Hunters to her side. How bad is it, Oisin?"

"Bad," he confirmed bluntly, waving for Mary to bring the Escalade up. "The lodge had power and phone wires running down to the city, plus satellite internet. No cellphone signal, but that was a selling point."

"I'm guessing *had* is the operative term here?" I asked.

"Wires were cut and the satellite dish hit with an antimaterial rifle less than half an hour after Mabona collapsed. We don't know what the hell is going on."

"The Masked Lords killed Ankaris," I explained quickly. "They used him as a conduit to attack the rest of the High Court. I don't know where the others are; all I could think to do was to try and protect the Queen."

"And thank the Powers that are that you came," Oisin told me. "Win tried to leave last night, but they blew her car up with rockets and shot her down with cold iron bullets."

I winced. Win Jernigan was—had been, I supposed—a Fae Lord, one of the most powerful beings in the world, short of a true Power. But yes, the sniper team that had almost taken us out would have sufficed to kill her if she'd been driving an unarmored vehicle.

"Mabona raised shields around this place to bar sensing and communication," he continued. "They're still up. She's the only one who can lower them, and she's been unconscious for days."

"So, you can't call for help, no one can walk Between to you, and there's almost certainly an enemy formation gathering strength nearby," I summarized.

"Bingo. I don't know what we do from here," he admitted. "There's a dozen of us here, but we were a general traveling security and support team. No heavy arms, and Win was the most powerful of us."

"Fortunately, I have backup," I said. "And, unless they've done something even more obnoxious than I can think of, I have a way to get them here."

———

Oisin moved one of the parked SUVs aside to let us park the Escalade inside the barricade, then closed it up behind us. An androgynous and young-looking fae emerged from one of the chalets at his shout, walking with an equally familiar poise.

I didn't know the Noble, but I recognized the power and grace of their status.

"Kilkenny, this is Christa Hase," Oisin introduced us. "Hase, this is Jason Kilkenny. He's like me: a Vassal and a Hunter."

"I know who Kilkenny is," Hase replied with a small smile and bow. "Greetings. I presume you're taking them indoors?"

"Aye."

"Hold up one moment," Raja suggested. He was still shoulders-deep in the SUV's backseat, the rippling muscles of his broad and uncovered back catching a lengthy admiring glance from Hase.

He emerged after a few seconds, holding the M60 in one hand and a box of ammunition in the other. He took a few seconds to link a belt from the box, into the gun then offered it to Hase.

"Cold iron–cored bullets," he told the noble. "Thousand rounds in the box, another box in the car if you need it."

The big asura grinned.

"Trust me that if you fire off a thousand rounds through this, *somebody* will hear to come to help you reload."

Hase chuckled and hefted the heavy weapon.

"Why didn't we have one of these, Oisin?" they asked the other member of the Queen's security detail.

"Because we figured assault rifles and Nobles would be more than enough to hold off any enemy who stumbled across us," the Hunter replied. "We thought the Queen's hiding spot was a secret."

"It wasn't, I'm guessing?" I asked.

"They were too damned ready," Oisin said grimly. "Maybe, *maybe,* they used the same link from Ankaris to find her that they used to knock her down, but..." He shook his head. "They were in place fifteen minutes after she collapsed, my brother. They knew where we were."

"And if they knew where Mabona was and had enough data on Tír fo Thuinn to attack Ankaris successfully, we have to assume they could locate *all* of the High Court," I said. "That's...not great, people."

"Go see the Queen," Hase told me. "I'm guessing you forced a link to find us, but unless you've seen her, you don't know how bad it is."

———

WITH OISIN PLAYING guard dog outside, I wasn't entirely surprised to find Niamh, his half-sister, inside. She was in the process of switching out IV bags on a mobile stand in the lobby, working from a well-equipped array of medical supplies...that were tossed all over the big decorative table next to the giant fireplace.

The fireplace in question was currently burning away, a carefully stacked and maintained pile of logs keeping the main lobby of the chalet warm.

"Niamh," I greeted the blonde Healer with a bow. "I take it you're not merely a random Healer the Queen happened to send my way, are you?"

She flushed, then returned my bow.

"I am Mabona's personal physician," she admitted. "I have been for, oh, about eighty years. I'd wondered why she sent me to take care of you back then, but my question seems to have been rather thoroughly answered since."

I nodded.

"That long. You met my father, then?"

Fae *really* didn't show their ages unless they chose to. Niamh actually looked a year or two younger than I was, but if she'd been Mabona's physician for that long, well. She was probably closer to ten times my age.

"I did," she confirmed. "I understand what Mabona and your mother saw in him." She smiled. "He was the kind of man to track a tenuous link into the middle of a snowstorm to look for someone he felt he was responsible for."

I scoffed.

"It's not snowing out there," I told her. "Not that much, anyway."

"You got shot at coming in here," Oisin pointed out. "Trust my elder sister's words, Kilkenny."

"She's here, then?" I asked.

"She's here," Niamh confirmed. "Just about to swap out the saline solution. It's not the only thing keeping her alive—she's a Power, after all—but it doesn't hurt."

"How bad is it, Doctor?" I said.

"Unlike anything mortal medicine has literature on," she told me. "I can heal almost anything, Jason. Curing cancer is a pretty standard method of recruiting mortal aid, right?"

I nodded. Our interfaces with the mortal world required utterly reliable people. Saving children and spouses from diseases humanity couldn't cure was a nearly perfect way of acquiring them.

There weren't enough supernatural Healers in the world to make a dent in the total cancer rate, but there were enough for us to be able to use it as a recruiting tool.

"And you can't do anything?" I said.

"This spell is unlike anything I have learned. I can only vaguely tell how it even *works*. All I can tell you is that it's attacking whatever makes her a Power."

"I need to see her," I told them. "I need to try to link from closer. This will be a lot easier if we can get her to lower her shields."

"We've tried everything," Oisin pointed out.

"I know," I confirmed, then tapped the spear. "But I have *Esras*, and the spear's proven capable of things I wouldn't have thought before. We may as well give it a shot, right?"

"And you have the right to see her anyway," Niamh told me. "Her Vassals need to know how bad it's getting." She paused. "Leave the others. This is for those who owe her Fealty only."

———

THE LARGEST BEDROOM in the chalet was just down the hallway from the lobby. Niamh led the way, rolling the replacement IV stand with her as we went.

A single armed guard stood outside the door, another Fae Noble, but he stepped aside as Niamh approached, opening the door for us.

The Healer went straight in and I followed more hesitantly. A young-looking man in dark gray scrubs was inside, checking over a display that was calmly beeping away next to a clearly improvised hospital bed.

There were monitors, IV stands and so forth, but they were hooked up to a regular-looking hotel queen-sized bed.

An IV line and an oxygen line were both linked to the tall woman in the bed. Sensor pads were festooned over her chest, and several clip sensors marked her fingers.

Mabona was a tall and statuesque woman, with the presence to cow armies even before she summoned her power. Right now, however, she lay utterly still in the bed, frozen.

I'd never thought of the Queen of the Fae as fragile, but that was the only word that could describe her today.

"Will she recover?" I asked softly.

"I think so," Niamh told me as she switched the IV line over to the new stand and bag she'd brought with us. "I think the spell is weakening. It's a temporary attack, one that will fade in time. Not quickly enough, though."

"We're talking days, then. Not hours, not weeks?"

"Probably days," she agreed. "*Maybe* weeks. This is outside my experience, Jason…which means it's outside anyone's experience."

She shook her head.

"She's our Queen. She's supposed to protect us, not be lying there broken while we try to survive."

"You have power here?"

"Gasoline generators in the basement. Oisin and the others have augmented them since we lost the power lines down the mountain." She shrugged. "We have enough fuel for two weeks of normal use. By the time the boys were done, that fuel will probably last us most of a year."

So, we had power but no communications. There was a satellite phone in the Escalade that *should* punch through, but it would also draw attention.

"Let's see if I can make a connection," I said aloud. I crossed to Mabona's bedside, *Esras* in my hand, and laid the spear against her. With my hand on it and the shaft resting against her left side, I used the weapon itself as a channel.

I'd pushed through much of her defenses before to be able to find her at all, but this was something else. This wasn't trying to pierce the exterior defenses. This was trying to break into the mind of a god.

Just because she was unconscious didn't mean her defenses weren't going to try and stop me. Like the shields she'd raised around the ski lodge, those defenses could be turned off only by a *conscious* Mabona.

This close, finding *her* was no problem. The connection that I'd worked so hard for from Calgary came instantly, the usual link between Vassal and Liege. That confirmed what Niamh had said.

I needed more than that. I needed to communicate with our Queen, to forge a link to her unconscious mind and see if I could get her to lower the defenses.

Letting people through those defenses would attract much less attention than using a satellite phone to send out a call for help and setting up the kind of massively powerful beacon Between it would take to open a path.

My first attempt to deepen the connection simply slid off. Mabona's defenses were powerful and subtle. I didn't even realize I'd failed for several seconds.

Niamh was already sliding a chair over to me, and I nodded thankfully to her as I sank into it.

This was going to be a long effort.

41

THERE WAS a limit to how much force I could apply to this endeavor, even if I *had* the power necessary to go past it. Too much energy applied to trying to forge this kind of mental link could damage us both.

Niamh's helper had switched out the saline drip bag again by the time I finally began to accept it wasn't going to work. I'd worn down a tiny sliver of a gap in her defenses and could feel that our link was stronger than it had ever been...but all it was confirming was that Mabona was deeply, deeply unconscious.

A Power like MacDonald might have been able to do more, but that wasn't going to happen. It didn't matter how much I trusted the old Magus; I wasn't going to allow another Power near Mabona in this state.

My Fealty wouldn't allow it.

Exhaling a long sigh, I nodded to the doctor and rose. I knelt by Mabona's bed and reached over to grip her hand.

"We're going to keep you safe," I whispered. "You, the rest of the Court, everyone. I'm going to finish what my father started, my Queen. This war will end."

She didn't react. I didn't really expect her to.

"My lord?" the doctor asked.

"I'm no lord," I replied. "I'm just her Vassal. And apparently, that's not going to be enough tonight. Keep her safe, Niamh."

"That's my job," she replied. "Well, to keep her alive, anyway. Keeping her safe falls on the rest of you, I guess."

I nodded. Healers weren't defenseless, but they weren't supposed to fight. Their powers didn't lean that way, in any case.

"We'll make sure," I promised. "I need to make a call."

———

MOST OF THE gear we'd brought with us had been moved into the front lobby now, taking over the one table that Niamh hadn't claimed as a medical prep zone.

The satellite phone was the largest piece, a backpack-sized chunk of technology that didn't need cellular coverage to reach the rest of the world. In theory, it was just as secure as the rest of our phones.

In practice, I wasn't confident in the ability of our phones to evade tracking by the Masked Lords—and *any* phone calling out of the middle of nowhere was going to attract attention.

"Any luck?" Niamh asked.

"A little, but not enough to make a connection," I admitted. "We need to send out a call."

"Half of our security here is secrecy," Oisin objected.

"And how much good has that done us, Oisin?" I asked bluntly. "Our enemy knows where we are. They know where Mabona is; they know she's weakened and crippled. The only people who *don't* know where we are are our friends."

"What do you want to do?" he finally asked.

"If I make a call directly to anyone, I'm betting I'm going to trigger a bunch of red flags," I admitted. "Instead, I want to use the satellite phone as a modem to link to the Fae-Net and put out a call on the Hunt channels.

"That'll alert my people in Calgary. If we set up a beacon Between, they'll be able to navigate here and avoid the snipers." I shook my head. "That's over a hundred Hunters, Companions, asura and shifters," I told Oisin. "If we can't hold with that, we're already fucked."

"We don't have the gear for any of that," Oisin admitted. "We were trying to hide ourselves from Between, after all. Why would we have brought a beacon?"

"That's all right. I brought one," I replied. "Kristal, can you and Oisin set up what we need with the satellite phone?"

"If he knows the codes for the Hunter sites, yep," she confirmed.

I looked at the other Hunter.

"I know them, brother," he conceded. "We'll make it happen. We have to protect the Queen."

"We swore an oath," I agreed. "I'll set up the beacon, but I won't charge it or move it Between until we've sent out the call. Let's minimize how long we're screaming to the world that we're here without having reinforcements."

Oisin nodded, then paused.

"A *hundred* Hunters?" he asked. "That'll make a good first wave, though that's more than I would have thought Ankaris would have assigned to you."

I winced. That was right; they were completely out of touch. I'd told him Ankaris had died, but not the rest.

"Much of the Hunt died with Ankaris," I told him quietly. "There's...maybe two hundred and fifty of us left. Grainne Silverstar is the Horned King now. She and I had a disagreement over the right course."

"I know Silverstar," Oisin said slowly. "How bad?"

"She executed a hunter for questioning her orders," I explained. "The Wild Hunt...is split, Oisin. She exiled me for defying her and half of the Hunt followed me.

"I can call on half the Hunt and my own Vassals...but that may be all the help that's coming."

———

MOST OF THE beacons I'd seen used to mark locations Between hadn't looked like much. The most common was a carved piece of rutilated quartz about the size of my fist.

We had at least a dozen of them bouncing around the house in Calgary, and anyone with the Gift of Between could charge one to show up. That wouldn't suffice to pierce the jamming effect that Mabona had layered onto the Between around her.

If that kind of beacon would have been enough, I'd have been able to step Between to her based on the link. To break through the security Mabona had created was going to take more—and I'd come prepared.

Instead of a single carved piece of rutilated quartz with natural gold veins, I had four fifteen-centimeter-by-three-centimeter clear quartz prisms. Each had a gold bar running up its six sides, forming a constant connection.

The fifth piece was one of the clearest pieces of pink rose quartz I'd ever seen, placed in a solid gold base that was designed to link into the prisms. Assembled, it made a tiny pyramid edged in gold and tipped in a pink crystal that caught the light from the fire and scattered it across the room.

I put it in front of the fireplace and touched *Esras* to it, focusing my gift into the four supporting crystals of the beacon. Energy flowed from me, down the spear and into the crystals. After a moment, they began to glow with a soft inner light that mortal eyes wouldn't have seen.

I held the link for a few more seconds, watching the light grow brighter. Once it was almost bright enough to hurt my eyes, I dropped the connection. The light muted a little bit, then steadied.

It wasn't active, but it was fully charged.

"How are we with the call?" I asked.

"Just about ready," Oisin reported. "Anyone specific we want to be reaching out to?"

"How about everyone?" I suggested. "The Hunt, the local Court, the Magus…"

I sighed. We couldn't call the Magus. I knew that even as I said it. It might be a good idea, but I could *feel* my Vassalage bond twinge at the thought of bringing another Power around my crippled boss.

"The Hunt and the High Court channels," I told him after a moment. "We need to keep this under wraps. We need reinforcements, but we also need to keep this quiet. No one outside the Fae community needs to know."

Oisin arched an eyebrow at Mary, who was helping sort through the additional heavy weapons we'd brought with us.

"She's with me and her bodyguard is with her," I said firmly. "Mary doesn't count. Raja is outside, but he owes me fealty. He counts as fae for this."

"I agree," he allowed with a chuckle. "Just checking in. There." He tapped the Enter key on Kristal's laptop and passed it back to her.

"As soon as we hook the modem up to the satellite phone, we'll have internet for a few minutes at least. Long enough to put out the call."

"The beacon is ready," I told them. "Once you trigger the alert, I'll step Between and activate it."

The good news was that we couldn't really be attacked Between. Attacked *through* the Between, yes, though any Hunter would feel the attackers coming, but even Hunters had problems finding the energy to fight Between.

There was a reason one of our capital punishments was to take the criminal Between and leave them there, after all.

"Well, I'd suggest you go place the beacon, my lord," Kristal told me. "We're good to go on this end."

I started to remind her I wasn't a lord but then sighed. Somewhere along the way, probably around the point I'd walked in on Mabona's staff and taken command without thinking about it, I'd lost that fight.

"All right. Let's make it happen."

———

STEPPING BETWEEN, the beacon in my hands began to pulse even more brightly. Part of the activation was just bringing it there, but I took a moment to study the "space" around me.

Between was always a cold and lifeless place, with a chill that struck even those with the Gift to walk here to the bone. The relation between it and the real world was always off, mis-scaled or otherwise warped.

Here, however, it wasn't even warped. It was distorted and fuzzy, like I was looking at even the Between through the bottom of a glass. Normally, I could get my bearings almost instantly Between.

In the middle of Mabona's "jamming," it was impossible. I could probably leave—pick a direction and walk until I did get my bearings, basically—but no one could find their way in.

Not without a beacon, anyway.

"The ground" was more of an idea than a solid thing Between, so I placed the beacon in midair where I could easily reach it. Then I channeled even more energy into the top rose quartz crystal, letting it grow even brighter than the clear quartz supporting it.

It hung there for a few seconds, and then the two lights blurred together into a single glowing spot that cut through the murk Mabona had gathered around herself.

The beacon was online and I sighed.

I'd just ruined the defenses my Queen had gathered, which meant I'd better replace them quickly. My people would be coming.

I had to hope that was enough.

I turned to leave Between and stopped when I realized someone had joined me. The newcomer was a stranger to me, a short creature barely taller than Eric but lacking the gnome's breadth. With the murk Mabona had conjured there, it took me a moment to realize they had tiny horns sprouting through their long brown hair...and a wide grin on their face.

There was only one creature in all the world that met that description. At least, when they *wanted* to.

"The Puck," I said slowly. "My...lord?"

"Puck will do," the first and oldest Power of the Fae High Court told me brightly. "It's a nice beacon, well made."

"How are you conscious? I thought they took down the whole High Court."

"I'm not conscious at all," the Puck replied. "This is a projection from a lucid dream, boy. Only you can see me, and I can't influence much of anything. If I strain too hard, I might do myself some serious harm."

"What do you need?" I asked carefully.

"You to do your job," they told me. "Mabona is the strongest of us. Two of the Ladies of the Seasons are dead, and the Masked Lords will come for her next, I think. Your call will bring them as well."

"I know."

"So, you've just rung the call to arms for the final battle of our little civil war, my dear boy. I'm watching, I'm listening. I'll give you what help I can...but it's on you."

They shook their head.

"It's *all* on you, Jason Kilkenny. Like it was on your father before you. Are you ready for that?"

"Hell, no," I replied.

The Puck laughed.

"Good. If you realize that, you might just survive this."

42

Stepping back into the real world, I shook my head. I wasn't sure if I was hallucinating the Puck or actually did have the oldest living fae poking along next to me.

They were still there after I returned to the lodge, but no one else seemed to notice them.

"Told you. Only you can see me," they assured me. "For now, at least. I can change that if I need to."

I couldn't even really respond now that I had people around me. The bastard.

"How long until our reinforcements start arriving?" Oisin asked. "We did just send up a giant flare, after all."

"We just rang the dinner bell for the fae-pocalypse, brother," I told him. "The Masked Lords probably knew where Mabona was, but they were working their way across their list. Now they know we're calling the Hunt here, they have to come here if they want to win."

I shook my head.

"Mabona is the strongest of the High Court, I'm told." Or had been told in the last five minutes, anyway. Assuming the Puck was real. "So, if we can save her, they're screwed. Mabona and the Horned King could build a new Court from ashes and the dead, so everything rides on them killing her."

"Or Silverstar," Mary pointed out. "If she abandoned her fortress like you said, then she's probably harder to find."

"They'll hope she'll come here," I said. "Hell, *I'm* hoping she'll come here. I may not like the woman, but she is the Horned King of the Wild Hunt now. I'll eat crow and apologize if it puts her and the rest of the Hunt on the right side of that barricade out there."

"But you won't give her the right of life and death over the Hunt," Oisin said quietly. "So, we'll see if apologizing would be enough."

"Regardless of what Grainne Silverstar thinks or wants, I am a Noble of the Wild Hunt and a Vassal of the Queen of the Fae," I reminded him, equally quietly. "Which means this is the only place I can be and this is a battlefield I cannot retreat from."

Further conversation was cut off as both Oisin and I felt the incoming arrival of people traveling Between.

"The beacon should direct them outside," I told them.

"Yup," the Puck confirmed for me. "I wonder if this round are friends or enemies, don't you?"

My dirty look at the Power's projection earned me some strange gazes from the others, and I shook my head.

"It's a long story. Let's go greet our guests."

"Is that going to be with words or cold iron bullets?" Raja asked, leaving me wondering if the asura warlord *could* hear the Puck.

"Depends on who it is, doesn't it?"

THANKFULLY, it was Riley and two troops of the Wild Hunt from my half of the organization. They brought a dozen shifters and another dozen asura with them, bringing the first wave to forty supernaturals.

From Oisin's expression, I don't think he'd truly believed he was getting reinforced until that moment. As the Hunters, Companions, shifters and asura swarmed out of Between and began inspecting the ski lodge, though, a degree of strain finally left his face.

"Riley." I clasped forearms with the Hunter. "How are we holding up at home?"

"I made sure the call came to me and not Damh," he said brightly. "The rest of the Hunt is prepping the heavier gear. Once they're equipped, Orman will wake up Damh and he can lead the way."

"We really need to start handing out some job titles," I murmured. "Damh's in command after me, but I think Amandine is technically the only one who's supposed be ordering around the troop captains."

We had one Guardian and one Noble. Chain of command amongst the troop captains went by respect—or in this case, who they figured had *my* ear.

Weird thought.

"Probably," Riley agreed. "Right now, though, everyone knows how it goes. Once the crisis is over, we'll sort shit out."

Hopefully, once the crisis was over, Silverstar and I could reconcile the two halves of the Wild Hunt. The schism amongst the Hunt's survivors was a clear and present threat to the security of the fae.

I turned to face Barry Tenerim and shook his hand next.

"I'm glad to see you lot," I told him. "Based off their last op, these guys are coming loaded with cold iron. You and yours are going to be a nasty surprise for them."

"I *love* being a nasty surprise," Barry replied with a grin. "How's my cousin?"

"Running things, as usual," I said. "Check in with her. I know protecting her is your first priority."

"Right now, it looks like the best way I can protect my charge is to keep this whole little fort intact," he said. "Could do with a few tougher walls or a tank. Or six."

"I could do with an army or a conscious god," I agreed. "But we've got what we've got."

"Oberis got the call as well, but I don't know what he'll have ready to go," Riley pointed out.

"Not much, most likely. The only fae organization that keeps troops ready to go is us," I reminded him. "And my Fealty won't let me inform the Wizard."

"We could use him," Riley said slowly. "But hell, I can feel *my* Fealty refusing, and my oath is to *you*."

"And mine is to Mabona, so you do owe her Fealty as well," I said. "We can't let another Power near our Queen while she's helpless. Even MacDonald might be tempted to take advantage."

"So, we're waiting for the enemy?" he asked.

"For now." I glanced over to where Raja was organizing his own people. "I do have one task for you right away, though. Hunters only, I think. There's a sniper team with an antimaterial rifle and at least a few rocket launchers stalking the driveway into this place.

"Deal with them."

Riley grinned and bowed.

"Consider it already done, my lord."

———

WE SPENT the next hour reinforcing the barricades Oisin and his people had assembled. Now that we had hands, such "simple" tasks as pulling the tables from the unused dining rooms and using them to reinforce the line of vehicles were possible.

Oisin had three Fae Nobles, also Vassals of the Queen, under his command. Their glamors helped us reinforce the barricades further, turning the horseshoe-shaped connected chalets into something close to a true fortification.

It wouldn't hold against anything resembling a modern military force, but we weren't really expecting to face that. There were limits to the resources that the supernatural community could field.

Even military-grade ordnance like the AMR and rocket launchers the sniper team had been using to besiege the ski lodge or the pair of M60s we'd now set up on the barricade was few and far between. Most supernaturals were limited to what a well-connected criminal organization could get their hands on.

I expected more of the mortal mercenaries we'd seen at Tír fo Thuinn, equipped with the gear you'd expect of mercenaries. They'd be supported by supernaturals armed with assault rifles, submachine guns and Gifts.

At the heart of it all would be the ritual team. Twenty-one Lords and Nobles, one of them carrying *Asi*. I wasn't sure what the range of their ritual was, but it couldn't be short. Not if they'd killed my father —and a Magus, for that matter.

I was operating on the assumption that if the ritual team could see it, they could kill it. The only real question was how much energy the ritual team had available. It would make a massive difference if the they had one shot available to them…or, say, ten.

"Amandine, we've got at least some people who were there when my father fought the Masked Lords, right?" I asked the Guardian. "I need to know more about what they did with this damn ritual."

"A few," she admitted. "Including me." She shivered. "I don't like to think about it, but if you need to know, I'll answer what I can."

"The ritual team they assembled," I said. "How much fighting were they doing other than focusing on that? I mean, we're talking about a collection of some of the most powerful non-Power fae alive. If they're free to get involved in the battle, it could be ugly."

She considered.

"From what I remember, they were defending themselves but not much more until *after* they'd fired their shot at Calebrant," she said slowly. "It seemed to be a 'one and done' kind of deal, where they had to rest afterwards and it took all of their energy."

"That makes sense. Powers are supposed to be unkillable."

"I'd agree. I don't know if that's safe to rely on, though," Amandine pointed out.

"Oh, I know," I agreed. "Once we locate the ritual team, we need to hit them hard and fast. That'll be the key point of the conflict. We'll need our best."

"We'll need you," she told me. "I don't think anyone will be able to go up against *Asi* without you and *Esras*. Artifacts like that…" She shook her head. "With that sword in their hands, they don't need to be Lords to be able to destroy anything in their path."

A new presence rippled through the Between, and we both inhaled.

"New guests," I said aloud.

"It's too soon for Coleman," Amandine reminded me. "Our people won't have been ready this quickly."

"I know. With me," I ordered.

———

"Where did they get the *horses*?"

It took me a moment to even register that it had been the projection of the Puck who'd asked the question, because I was thinking it myself and I was quite sure everyone else was too.

Twenty-four massive pure white horses emerged from the Between in a neat double file, each easily six or seven feet high at the shoulders.

The women on their back—and they were *all* women—were not cut to the same scale. Even from a distance, though, I could tell they were carved from iron and stone. They wore regular casual clothes—and finely crafted silvered chainmail hauberks over those clothes.

Each bore a silver-hilted sword over her shoulder, and the horses were carrying an assortment of weapons, ranging from a massive two-handed greataxe to a World War II–vintage Browning machine gun.

I knew *what* they were, but I wasn't sure *why* they were there until the leader dismounted and embraced me.

Inga Strand had trained me in the use of my Gifts as a favor to the Queen. She'd been a Valkyrie and then been a Hunter once the Wild Hunt had absorbed the various other military forces of the Fae and Aesir.

She was retired now, after two centuries of service. No one who'd ridden as a Valkyrie remained in the Wild Hunt—two hundred years was more than enough for even a fae to decide they needed to try something new with their lives.

"Kilkenny," she greeted me. "We heard the call. Looks like you were doing okay, but I figured you wouldn't mind the help."

I returned her unexpected embrace as I looked over her companions. Like Inga, they all could have passed for a solidly fit middle age among mortals. Among fae, that meant they were all easily into their third century.

"You brought the Valkyries," I said slowly.

"All I could call in short order," she confirmed. "We're retired now, but…it seemed like you could use the hands."

"Everything might ride on tonight, Inga," I told her. "Thank you. I...I never expected you to come. You're retired, after all."

"Retired or not, I'd rather not see these *morons* burn the Covenants of Silence down around our ears!" she said fiercely. "Where would you have us, Lord Kilkenny of the Hunt?"

"My lady, you've fought more battles than I've seen movies," I pointed out. "I'd use you as a mobile reserve, but you know this dance better than I do."

She smirked.

"You're getting better at this," she told me. "Ankaris was right to recruit you."

"You know what happened to him." I wasn't asking. There was no way she'd be here if she didn't know.

"I know. I won't say he made a mistake with Silverstar, but I think everyone would have been happier if you'd been with the Hunt for a decade or so before anything happened to Ankaris."

There was an implication there I didn't dare try and unpack, so I stepped back and bowed to the other Valkyries.

Respect cost very little, and one did *not* disrespect multi-century-old Hunters.

They were dismounted and arranging their weapons. The one with the WWII Browning turned out to have a harness for mounting the big gun on her horse, the animal seeming surprisingly unperturbed by the process of being turned into a mobile weapon platform.

I was so distracted by the Valkyries that it took me a few seconds too long to sense the incoming presence of the *next* people to arrive from the Between. They didn't arrive calmly or politely, either, with Between ripping open to spill out rapidly deploying fire teams.

If I hadn't recognized them, we might have had a firefight right there.

"Hold fire, hold fire!" I barked. "It's the Wild Hunt."

Coleman wouldn't have been there yet—and Coleman wouldn't have shown up nearly as aggressively. Fire teams of Hunters and Companions formed a rough perimeter in the outdoor parking lot, clearly prepared to fight the people I'd arrayed to defend the Queen.

They weren't starting a fight, though, and I waited for what had to come next, the only reason multiple troops of Hunters I wasn't expecting would have shown up like this.

She arrived in the center of the perimeter her people had established, clad in reforged green armor and the horned helm of her rank. Walking out of the nothingness of Between, she surveyed us all with distaste.

Grainne Silverstar, Horned King of the Wild Hunt, was there.

43

THE PARKING LOT made for a solid impromptu assembly yard for the troops we'd been gathering, and now it looked like it might make for an effective battlefield.

Silverstar picked me out of the people waiting and clearly stalked directly toward me.

"Stand back," I murmured to Amandine and Inga, gesturing for them to fall behind me as I walked forward to meet the Horned King.

The perimeter her Hunters had formed drew back slightly to allow her to walk through, and I waved my own people back. We halted about ten feet apart in a rapidly growing empty space in the center of the parking lot.

"Your Majesty," I greeted her, inclining my head. "You received our message? I'm grateful that you could come. With the Masked Lords threatening the Queen, every hand, every fae, is needed to keep us together."

"The Queen lives, then?" Silverstar asked. "I've been seeking the High Court, but every one of them we've found is already dead. We are growing short on Powers, Kilkenny."

"I am her Vassal," I said. "She lives and we stand to protect her.

Unfortunately, the Masked Lords know where we are. This lodge was under siege already before I arrived."

I shook my head.

"My call for aid inevitably has warned them that we are preparing to defend her, but we had no choice."

"I understand," she allowed. "You seem to be missing a few Hunters who followed you into treason, Kilkenny."

"They're coming," I said calmly.

"She's missing a few of her own, too," the Puck said softly. "Don't ask why. You'll make her suspicious…but I wonder if these are only the ones she trusts completely."

He was right. There were only two troops of Hunters here…thirty-six fighters. Eighteen should have been Companions, but it looked like instead she only had nine Companions and twenty-seven Hunters.

Why? Was the Puck right? Had she brought only the ones she trusted completely?

And if so, what was she trusting them to do?

"You are not forgiven your trespasses, Kilkenny," the Horned King told me, her voice iron. "But we have a greater enemy today. Will you put aside our conflicts and stand together to defend our people and our Court?"

If she was willing to make peace for now, I was fine with that. So long as she didn't try to execute any of my Hunters, at least.

"My Queen is in danger," I replied. "I will accept any aid to make certain she is safe."

She slowly bowed her head to me.

"Then we stand together," she told me. "My Hunters will reinforce the defenses. Do you have any intelligence on when the enemy are coming?"

"Not yet," I admitted. "We removed their agents on the scene, however, so I can't imagine they'll wait long."

"Some of what we have learned may be of value," Silverstar suggested. "Shall we speak inside, out of the cold?"

"All right."

The cold in this conversation had nothing to do with the temperature, and I wasn't sure that going inside would help it at all. None-theless, it cost nothing to be polite.

———

WE LEFT Silverstar's people outside, but Inga calmly followed us in. From the way Silverstar quailed when the Valkyrie fixed her with a harsh gaze, I wasn't the only one in this room that Inga had trained.

I traded a quick glance with Niamh as we entered the chalet lobby. She coughed, tapped the base of her throat with two fingers, and then disappeared back toward Mabona's room.

It took me several seconds to realize she was reminding me about the tiny vial of quicksilver I wore around my neck. While I'd replaced the dose of heartstone-infused mercury after using it, the stone vial and leather cord I stored it in had been delivered to me by Niamh.

She'd only delivered under Mabona's direct orders and had never approved. If she was reminding me about it now...

Yeah, Niamh did *not* like Silverstar.

"You said you might know something useful?" I asked Silverstar as she promptly proceeded to the bar and, without asking, started mixing herself a drink.

"We tracked the amphibious vehicles the bastards used to attack Tír fo Thuinn," she told me, then swallowed down a mouthful of what-ever hellishly alcoholic beverage she'd just put together. "They were launched from a retrofitted merchant ship, French registration. A few pointed questions to the captain later and, well..."

Somehow, her phrasing left me doubting that the captain of the merchant ship was still alive.

"And?"

"They docked at a port in France after the attack. Doesn't matter which one, really. There were transport planes for them there, heading to North America. The Masks already knew where they needed their mercenaries."

"Assuming they brought their gear on those planes and managed to sneak by customs, they would be in the mountains by now," I concluded. "If they're relying on conventional transportation for their mercenaries, that limits how subtle they can be. We'll want to send scouts to watch for them."

"Of course," she agreed. For a long moment, she stared at her drink in silence, then she downed the whole thing.

"I need to see Mabona," she told me flatly. "You can talk all you want, Kilkenny, but I've seen three dead members of the High Court now, *including* my own boss. I can't just take your word that she's still alive."

"You know damn well we won't let you see her if she's injured," I replied. "Our Fealty won't permit it."

"Handy excuse, that," Silverstar said. "Right now, Kilkenny, I don't know if she's still alive or if *you've* set this all up as a trap for me and the last loyal members of the Hunt."

"I am *also* a Vassal of the Queen," Inga reminded her. "Mabona lives. You know the value of *my* word, Your Majesty. You know the worth of a Valkyrie."

Silverstar sighed.

"I do," she conceded. "But I also must see her with my own eyes. It is hard to believe that the High Court were struck helpless, even having seen them felled by the hands of our enemy."

"It cannot happen," I said quietly. "I understand your concern, Your Majesty, but even were *I* to permit, Mabona is under the guard of other Vassals. *They* will not permit it."

"Your stubbornness will be your undoing, Kilkenny," the Horned King said conversationally. "If you are ever to return to the Hunt, you must learn *obedience*."

"My first Fealty is to Mabona. Then to the ideal of the Wild Hunt." I smiled thinly at Silverstar. "Only at a far distant third is any need for obedience to the Horned King."

"Shame."

I never saw her move. One moment, she was putting the glass back on the table; the next, a trio of daggers were flashing across the room at me.

Inga was faster. The Valkyrie was between us before Silverstar had finished throwing the daggers, her own sword flashing through the air so quickly, all I saw was a glint of silver.

She blocked two knives. The third hammered into her shoulder with inhuman force, hurling her across the room. I could *feel* the cold iron in the blades, too.

I was mostly certain that Inga's armor had saved her life…but she was out of this fight.

———

THE FIRST ATTACK had come without any warning. Without Inga's intervention, Silverstar might have killed me right there. The second attack I *knew* was coming, and *Esras* flared to life with my power as I backpedaled away from the Horned King.

She snarled and flung blades of glamor at me. I shielded myself against them with force, scattering the glamor to pieces.

"What the hell?" I demanded. "Whose side are you on?"

"There are probably smarter questions you could ask," the Puck noted from their new position sitting on the bar. "Though I'll admit none come to mind."

"Mine, you fool," Silverstar told me. "Ankaris was all set to declare *you* his heir! All of my work, across *centuries*—across *three* Horned Kings!—to be tossed aside on some whim of bloodline and family."

"Oh!" The Puck exclaimed, sitting up straight. "I was getting suspicious of her, but I hadn't known that!"

"Shut *up*," I hissed at the not-quite-hallucination as I deflected a blast of force and flame into the bar.

"So, what, you weren't one of the Masked Lords until now?" I demanded.

"Of course I was one of them," she told me, accompanying her words with another barrage of force. This one nearly overwhelmed my shields, pushing me several feet backward. "I helped *create* them! Ever since I learned Calebrant had knocked up his damned changeling floozy and broken *that* Covenant!"

My mother had been dead for years. It probably shouldn't have made me that angry to hear her called that, but it did.

I flung *Esras* forward, calling Force and Fire as I channeled my Gifts down the length of the spear. Pale-green flames blasted across the room at Silverstar, but she knocked them aside with laughing ease—and smashed me to the ground with glee.

"I should have succeeded *Calebrant*," she bellowed as she advanced on me, her silver-hilted sword in her hand. "Even Ankaris stole what should have been mine, but I saw what they did not. I saw that the High Court had weakened the fae, emasculated us. *We were gods once.*"

I started to struggle upward, but she smashed me down with another calculated blow of Force. Not every silver-hilted Hunter's sword had a cold iron blade...but Silverstar's certainly did. I was less vulnerable to cold iron than most fae, but it would still kill me very, very dead.

"You betrayed us," I ground out. "You betrayed *my father.*"

"You fool boy. I *killed* your father," she told me. "I lured him into the path of a spell he might have dodged. And he betrayed *me.*"

She had my hands pinned and my power contained, but I could still exercise some level of the Gift of Force. Not enough to escape. Not enough to attack.

But enough to flip the tiny stone vial hanging around my neck up to my lips and pour the quicksilver into my mouth.

New power flowed through me as I swallowed the drug. Quicksilver was a combat drug for us, supercharging our physical and magical prowess. The last time I'd taken it, I'd jumped Between through the strongest barriers a Magus could raise.

This time, I slipped Between through the magical bonds Silverstar had wrapped around me—moments before her sword would have stabbed through my chest.

I only had time to seize a single breath of Between's ice cold air. There were other defenders between Silverstar and Mabona, but the Nobles assigned to guard the Queen's door wouldn't expect the Horned King to attack them.

She was waiting for me when I stepped back into reality, Force slicing across the room at neck height as soon as she saw me.

I expecting something similar, though, and interposed *Esras*. The ancient spear's magic laughed at her attack, snuffing out the blade of Force instantly.

I moved with the spear, letting the quicksilver flow through my veins as I channeled Force around my limbs. My strike was the fastest I'd ever moved, with every scrap of the quicksilver's extra energy and Inga's training behind it as I tried to put *Esras's* millennia-old spearhead through Silverstar's chest.

She sidestepped even faster than I struck, her sword and power slashing toward my face. The quicksilver allowed me to drop to the floor, sliding past her on the waxed hardwood and crashing into the bar.

"Um. The floor is *not* going to help you win this fight," the Puck told me from their seat on the bar. "Sadly, neither am I. But…ah, you are still going to need help."

"Shut. *Up.*"

The last thing I needed in a fight I was losing was a sarcastic peanut gallery. I could hear gunfire outside as well, so either the Masked Lords' main assault had chosen the *perfect* time to show up—entirely possible, since it appeared that Silverstar was in command of the Lords —or her people were turning on mine.

Esras had slipped from my hand as I fell, and it skittered away from me as I reached for it. From the overwhelming sense of impotent anger I picked up from the spear as it moved, it definitely wasn't *it* doing that.

Of course my spear decided to complain about its abandonment issues while it was being stolen from me.

It flashed across the room and landed in Silverstar's free hand.

"Quicksilver," she noted aloud. "Might have been enough if you were more experienced, but you were never a match for me, Kilkenny. Not even with the spear in your hands. I have learned and trained and fought for far longer than you've been alive.

"You should never have been born, and the spear should never have been bound to you." She smiled. It wasn't a pleasant sight. "Fortunately, it now falls to me to correct those errors of your father's."

"Okay, apparently, I'm being too subtle," the Puck snapped. "*Run,* you idiot!"

Sarcastic semi-hallucination or not, I could follow those instructions. Of course, it wasn't like Silverstar was willing to just stand there and *let* me.

GLYNN STEWART

I ran for the door and took a buffet of Force to the face that flung me back across the room. If I hadn't had quicksilver running in my veins, I probably would have broken limbs when I landed.

As it was, I used Force to land on my feet next to the hallway leading to Mabona's room. A second blast of Force sent me flying down the hallway, smashing into the spare IV stand sitting outside the door.

The Nobles who should have been guarding the room were gone. That...seriously screwed up my plans, and it took me a moment to realize where they were.

Niamh had taken them inside the room and wedged the door shut. With a Healer and two Nobles on the other side, she could probably hold the room for a while, even against Silverstar.

Her paranoia had proven well founded. On the other hand, if those Nobles had been out *here*, we probably could have taken Silverstar together.

She stepped into the hallway, green armor glowing brightly with her power as she raised *Esras*. The spear was almost useless to her, but she could still use it as a weapon.

While I was quite certain the spear would conspire to miss if she threw it, she could definitely stab me with it. And stabbing me with *Esras* would definitely break the blood bond.

Which appeared to be her plan. I dragged myself up the wall to face her, *feeling* Mabona's presence on the other side of the thin plaster and wondering how long Niamh and the Nobles could hold Silverstar off if I failed.

"If you can hear me at all, my Queen, I need you," I muttered under my breath, focusing on my link to Mabona. "Now would be a *fantastic* time to wake up."

She didn't wake up. I hadn't really been expecting her to.

The Puck appeared next to me suddenly.

"Wrong question," he told me. "And we're out of time for me to keep being mysterious."

A wooden staff twice their height appeared in their hand and they slammed it into the ground. From the way Silverstar recoiled, she might not be able to *see* them...but she heard that.

"Mabona! Sister of my Court! Child of my blood! Lend your Champion your power!"

My link to Mabona seemed to warm. A tiny shred of consciousness flickered into being on the other side of the wall. She wasn't awake. But somewhere deep in in her dreaming state, she heard the Puck's words.

And answered their call.

Silverstar charged down the hall, power augmenting her every step...and fire flashed through my veins as I sidestepped her. My link to my Queen was no longer warm. It was *searing*, pouring liquid fire into my veins and muscles as I moved with an unconscious grace I'd often seen and never matched.

Force flashed from my hands and *hammered* the Horned King into the wall. *Through* the wall, leaving her armored form to crash into one of the empty rooms we'd raided for furniture to build the barricade.

Esras jumped back to my hand with a will of its own, settling into my grip with a mental purr.

Silverstar was back on her feet as I struck again, deflecting my blow of Force into the wall with a broad grin.

"A fair fight, then, it seems," she snarled. "I'm going to rip your spine from your flesh!"

"*Finally*," the Puck barked. "Now, Kilkenny, fight for your Queen!"

44

I HONESTLY HAD no idea what to even *do* with the amount of power singing through me at that moment. That hesitation nearly killed me for, oh, the fifth or sixth time that fight.

A screaming blizzard of Force and Glamor-blades crossed the wrecked room in fractions of a second—and the floor beneath my feet disintegrated just as it hit. I conjured a shield to protect myself, but with no footing to secure myself, I went flying through the wall behind me.

And the wall behind that. And the one behind that.

The only reassuring thing was that I managed to focus enough power to yank Silverstar along with me, and we both planted ourselves in the concrete of the parking lot with a resounding crash.

Whatever gunfire had been sounding outside had resolved itself now, and I didn't have time to really study to see who had won. I left cracks in the cement as I bounced back to my feet, Mabona's power fueling my own Gift of Force as I hurled myself at the Horned King, spear first.

She parried the spear with her sword, a blur of Force and ice crashing at me as she moved.

Everyone except her seemed to be moving so slowly. I dodged the ice and sent flame hurtling at her. She smashed it into the ground, the concrete melting under the heat of my attack and giving me an idea.

As she conjured another attack, I returned the favor of what she'd done to me. The ground beneath her feet vanished and a tornado of fire surrounded her, superheating the concrete and stone as she fell into the hole.

Steam and molten rock filled the gap in the ground—but she vanished Between to avoid the crudely assembled trap.

I stepped sideways as she emerged, dodging a flurry of glamor-blades that hurtled into the already half-wrecked wall of the chalet. I sent Silverstar flying after her blades with a blow of Force, twisting her own glamors and the debris of the wall into a series of spikes.

She didn't manage to slow herself in time. The glamors disap-peared but she still slammed home onto a dozen or more spikes of rough wood yanked out of the chalet's wreckage.

They weren't cold iron and they couldn't kill her, but it looked and sounded like it *hurt* as they punched through and splintered around her armor. I charged her with *Esras*, and she barely managed to twist aside. I sank the spearhead into the debris, barely yanking it free as Silverstar leapt free and swung her sword at my head.

I ducked the blade and dodged backward. She was bleeding from half a dozen wounds where the impact had broken her armor. Even as I watched, however, the wounds were sealing. Even the armor was repairing itself, the ancient enameled metal knitting itself back together.

"You are a *giant* pain in my ass," she bellowed. "You will die, Jason Kilkenny."

"You are a traitor to the fae," I reminded her, loudly. There were a *lot* of people watching this fight without getting involved. With Mabona's power singing through me, I probably didn't need their help —but if I failed, they needed to know she couldn't be allowed near the Queen.

"Maybe to the High Court," Silverstar told me. "Never to the fae. All I have done is for the fae!"

"All you have done is for your own power," I replied. "So much blood and death, Grainne Silverstar. All in pursuit of…what? A crown? An antlered helm that didn't even make you a Power?"

"I will be a Power when *you are dead!*"

It was the fastest she'd moved so far, a blur of motion and death and power that I knew I normally wouldn't even have *seen*.

With Mabona's will driving me, I met her halfway. *Esras* flashed through the air with lightning speed, and Grainne Silverstar, Horned King of the fae, stopped in mid-charge.

The spearhead had emerged from her back, dripping blood as she slumped to the ground.

"It's…" She coughed, falling to her knees. "It's iron enough, isn't it?"

"It was forged to kill fae," I told her. "I think I'm keeping my spine today, Silverstar."

"You're still fucked. The rest are still—"

She fell forward against the spear, the last of her breath leaving her as she died.

———

THERE WAS a strange silence to the world after that. Mabona's power slowly ebbed from me, the purpose for which it had been lent to me complete. I couldn't tell if the Hunters and others gathered around me were speaking or not.

If they were, it was muffled, as if a great distance had just fallen between us. My world had shrunk to myself, *Esras* and Grainne Silverstar's body.

Mabona's power was gone, but my blood still felt warm. A new heat filled my body, radiating out from my core the same way my fire always had, except…my faerie fire had barely been noticeable when it did that.

Now it felt like I had the *sun* buried inside my chest. It didn't hurt —but it felt like it should have? It felt like I should have been glowing, surrounded by a storm, not by this sudden silence.

The Puck was suddenly there, stepping through the wreckage we'd made of the ground with a delicate grace. There was something more to the Puck than there had been before, and I realized that everyone around me could see the Puck now.

"You keep what you kill," the Puck quoted at me. The Power's voice was gentle, but it cut through the strange silence like a knife. The fog lifted, and now I could tell that everyone around me *except* the Puck was silent in shock.

"What?" I demanded. I vaguely recognized the quote but I didn't see the relevance.

"What?" the Puck replied. "I watch movies." They knelt and picked up the antlered helm.

"I don't understand." I admitted.

"You keep what you kill," they repeated, their bright green gaze locked onto me. "By ancient rights, by blood, by iron, you are her heir."

The only "her" relevant here was Grainne Silverstar. I couldn't be her heir. Her heir would be...

The Puck didn't seem to grow at all, but they were somehow tall enough to place the antlered helm on my head while I was distracted. A flash of their power swept the ancient green armor from Silverstar and onto me and I stared at him.

"Jason Alexander Odysseus Kilkenny Calebrantson," the Puck said formally. "Child of the blood of Lugh. Bearer of the spear *Esras*. Slayer of the Horned King in righteous single combat.

"The antlered helm is yours. The Wild Hunt is yours. *You* are the Horned King now."

I wanted to argue. Wanted to deny. I couldn't be the Horned King! I wasn't even wholly fae!

But the burning sun in my chest told me the true story. The warm acceptance radiating from the ancient regalia of the King told me the true story.

The Hunters and Companions and asura and Nobles kneeling around me in an ever-widening circle told me the story.

They could see the Puck. That probably helped. It was one thing to defeat the Horned King and claim the helm. That was what *made* me King, I think. But it helped to have *another* Power crown you.

"Powers that are," I breathed.

"Don't swear by yourself," the Puck advised. "It's not a good look." The projection shivered. "That...took more than I hoped. We'll meet again, Jason Kilkenny."

They disappeared and I found myself looking at *my* Hunt.

Fuck me.

45

THE VAGUE SENSE of distance didn't fade. Neither did the burning star in my chest. Everyone was staring at me after the Puck disappeared and I slowly moved forward. I could *feel* the aura of power radiating out from me.

I had never realized that Mabona in full "terrifying goddess" mode was her *default*. It took effort to suppress that overwhelming aura, and I didn't even know where to begin.

For now, however, it worked.

"I heard gunfire," I said. "What happened?"

"The Hunters Silverstar brought with her attacked on some signal we didn't see," Riley told me. "The Valkyries stopped them."

I saw that now. Two troops of the Hunt were disarmed and sitting on their hands, surrounded by the big horses and watched by armed women.

"How bad?" I asked.

"We lost three Companions," he said grimly. "The shifters took the brunt of it, though, and..."

"And we're fine," Mary told me, slipping into the conversation. "Barry was feeling paranoid about the newcomers and put his people closest to them. They weren't carrying silver."

And while most shifters lacked the many and varied Gifts of the fae, they were even harder to kill than we were. I took a moment to kiss Mary, trying to put as much reassurance into an embrace and a peck on the lips as I could.

I didn't know what was going to happen now, but I wasn't giving her up unless I had to.

She leaned into me, somehow managing to reassure *me* as I was trying to reassure her.

There was a reason I loved this woman.

"Thank you," I whispered.

Mary stepped back and nodded firmly to me, gesturing for me to keep going.

I walked past everyone to where the Valkyries waited with their prisoners.

"Inga is in the building," I told them quietly. "Bring her to me. I believe she lived, but I owe her."

The oldest-looking Valkyrie bowed and disappeared in silence. The rest parted the horses as I approached the prisoners.

"You are traitors to the Hunt and the fae," I told them gently. "You followed Grainne Silverstar into treachery and turned your arms and Gifts upon your siblings of the Hunt. There are penalties laid out for such things."

The Cold Death was hard to inflict on a Hunter, but I could sentence the Companions to it. The Hunters we would simply have to execute.

I *really* didn't want my first act as Horned King to be a mass execution.

"What do you have to say for yourselves?" I asked. "There will be enough death today, I think. What reason can you give me for mercy?"

There were thirty fae in front of me. I could use every one of them to stand against the assault I knew was coming, but that was only if I could trust them not to shoot us in the back.

They were silent for several long seconds, then one of them coughed.

"We were bound by Fealty," she said in a thick Irish accent. "We didn't know what cause she'd chosen until it was too late. Once bound, we cannot defy. You know that."

I did. If they had been sworn Vassals, they were damned limited in how much they could stand against Silverstar. That would explain why she'd been willing to trust this group with betraying the rest of the Hunt, and left the rest of her loyalists behind.

"And now?" I asked.

"We will not be traitors," the woman replied. She glanced around at the others. "I will swear Fealty to you as the new Horned King. Be bound, as I was bound before." She shook her head. "It seems a fair trade for a life."

I nodded to her and looked at the rest.

"Well?" I said. "I'll make that offer to you all. Swear Fealty and be bound as my Vassals, and I will spare you the punishment for your crimes. I will grant you the assumption that Silverstar left you no choice."

There were oaths and formalities I could insist on, that I would have needed an hour before. Now...now I only needed their consent.

And I had it. My power swept over them, releasing the bonds around their wrists and imposing new bonds on their Gifts and their minds.

"You are mine now," I told them. "The Vassals of a Power."

Ankaris and Silverstar had been the Horned King, but they had not been Powers. They had lacked an extra spark, an extra piece of power that had belonged to Calebrant...and that instead of passing on to them, Calebrant had passed it on to the son he wasn't supposed to have.

He'd passed it to me, and it had made me one of the only Changelings to ever classify as a Noble. And now, with the mantle of the Horned King settling upon me, that spark made me what Ankaris and Silverstar hadn't been.

A Power of the Fae High Court.

———

THE VALKYRIES BROUGHT Inga out shortly afterward, and it wasn't looking good. Before today, I could sense cold iron at a distance but not with any great detail.

Now I could tell that the cold iron blade had fragmented and several pieces of our ancient bane had made it through Inga's armor. Not enough to instantly kill her, but enough that it *would* kill her—and would frustrate, say, Niamh's healing gift.

Niamh was with them as they brought her out and she looked at me helplessly.

"There's cold iron in her bloodstream," she told me, stating aloud what I'd just sensed. "I can't do anything. She has...an hour. Maybe less. I could wake her up, I suppose, but that would cost her time."

A stimulant would wake the Valkyrie up despite the blood loss. It would allow her to say goodbye, but it would kill her even faster.

For all that we were nearly unkillable and wielded powers only barely imaginable by mortals, we were in some ways so very, very, human.

"I think I can help," I said quietly. "I know I have the power now, but this isn't something I've done before. Can you...can you guide me?"

The one time I'd been involved in healing someone, I'd linked minds with Talus to allow him to use my iron-seeker Gift to pull cold iron chunks out of Robert. That had been pure telekinesis, leaving the healing to the young noble's own powers, but the pieces of cold iron had been larger.

Niamh clearly realized what she'd missed as she studied me.

"I can do that, my lord," she told me. She offered me a hand, hesitantly.

I took her hand gently.

"Thank you," I said. "I owe Inga."

I channeled power. The burning star in my chest leapt to brightly cheerful life, sending energy surging down my hands. I linked with Niamh without even realizing what I was doing and leaned on her knowledge, her skill.

My power could locate the cold iron and move it, but extracting it without injuring Inga required a delicacy I'd never learned. Niamh's healing gifts couldn't touch the cold iron, but all of her powers required that same delicacy.

Together, we found each tiny piece of cold iron and extracted it with a delicate blade of telekinesis. Flesh knit behind us as we worked, removing fragment after fragment of metal from the woman who'd saved my life.

It seemed like an eternity, though it was probably only about five minutes, before Inga opened her eyes and looked up at us.

"That hurt," she said in her Swedish-accented English. "And you...saved me."

"There was iron in your blood," Niamh told her as I released the bond between us. "Only a Power could have saved you. But..."

"Jason is the blood of Lugh, and if he's still here, he defeated Silverstar in single combat," Inga said instantly. "My lord. Your Majesty," she corrected herself.

"Did everyone see this coming but me?" I asked plaintively.

"Probably," she replied. "Help me up, Jason. I'm guessing we still have a battle left to fight?"

"Whenever the Masked Lords decide to show up, yeah," I told her. "Though I suppose they could go into hiding again."

I snorted.

"I doubt I'm that scary, though."

46

"They're coming."

Damh Coleman's arrival had brought more than just hands and guns. He'd also brought a full set of military-grade radio headsets that we'd passed out.

I now had Hunters on both the road and scattered throughout the mountains around us. I didn't expect the Masked Lords to try and sneak around us, not when they had several hundred mercenaries to deploy.

"What are we looking at?" I asked.

"Looks like a convoy of trucks. Rental pickups and minivans, mostly. They probably got them all out here two or three at a time, because it's damn obvious they're rolling a small army up the hill now."

"All right. Pull the nearest teams together and set up a blockade behind them," I ordered. "No one escapes, people. I prefer prisoners to corpses, even for the Lords themselves, but no one runs. You hear me?"

"No one ever outruns the Wild Hunt," the troop captain told me. "We'll be in position shortly."

He paused.

"They'll be knocking on your door in about five, maybe ten minutes if they drive right up."

"We'll be waiting for them. You just make sure the door stays shut behind them."

The channel clicked closed and I looked at the others.

"Make sure we're set up," I ordered loudly. "We're on the final countdown now."

"We have a plan?" Raja asked. "I mean, beyond pointing a god at them and laughing?"

I winced.

"I am *not* a god," I told him pointedly. "And I have no damn idea what I'm doing with this level of power yet, either.

"My plan is to hold the walls until they bring out *Asi* and the ritual team. At that point, I'm going to go meet them and we get to see how well their ritual works while we're fucking their shit up."

Raja grinned and shucked his long trench coat. The cold iron sword I'd given him was sitting on the ground next to him and, he picked it up while flexing his now *very* visible muscles.

"Aren't you cold?" I asked the shirtless Indian.

"Absolutely freezing," he confirmed brightly. "But Bollywood left me with an image to live up to! I can't let those shirtless mortal hunks look *better* in a fight than I do!"

I shook my head.

"These are the people who killed your families," I reminded him. "Are you going to be...steady?"

I couldn't quite think of a way to phrase "Are you going to go mad with bloodlust and kill everyone, even when I'd rather have prisoners?" that was polite.

"Not really," he admitted. "But we won't kill anyone who surrenders. We swore Fealty and you gave your orders, my lord."

I couldn't even argue with the *my lord*s anymore. Now I got to argue with people calling me a god.

It wasn't an improvement.

"Let's see what our friends decide to open with," I said aloud. "I'm guessing it would be far too optimistic, hoping that Mabona wakes up before they get here, wouldn't it?"

Raja chuckled.

"If anyone could wake her up, it would be the new Horned King. I take it that didn't work?"

"They attacked what makes her a Power," I said with a sigh. "Until that link heals, she won't wake up."

Which meant that this fight was mine.

Well, mine and my small army's.

———

THE VEHICLE CONVOY came to a halt at the entrance road to the lodge, where their sniper team had tried to take us out. I was tempted to try and disrupt their deployment, but I also was relatively certain that the Masked Lords themselves weren't in the array of cheap rentals.

They would be coming from the Between when they were ready. Everyone else here was pawns on the board, especially the human mercenaries.

If we took out the Masked Lords and reclaimed *Asi*, this war was over. If we wiped out their assault force but the Masked Lords escaped with the sword, all we'd achieved was a pile of corpses.

So, we let them come. Hunters lurked in the trees, following their progress.

"We're looking at about a hundred and fifty mortal mercenaries, presumably armed with cold iron rounds for their assault rifles," Amandine reeled off to my impromptu command staff. "Sixty fae scattered throughout, with rifles and blades. We're reporting everything from a couple of will-o'-the-wisps to at least one Masked Noble in command."

"One Mask isn't their ritual team," I concluded. "How do we draw them out?"

"I think we have to throw back their first attack," the Guardian told me. "Might help for bringing them out if we have the Horned King being obviously involved?"

"Probably." I shook my head, the weight of the heavy antlered helm a new distraction. "That will leave them with a long list of unanswered questions, given that I think Silverstar was one of their core members. They *know* the Horned King is on their side."

"Well, that'll be quite a shock for them, won't it?" Mary replied, reaching out to squeeze my hand. "Are you ready for this, love?"

"I have to be," I told her, squeezing her hand in turn. "How long do we have?"

"Depends on how careful they're being. Scouts aren't reporting any real heavy weapons, so it's going to be pretty straightforward," Amandine said. "No grenade launchers, no mortars. Just rifles and body armor."

"So, the only difference from the usual affair is the numbers and the mortals," I concluded. "Think they're expecting the machine guns?"

We only had four of them, but that was still four more machine guns than I would have expected to see in a fae battle formation.

"If they're smart, they're allowing for the possibility," Raja said. "These people stormed the citadel of my order. Do *not* underestimate them."

"And Tír fo Thuinn," I added. "These people hit two of the most secured and heavily fortified supernatural bases in the world and won. This is all looking *very* low-key compared to what I expected."

I considered the situation.

"It's more than the ritual team," I concluded aloud. "They've got a whole second wave coming via Between—and we need to be ready for them."

THE MERCENARIES MIGHT BE UNDERQUALIFIED for the fight they'd been recruited for, but they definitely knew their business. They made it to the edge of the forest in good order and took time to survey our crude fortifications before they did anything.

We'd kept everyone out of sight, but they definitely figured we were there. They stayed out of sight for several more minutes, and then half of them opened fire.

It wasn't wild automatic fire and it wasn't carefully aimed shots. It was an unhurried metronome of single shots taken at the top of the barricade and anywhere else they thought we might stick our heads up.

The other half started advancing at a run. They made it about a third of the way across the open space and then threw themselves down in the snow before they opened fire.

"I think that's close enough," I murmured as the second set of troops began to charge forward. "Watch yourselves. Those bullets are cold iron."

We'd expected as much, but as they ricocheted off our defenses, I could sense enough to be certain.

"Gunners!" Raja bellowed. "With me!"

He was first up, the ammunition belt for the big M60 slung over his shoulder as he braced himself and opened fire. The mercenaries targeted him as he rose, bullets slamming into his golden skin—but the same cold iron rounds that would have been nearly instantly deadly to my fae *shattered* on the asura's skin.

The second machine gunner was also an asura. Not quite as large or impressive as Raja, perhaps, but large enough—and his golden skin was just as bulletproof.

The third gunner was the only werebear in the group, Barry's second-in-command. Almost as large in human form as in bear form, he was the only one of us capable of hand-firing a massive M2 machine gun.

We'd brought a tripod mount for the weapon, but Richard decided he made a better support system.

The fourth machine gun was the WWII vintage version of the same gun, mounted on the giant horse that nimbly leapt to the top of the barricade with her Valkyrie rider on her back.

As the three big men opened fire with their machine guns, the Valkyrie's horse danced along the barricade like she was on a dressage field, delicately leaping and hopping over the streams of fire from the other machine guns. Her rider seemed to instinctively know what the horse was about to do, adjusting her fire to account for the motions.

The second wave of mercenaries went down. They probably

weren't all dead, but even the ones who hadn't been hit knew better than to be upright while that hail of death swept the field.

Both groups started to focus their fire, trying to bring down at least one of the machine gunners.

I don't know what the Valkyrie's horse *was*, but it was apparently just as bulletproof as the asura. As the horse and the golden-skinned warriors alike shrugged aside bullets, Richard just calmly took the hits, bracing himself against the impact of bullets that inflicted injuries he healed in seconds.

"Now," I ordered conversationally.

The Companions and the rest of the asura stepped up to the wall. They only had assault rifles, but that was all our attackers had. The exchange of fire wasn't going entirely in our favor—even Raja or Richard could only take so many hits before they went down, at least temporarily, but the mercenary advance was halted.

Then the supernaturals that had been deployed with the mortals acted. A wash of green faerie fire appeared out of nothingness, sweeping across the snow toward us like a tidal wave. Telekinetic shields started blocking bullets and lightning crackled as the fae started to push back against our attack.

I jumped to the top of the barricade, *Esras* in my hand. I didn't let my brain slow down to boggle at the leap I'd just made—that wall of fire was going to be a problem.

I snuffed it out with a gesture of the spear, then duplicated the trick it seemed that *everyone* had pulled on me in the last year. I conjured a dozen blades of glamor and sent them hurtling at the telekinetic shields the fae had conjured.

Glamor shattered against the shields, but the glamor was only a cover for darts of force that ripped through the shields like they weren't there.

A new shield appeared out of nothingness, covering my people from the incoming fire as best I could without blocking our return fire, and for a moment, that was it.

Then the fae conjured a new defense, a swirling storm of Fire and Ice and Force that filled the air between the attackers and our defenders. I contained it, holding it in place.

The intent wasn't to attack us now. That storm was just cover, and it worked. While I struggled to contain the magic woven by over forty fae, they helped their mortal mercenaries retreat. By the time I collapsed the storm cloud, they'd abandoned the field.

And if I'd intentionally taken longer to destroy their spell than I needed to, well, no one was ever going to know but me.

47

A PEACEFUL QUIET descended across the mountains. The field in front of the chalet was a warzone, with snow and mud churned up with blood and ashes, that gave the lie to that peace.

"Get the wounded back to Niamh," I ordered. "Richard, how are you holding up?"

The big shifter had a *lot* of holes in his heavy winter coat, but he shook himself like a wet dog and threw me a thumbs-up.

"I could really use a burger, but otherwise, I'm good," he told me.

"Someone get the man who just regenerated thirty bullet holes a sandwich," I called with a shake of my head.

"Raja?"

"I'm fine. Basant will need some bandaging and to pass the gun over to someone else," he said, with a firm glance at the other asura. "He's no good to our liege lord dead, is he?"

Basant wilted a bit under Raja's glance and allowed one of the shifters to lead him away to get his injuries checked out. Cold iron bullets weren't armor-piercing, but they were close enough to do a number on even asura who weren't careful.

"No dead," Damh reported. "It looks like our opponents pulled back their wounded as well, but they definitely lost more than they could afford."

"I doubt the Masked Lords will weep for their mortal pawns," I replied. I might. I certainly felt bad enough for the poor bastards. They had no idea what kind of war they'd wandered into the middle of.

"Or their fae pawns, for that matter," Inga said gruffly. The Valkyrie was still weak, but she was conscious and recovering. She couldn't take part in this wave, but she'd be ready if the battle dragged on. "Even Silverstar's Vassals were expendable."

"Much as I would *like* prisoners, I'm not going to feel particularly bad if none of the Masked Lords surrender," I said grimly. "This needs to end, people. We can't continue to run our society knowing that some of its *leaders* are rebels."

"I don't suppose we're expecting more reinforcements?" Amandine asked.

I shook my head at the Guardian.

"It's possible," I allowed. "The problem is that I can't *trust* anyone. I'm reasonably sure I can trust Oberis and his people...but I'm *also* relatively sure the Masked Lords still have at least one agent in his court."

"So, we fight them with the Hunt and your personal Vassals?" she said.

"Exactly." I hefted *Esras* and felt the tenor of the world around me. The way that all of reality seemed to be...malleable to me now was still strange.

"They'll be here soon," I observed aloud. "They know I'm here now and what I am. What my father started, it falls to me to finish—so, if they want to win their little war, they have to come for me."

"We'll be waiting for them, my King," Amandine told me firmly. "The Wild Hunt has faced this enemy before and we taught them defeat once."

With the attack on Tír fo Thuinn, the honors between the Hunt and the Masked Lords were roughly even, but I kept my peace.

She was right, after all. With my father at their head, the Wild Hunt had beaten the Masked Lords once. With me at their head, they would do so again.

If they didn't, the failure was probably mine. My father, after all, had been a Power for almost a century before he'd fought the Masked Lords.

It was looking like I might have a whole three hours of experience as a Power before I fought them.

———

THE ARRIVAL of the next wave of the Masked Lords' attack was a hammerblow to the head of everyone with the Gift of Between. We could feel arrivals, but this was something else entirely.

This wasn't a few dozen Hunters bringing one Companion apiece. This was twenty-one Lords opening a *tunnel* through the Between, creating a passageway from wherever they'd been preparing to the field in front of the chalet.

If we hadn't had the warning, it would have been a disaster. They opened their attack with a salvo of grenades and light mortar rounds *out* of the Between. I threw a shield of Force up as soon as I realized just how large an opening they were creating, and barely managed to hold off the onslaught of explosives.

Explosives were followed by a brutal barrage of gunfire and Gifts as another hundred fae came storming out of the tunnel. Fire and lightning hurtled at our barricades from multiple directions as they spread out to cover as many angles as they could and the previous attackers joined the assault.

Our machine guns returned fire and our people added their own Gifts to the fray, but the mortars rapidly proved a serious problem. Grenade launchers had a bit of an arc and we could shield against them.

The mortars were firing dozens of meters into the air and descending behind our positions.

"Shield *up!*" someone shouted, and I expanded my defenses. Shells were falling from the sky and exploding against the telekinetic shields we were covering our position with.

Not every shell had cold iron fragments in it, but enough did that the shield was a strain even for me. I was protecting multiple angles against multiple attacks *and* suppressing the Gift attacks at the same time.

Gunfire echoed next to my ear as someone stepped Between *inside* our fortifications. Unfortunately for the Hunter who'd sworn service to the Masked Lords, Mary was waiting next to me, and his lunge at me ended in a spray of point-blank submachine gun fire.

"I've got your back," she told me. "Keep covering everyone."

This was the full-bore assault, the hard and fast hammer that had overwhelmed the defenses of Tír fo Thuinn. There'd been four times as many Hunters and Companions to protect that ancient fortress—but they'd been taken by surprise.

We weren't.

I flung back the Gift assault, clearing the path for our own Companions to fill the air with a storm of power that smashed the lead elements of the assault force back. That gave me a few seconds to locate the mortars.

I didn't have time for subtle. I focused my will on the weapons' position and told the world to make them go away.

One moment, half a dozen portable light mortars were pounding our position and several more were being set up. The next, a dozen guns and two dozen fae were just...gone. Ash and dust drifted in the breeze as my will simply *obliterated* them.

I was no longer a changeling with specific Gifts at Noble levels of power. I was a *Power,* and even I had no idea what that meant.

I unleashed another wave of destruction at what looked like a core assault group, scattering the Nobles who tried to defend against it. They protected their people, but only at the cost of physically being strewn across the battlefield.

Even inexperienced and unaware of my powers and limits, I realized there was no way this assault could succeed so long as I was there. All of this was a distraction, a side show to what had to be coming...now.

I *stepped* Between as I felt the arrival coming, emerging on the mountainside above the battlefield and spraying the attackers' left flank with fire.

My goal wasn't really to defeat them or kill anyone. My goal was to attract the attention of the newest arrivals.

Twenty-one figures in cold iron masks were suddenly standing in the middle of the battlefield. I could feel the potential power rippling off them from here. The ritual was already mostly complete, ready to be fired off. A second, smaller group of masked Nobles was shielding them from the battle.

All told, thirty Nobles and Lords of the fae stood in the center of the battle, ignoring everything except me.

The woman in front raised an ancient-looking sword and pointed it at me. There was no warning, no threat, no rise in the increase in potential.

Only the fact that I *knew* what was going on let me realize that she was attacking. Surprise was a powerful tool, and I could easily see how they'd managed to strike down my father and Ankaris.

I stepped Between as the blade leveled at my heart. Even from outside reality, I *felt* the blow strike home, an unimaginably powerful bolt of force hammering into the mountain where I'd been standing.

The ritual didn't attack a Power. It attacked the reality *around* a Power, finding and twisting, distorting the link to the world and magic that *made* a Power a Power.

But I was Between. There was no link for the magic to hit, so it unleashed its force on the mountainside. I couldn't tell if that was all they had or if the ritual had a second shot...and there was only one way to find out.

I stepped out of the Between back onto the mountainside.

That was a mistake. The spell hadn't hit me, hadn't had the inextricable link between Power and reality to sever, so it had spent all of its energy in a more...kinetic fashion.

On a mountainside of stone and snow. In avalanche country. The ground gave way under my feet as I tried to find my footing, and I realized the *entire* mountain was coming down.

Right at the ski lodge. They might have failed to kill me, but it looked like the Masked Lords were about to do a good job of murdering my people instead.

Except that I was, inexperienced and unprepared or not, a Power.

I let myself fall as I reached into that link with reality and *changed* what was happening. The mountain was still falling, yes, but it wasn't falling on the chalet. By a "fluke" force and wind and angles, the rock-slide was going to miss the lodge.

The Masked Lords took too long to realize I'd redirected the avalanche. They tried to shield themselves, but it was far, *far* too late.

I smashed their shield to pieces anyway. They probably had enough time to realize what I'd done before several thousand tons of rock and ice descended on them.

They definitely didn't have enough time to *do* anything.

48

It took me fifteen minutes to find *Asi* in the debris. My people were focused on taking the survivors of the Masked Lords' army into custody. None of the Lords themselves had survived. A Power-guided avalanche made for a terrifyingly deadly weapon.

And it looked like most of the fae had been bound by Fealty. The deaths of their lords had freed them from those bonds, so they were willing—even *desperate*—to surrender to anyone who'd let them.

My orders had been very clear and my people were being surprisingly obedient. Even the asura were calmly taking prisoners, focusing on making sure we got everyone who was still alive out of the snow.

The battle was over. No one was going to freeze to death out there on our watch.

Once I was sure that the survivors were in hand, I searched for the pulsing energy signature of the ancient blade and then starting digging.

None of the bodies I uncovered were intact enough to really deserve the title. I'd thrown the heart of the mountain at the Masked Lords' ritual team. They'd been smashed flat.

The sword, however, was intact. I'd known that from the beginning, and I could feel it and *Esras* "communicating" as I got closer. The two weapons were much of a kind, really, and the degree to which they clearly recognized each other was fascinating to me.

More than anything, though, I wasn't leaving *Asi* buried there. I couldn't responsibly leave one of the most powerful artifacts in the world *merely* buried under a few meters of ice and rock.

I pulled the old sword out and levitated myself back up to the surface. Holding the two ancient weapons in my hands, I looked at the hole I'd dug for a long minute.

Then I collapsed it in on itself. The Masked Lords would be buried where they died. We would eventually need to pull out the bodies and check under the masks. Enough people had died in this chaos that there would be an open question of who the rebels had been otherwise.

For now, however, they would stay there under the ice.

I walked back toward the chalet and was unsurprised to find Raja waiting for me halfway.

"We've found everyone who's still alive, I think," he noted calmly. "Probably about half of them at best. They weren't expecting to fight a mountain."

"Perhaps they should have." I considered the asura warlord silently for a few seconds. "You have your revenge, Raja Venkat Asi. What now?"

He winced.

"I don't know," he admitted. "I didn't swear Fealty to you contingent on anything, my lord. I am yours to command."

"Huh." He wasn't looking at the sword in my left hand but I knew he'd seen it. There was no way that Raja wasn't aware of what I was holding.

"Catch." I tossed him the sword.

He caught it, staring at it as it glowed happily at being in contact with him.

"I failed that oath," he told me. "I failed my family. I failed the sword. I am your man now."

"Then in my service, guard that damn thing," I replied. "I'll keep you with me and the Hunt if you want to stay, but there's no one else better qualified to stand over *Asi*. Though I'll note that if you fall back into mercenary assassinations, there will be *words*."

His fingers clenched on the hilt.

"Never again," he told me fiercely. "I will serve to my death, but I will see the sword guarded. And there will be no distractions for his new protectors."

"Good." I walked past him toward the chalet. The battle was over, but I still had work to do today.

———

Oisin's people were clearing away the SUVs, though the Queen's guard were still clearly maintaining a watchful eye. The Hunter Noble himself was sitting on the front hood of an SUV that was never driving again.

"Oisin. How are your people?" I asked.

"Alive, thanks to you," he replied. "The Queen is still out, though. Any idea how long it'll be before she wakes up?"

I shook my head.

"Ask Niamh?" I suggested. "She's spent more time being a Power's physician than I've spent being a Power. By a couple of orders of magnitude."

He nodded.

"Fair enough. Not how you expected the day to go, huh, boss?"

I paused, then sighed.

"I guess I am your boss now, aren't I?"

"One of two," he confirmed. "And with Mabona still unconscious, it's all your call."

"I don't see a reason to move her," I told him. "I'm going to get some of my people moving back towards both Calgary and Tír fo Thuinn, but we'll be keeping a close watch on this place.

"I'm certainly not going anywhere until she wakes up," I said with a grimace. "I need to make sure there's someone around to take charge of this giant mess. Speaking of people in charge, do you know where Amandine and Damh ended up?"

"They're running your people ragged from over there," Oisin pointed.

"Thanks."

The four fae who'd ended up acting as the Wild Hunt's command staff—Damh, Amandine, Riley and Inga—were gathered around the Escalade, talking to Mary.

I walked over to them, hugging Mary as I traded nods with the rest. "Where are we at?"

"Digging," Amandine replied. "There's no road left out of here, if you hadn't noticed. Someone dropped a mountain on us."

"That was them," I said. "I just made sure it didn't fall *directly* on us."

"Which is appreciated."

"In any case, any problems getting people to fall in line?" I asked. "We've been going on 'people know who Jason trusts' for most of this."

"Nada," Riley replied. "That's been enough."

"It won't be for long, not as we try and put this mess back together," I told them. "So, let's make it clear." I pointed at Damh and Riley. "You two are Second and Third Guardians.

"Riley, I want your butt and three troops of Hunters and Companions back at Tír fo Thuinn," I told him. "Double-check the fortifications, renew the cloaking spells." I sighed. "Bury any of our dead that Silverstar left there."

"Yes, my lord."

"Damh, I want you to take two troops back to Calgary," I continued, turning to my first Hunt subordinate. "The house is now going to be an official Wild Hunt base. You need to petition Oberis and MacDonald for permission, but I doubt they'll give us trouble.

"Once we've got leave, we'll move more of our hands back to Calgary. I don't want to have the entire Wild Hunt floating around here." I shook my head. "We need to keep a careful eye on Mabona, but too many fae here is going to draw attention."

"Can do," he confirmed.

I turned to Inga.

"You're retired," I pointed out. "So are your Valkyries."

"Your point?" she replied.

"I'm not giving any of you orders, but I would be grateful beyond words if any of you would be willing to return to the Hunt for a year or two."

"I'm in," Inga said instantly. "You need someone to keep an eye on you. Most of the rest will probably follow suit. We like our retirement, but we still feel our duty as well."

"Good. You're a Guardian now," I said briskly. "Get as many of the other Valkyries on board as you can, but there's no obligation here. I'm not drafting *anyone*, am I clear?"

"Perfectly. And thank you."

There was more to declaring people Guardians than words. As I gave them titles, I focused power through them.

Only Inga of the three I'd just promoted had been of Noble power level before. Unless I'd severely misjudged what I was doing, they all were now. Guardianship had its perks.

"And me, my lord?" Amandine asked.

"You're First Guardian," I told her. "You and Inga will stick with me while we play babysitter for the Queen of the Fae—and start looking to see where the hell the rest of the High Court went."

From what the Puck had told me, at least some were dead.

"And me?" Mary asked softly. I looked at her and swallowed hard. This was going to be awkward.

"I think you and I need to talk alone," I said, equally softly.

———

WE STEPPED into one of the chalets that had been going unused. There was wood in the fireplace, currently unlit, but the room was warm enough. The entire lodge was extremely well built.

I grabbed one of a pair of comfortable chairs and waited for Mary to take a seat across from me.

"So, what, my boyfriend is now a god?" she finally asked.

"A Power. The line is fuzzy, but since at least some of the entities we would historically have called gods were definitely Powers..." I sighed. "It's an inaccurate but not invalid descriptor. Of course, I have no idea what the hell it means or what I can do with any of this yet."

"Right now, I think it's probably important that it means you're all but immortal, aren't you?"

"Given the recent turnover in the Fae High Court, that's not an assumption I'd cling to," I told her. "But, yes. The Puck is estimated to be at least five or six thousand years old."

Mary leaned her head on her hands and studied me.

"Shifters live maybe two or three hundred years," she pointed out. "Double that for an Alpha or Alpha-candidate or a shaman. So...six hundred years for me. Six thousand for you. See the problem?"

I did. My true likely life expectancy was much shorter, but I could see the problem.

"And if I don't care?" I asked carefully. "You are the woman I love, the second mind and set of eyes that got us this far alive. If I have six months with you or six millennia, it doesn't matter. They're with you. They're us, together."

"Six months would probably require one of us dying," she pointed out.

"Or you deciding that you don't want to put up with a Power for a boyfriend," I said. "I'm not leaving you, Mary. I love you."

She sighed.

"And what happens when I can't keep up?" she asked. "When I'm not an equal partner to a freaking god, or I start aging? Even shifters age, Jason...and I'm not sure Powers do."

"I don't recall you needing to be able to throw cars or walk through walls to be my partner before this," I reminded her. "You're smart, my love. You see things a way I don't...and I don't think that's going to get any *less* useful now."

I knelt in front of her chair and took her hands in mine.

"And as for the rest, I *am* a Power," I pointed out. "If you want to be a shaman? I can probably make that happen. If you want to live an extra few millennia? I can be selfish enough to make that possible."

"Seriously?" she looked down at me with surprise.

"Well, I'll have to ask Mabona or the Puck *how*, but I know it's *possible*," I agreed. "Any time I can get with you is precious, my love, but I will *make* time with you if you'll let me. I won't force anything on you, but if you're prepared to stay by my side, I see no reason to let who we *were* limit us."

She finally leaned forward, resting her forehead against mine.

"I hadn't thought of it that way."

"We need a vacation," I told her. "I don't think I've stopped running since I hit the ground in Calgary a year ago."

Mary chuckled.

"I love you, but how are you going to pull *that* off?"

"I have competent subordinates who know where to find me if they need to," I said. "I'm thinking we just fuck off once Mabona's awake. Leave them a week or two to arrange a wedding."

I coughed.

"If...if that's what you want, I suppose."

Mary's chuckle turned into a full-throated laugh.

"If that was meant to be a proposal, my love, you are *terrible* at this."

I laughed—and conjured a ring out of thin air. It was a simple thing, plain gold...but it was more than that as well. This had never been forged or cast by mortal artisans. It was a thing of *my* power and *my* will far more than it was a thing of gold.

"Mary Tenerim, will you marry me?"

49

It was another week before Mabona finally woke up. She was out for eleven days total before Niamh came and collected me from the room I'd coopted as my own.

"She's awake and asking for you," the Healer told me. "I'm not sure how much she knows about what happened—she certainly seems just as confident as ever."

"I would guess she knows at least a bit," I told Niamh. It had been Mabona's power I'd used to defeat Silverstar, after all.

"I'll be there in a minute."

The Healer bowed and withdrew, leaving me to turn a tired smile on the video screen.

"Many things change, Lord Oberis, but that I will answer the Queen's call does not," I told Calgary's Fae Lord.

"Go, Kilkenny," he told me. "I know what's happened the last two weeks. I don't think Mabona does." He smiled. "Confidence is an easy thing to fake with practice, my dear friend. You'll learn."

"I'll have to," I admitted. "We'll speak again soon."

"Don't worry about me," Oberis told me. "Grandfather and I have everything under control."

"That's what I'm afraid of," I said. The concept of what Oberis and

Enli would consider appropriate for my wedding was mildly terrifying.

Nonetheless, I shut down the laptop and went to Mabona's room.

For all of the confidence she was projecting, she was still the second most fragile-looking I'd ever seen her. She was slowly helping Niamh remove the sensors and wires attached to her, but looked up as I came in.

"Jason," she greeted me, then paused. "Your Majesty," she corrected.

"Last I checked, if there was anyone on the planet who didn't need to give me that title, it was you," I told her. "But yes. Ankaris left the antlered helm to Grainne Silverstar, who betrayed us."

"I killed her—with your help—and inherited."

Mabona was silent for several seconds.

"Leave us," she ordered Niamh. "This is now a matter for the High Court."

The blonde Healer bowed and retreated, closing the door behind her.

"The situation?" she asked sharply.

"The Masked Lords are dead. *Asi* has been retrieved and is currently in the hands of a Vassal of mine." I shook my head. "The Wild Hunt is battered but unbroken. It will take us time to recruit back to strength, but my Guardians are already preparing our new base in Calgary and the fortress at Tír fo Thuinn for new recruits.

"Now that you're awake, I no longer need to keep five troops of Hunters and Companions here," I concluded. "That will allow them to get to work while I see if it's possible for me to rest."

Mabona snorted.

"You're your father's son," she told me. "*Rest* is not in your vocabulary. And you don't have time. You aren't the not-quite-Power Ankaris was—or that Silverstar would have been, I guess. I never met her as the Horned King."

"No. My father's blood, *Esras*, the regalia and mantle." I shook my head. "I am a Power, my Queen. And no longer your Vassal."

The relationship existed still, technically, but the magical bond was gone.

"No. Now, more than ever, you must be my student."

She was suddenly standing. There was no motion between. One moment, she was half-naked in the bed; the next, she was standing next to me, clad in a dark green floor-length gown.

"What you have come into cannot be lightly controlled. You must learn your Gifts."

"I will," I promised. "In time. Right now, I've been waiting for you to wake up and take charge of your own affairs. Now I'm going to go take a vacation."

"You can't be serious!"

"My Guardians can find me wherever I go," I told her. "*You* can find me without much difficulty. And I need time to understand just what has happened to me."

There was no knock, but suddenly we weren't alone in the room. The new member was a tall and slim androgynous fae with long copper-red hair.

The advantage of what I was now, I supposed, was that I didn't need to pick out the horns in the Puck's hair to know who had joined us.

"You're awake as well, I see," I noted.

"We were all taken down as one by the attack on Ankaris," the Puck observed. "We all awoke at roughly the same time. Like Mabona, I had to let a Healer fuss over me before I made my way here."

"When did you two meet?" Mabona asked, then paused. "Wait. I remember now. I channeled my power to help you fight Silverstar." She shook her head. "That's a weird feeling."

"You should have been more capable," the Puck noted sharply. "All of you should have been. It seems that young Kilkenny is not the only Power of the High Court who will need lessons."

"And that is why this idea of his to just up and disappear is madness!"

"The Masked Lords are broken," I said quietly. "The war is over. The High Court is damaged but intact. The rest of the courts are in turmoil but at peace. A week, ten days. I won't be missed. I'm taking Mary and finding a beach somewhere. Hawaii sounds nice."

That got a small smirk from Mabona, but she wasn't done yet.

"I need to get my feet under me. Catch up on affairs. We need the whole High Court to pull this together."

"In that case, we don't need Kilkenny until we've replaced our other losses," the Puck pointed out reasonably.

"You're supposed to be helping," Mabona told the Puck. The smirk wasn't hiding nearly as hard, though.

"I can recommend some good beaches in Hawaii," the Puck told me in answer. "You aren't the first Power to need a vacation away from all of this on being elevated. *Someone* was the model for half the paintings in Venice for a year, after all."

"Fine," Mabona said with a sigh and a barely concealed blush. "You'll need the time with Mary, anyway. Maintaining a relationship across this kind of transition is difficult, and the Puck is right. We lost more than Ankaris, which means I need to hunt down more heirs than just you.

"But if we need you…"

"You can find me," I told her. "I want to go rest on a beach, my Queen, not let the world burn down. My Guardians will be able to find me, if nothing else. I even have a cellphone—and *I* check my voice-mails, even if I don't always answer."

"I can see that the young one is going to be an…interesting addition to the Court," the Puck observed. "I look forward to it."

JOIN THE MAILING LIST

Love Glynn Stewart's books? Join the mailing list at

GLYNNSTEWART.COM/MAILING-LIST/

to know as soon as new books are released, special announcements, and a chance to win free paperbacks.

ABOUT THE AUTHOR

Glynn Stewart is the author of *Starship's Mage*, a bestselling science fiction and fantasy series where faster-than-light travel is possible–but only because of magic. His other works include science fiction series *Duchy of Terra*, *Castle Federation* and *Vigilante*, as well as the urban fantasy series *ONSET* and *Changeling Blood*.

Writing managed to liberate Glynn from a bleak future as an accountant. With his personality and hope for a high-tech future intact, he lives in Kitchener, Ontario with his partner, their cats, and an unstoppable writing habit.

VISIT GLYNNSTEWART.COM FOR NEW RELEASE
UPDATES

f facebook.com/glynnstewartauthor

OTHER BOOKS
BY GLYNN STEWART

For release announcements join the
mailing list or visit **GlynnStewart.com**

STARSHIP'S MAGE
Starship's Mage
Hand of Mars
Voice of Mars
Alien Arcana
Judgment of Mars
UnArcana Stars
Sword of Mars
Mountain of Mars
The Service of Mars
A Darker Magic
Mage-Commander (upcoming)

Starship's Mage: Red Falcon
Interstellar Mage
Mage-Provocateur
Agents of Mars

Pulsar Race: A Starship's Mage Universe Novella

DUCHY OF TERRA
The Terran Privateer
Duchess of Terra
Terra and Imperium
Darkness Beyond
Shield of Terra
Imperium Defiant
Relics of Eternity
Shadows of the Fall
Eyes of Tomorrow

SCATTERED STARS

Scattered Stars: Conviction

Conviction

Deception

Equilibrium

Fortitude (upcoming)

PEACEKEEPERS OF SOL

Raven's Peace

The Peacekeeper Initiative

Raven's Course

Drifter's Folly (upcoming)

EXILE

Exile

Refuge

Crusade

Ashen Stars: An Exile Novella

CASTLE FEDERATION

Space Carrier Avalon

Stellar Fox

Battle Group Avalon

Q-Ship Chameleon

Rimward Stars

Operation Medusa

A Question of Faith: A Castle Federation Novella

SCIENCE FICTION STAND ALONE NOVELLA

Excalibur Lost

VIGILANTE
(WITH TERRY MIXON)
Heart of Vengeance
Oath of Vengeance

**Bound By Stars: A Vigilante Series
(With Terry Mixon)**
Bound By Law
Bound by Honor
Bound by Blood

TEER AND KARD
Wardtown
Blood Ward

CHANGELING BLOOD
Changeling's Fealty
Hunter's Oath
Noble's Honor
Fae, Flames & Fedoras: A Changeling Blood Novella

ONSET
ONSET: To Serve and Protect
ONSET: My Enemy's Enemy
ONSET: Blood of the Innocent
ONSET: Stay of Execution
Murder by Magic: An ONSET Novella

FANTASY STAND ALONE NOVELS
Children of Prophecy
City in the Sky

Made in United States
Orlando, FL
02 June 2023

33739805R00193